# REVELATION

ELLERY KANE

Book Developmental Editing/Consulting:
AnnCastro Studio with Ann Castro, Katrina A. Martin, and Jae Gravley.

First published by Dog Ear Publishing
4011 Vincennes Rd
Indianapolis, IN 46268
www.dogearpublishing.net

ISBN: 978-1-4575-4402-6

This book is printed on acid-free paper.



Printed in the United States of America

For my mother . . .

because my story begins with yours

"The events in our lives happen in a sequence in time,
but in their significance to ourselves, they find their own order . . .
the continuous thread of revelation."
—Eudora Welty

# PROLOGUE

THE FIRST TIME I SAW, I knew. Just like when old bones can sense a change in the weather. What I saw—what I still see—cannot be unseen. Some things are like that, I guess. Uninvited guests, they took up permanent residence in my mind, returning again and again without warning. Elliot's lifeless face. My mother's chest exploding red. The crimson trail of Shelly's blood in her bedroom. My mother would've called them flashbacks, but it felt a lot like being haunted.

It was early December, a day like any other. I was running my usual route with Artos trotting beside me. I heard the truck before it rounded the corner. Loud men's voices, raucous and unhinged, started barking at me from a block away. I yanked Artos into the ditch, but the truck swerved toward us, narrowly missing my foot. Words of outrage stuck in the hollow of my throat, where they died, unspoken. The men inside—at least ten of them—cackled through black bandanas as the truck screeched down the street. One of them hung from an open window, casually waving a rifle in his hand, as if he was greeting the neighbors.

I was fixed, frozen in mid-stride like a broken toy, until Artos pulled at his leash and jolted me forward. Up ahead, the truck stopped. Two children scurried across the road like small animals. For a moment, the world was still, waiting. And then, he fired.

## CHAPTER ONE

# MR. RIGHT

"I CAN'T BELIEVE YOU TWO," I muttered, glaring at Edison and Elana. They were sitting side by side on Mr. Van Sant's leather sofa. "Did you really think I would like that guy?"

Edison snickered, prompting a swift elbow from Elana. "What's wrong with Teddy?" he asked. "He's named after a dead president, you know. That should count for something."

I rolled my eyes, contemplating my long and unpleasant evening with Theodore Bryce Griffith III. "Yeah, and he thought the Guardian Force was a rock band."

Edison grinned. "An honest mistake."

"Sorry, Lex." Elana patted my knee across the coffee table. "I told Edison he wasn't right for you."

"But then again, who is?" Edison retorted. "You're sort of particular."

I shrugged, feeling guilty. It wasn't their first failed attempt at matchmaking. In the two and a half months since Quin left, Edison—at Elana's urging—had introduced me to a long and distinguished list of his former classmates. She insisted it would be a "welcome distraction" for all of us.

"I don't need any distractions," my protest halfway believable. Only Artos knew I slept in Quin's T-shirt, wishing it still smelled like him.

So first, there was Eric, *Mr. Wandering Eye*, who flirted with Elana on our double date. That one didn't end well. Next was James, *Mr. Isn't It True That.* The son of another prominent defense attorney, his conversational skills consisted mostly of his father's cross-examination techniques. Last week was Percy. With a name like that, it was doomed from the start. I let him kiss me anyway, hoping his lips, soft but inept, would do something to me, erase something indelible inside me. Afterward, he stood there almost, but not really, looking at me, and I realized I was exactly the same. It was unsettling, but strangely comforting. Before I could protest, he kissed me again.

Elana shook her head. "She's just waiting for Mr. Right."

"I told you. I don't want to date anyone."

"Not entirely true," Edison countered. "I think we all know what's going on here, Lex." My stomach churned as I conjured Quin's face. "You've already got a boyfriend. It's obvious." He gestured toward my cell phone on the coffee table. Inwardly, I was relieved. "Some mystery man has been texting you all night." With a sly smile, Edison leaned toward the table and reached for my phone, but I beat him to it. He laughed.

Elana was not amused. "Who is it, Lex? You know you can tell us."

"I know." But when I imagined myself saying it out loud, it was inconceivable—the kind of secret you bury so deep that releasing it would mean uprooting an entire part of yourself. *Augustus. I've been texting Augustus.*

## CHAPTER TWO

# PUBLIC MENACE

"BE CAREFUL." Elana's voice was muted by the car window, as I pulled away. She held her jacket like a tent over her head to avoid the light rain that was beginning to fall. Already damp, her auburn hair stuck to her cheeks. She gave a small wave before ducking back inside.

*Slow down*, I reminded myself, tapping the brakes as the car rumbled across the Golden Gate Bridge. Lights flashed red ahead of me, signaling a mandatory military checkpoint. A soldier—flashlight in tow—approached. Lowering my window, I felt the wet air rush in and pepper my face with cold droplets. I steadied myself and prepared for his questions.

"Hello, Miss. Could I see your driver's license and registration, please?" I handed him both with a demure smile, casually studying his forearm. Tattooed. Just like all the others.

"You live over in Tiburon, huh?" I nodded. "Is that where you're headed?" Another nod. "Use any EAMs this evening? Onyx?" He shined the light across my face, pausing to consider my eyes.

"Uh, no. No, sir," I stuttered. Though these checkpoints were interspersed throughout the Bay Area and had been operational for almost a month, I still felt unnerved with each pass-through. *This is what it's like to have a secret.*

The soldier held up a picture, protected from the rain by a plastic sleeve. In bold type, it read, *Wanted Fugitive For The Crimes Of Burglary, Illegal Drug Trafficking, Embezzlement, Racketeering, Public Corruption. Do Not Approach. Considered Armed And Dangerous.*

"Have you seen this man?" he asked.

"No." *Not since last week.*

Oblivious to my wordless drama, he waved me through. "Travel safe," he called out as I pulled ahead, tires sloshing. In my rearview mirror, I watched him approach the next vehicle and another. A string of headlights trailed behind me—same questions, same answers. I could only wonder which of them, like me, had something to hide.

* * *

I parked a half mile from the marina, tucked my father's gun inside my waistband, and ran the rest of the way. The rain had subsided to a cold mist. I shielded my face with my sweatshirt as my feet splashed ahead blindly. Never the same way twice—that was our agreement.

Near the water, I slowed my pace, taking a cautious glance around. There was no one. The only sound came from the boats—their hulls creaking and plaintive as they rocked on the waves. I passed the small fishing vessel where I'd found him and took a tentative step onto the bow of my pretend houseboat. Each time I came here, I imagined Quin's voice in my head. *Our houseboat? Seriously?*

The door was ajar. "Hello?" My voice was half croak, half whisper. I slipped inside, shutting out the bitter night air. From behind me, the click of a flashlight illuminated the cabin. I jumped.

"It's about time." Augustus was sitting on the bed, cradling his gun. Snake-like, his eyes followed me without blinking. In a week, his beard had grown even thicker. Beneath it, I imagined his face, like the rest of him, was gaunt. "What took you so long?"

I opened my backpack and handed him a foil-wrapped pimento sandwich—his favorite, apparently. "A simple *thank you* will suffice," I said as I unpacked the rest of his supplies, secreted from our old stockpile—crackers, cans of soup and vegetables, medicine. In the awkward silence between us, I could hear Augustus chewing and swallowing, chewing and swallowing.

I closed the cabinets and turned toward him. "They're still looking for you." He gave no response. I gestured to his beard where a glob of pimento lingered. "Xander gave another press conference yesterday. He keeps trying to convince everybody Zenigenic is innocent in all this."

"Hmph." Augustus grunted thick with contempt, wiping his mouth with his shirtsleeve. The shirt, borrowed from my father's closet, was at least two sizes too small for him.

"Your name came up again—in case you were wondering." Augustus said nothing, but took a long swig from a bottle of water I brought. "Xander said he's fully cooperating with police. He called you a menace. A public menace. And he's blaming you for Onyx, along with everything else." Since Augustus had disappeared, he'd become a convenient scapegoat for all Xander's transgressions. "He wants you—if you're alive, that is—to turn yourself—"

"Enough!" Augustus slapped his palm against the bed. For a moment, his eyes were intense, seething, like the Augustus I knew. Then as fast as the fire ignited, it was doused. He grimaced and leaned back against the cabin wall.

"Take it easy," I cautioned. "Your shoulder's still healing." When Artos discovered Augustus in the fishing boat, his wound was already infected, the edges blackened like a rotting apple.

"Your fault," he muttered.

"My fault?" His persistent refusal to accept any responsibility for his predicament was expected—typical Augustus. Still, it rankled me. "You can't stay here forever, you know. I hope you haven't forgotten what we discussed. You still haven't told me what you've got on Xander, and I'm not doing this because I—"

"I know, I know," he interrupted. "You despise, detest, and abhor me. You wish me a long and painful death, etcetera, etcetera."

I rolled my eyes at him. "Good. I'm glad you remember." I handed him a new disposable cell phone from my pocket. "Start using this one . . . just in case. And don't text me unless it's important." I narrowed my eyes at him. "Life-or-death important, not pimento-sandwich important."

Augustus mocked me with a military salute. "Yes, ma'am."

"One more thing," I said, nudging the cabin door open with my hip. "There's a razor and shaving cream in the drawer. You might want to use it."

## CHAPTER THREE

# CRUMPLED

I SPED HOME, eyes alert to anything that moved. It was almost midnight and well past the newly established curfew. Except for the pulsing red light from the alarm my father recently installed, the house was dark. Its cavernous, black eyes watched me. Artos met me at the door, sniffing my shoes with vigor, the lingering scent of Augustus teasing his nose.

Even before I read my father's note that was scribbled on a pad in the kitchen—*Gone to work on a story . . . be back soon*—I knew he wasn't there. His jacket and *Eyes on the Bay* press pass that usually hung on the door hook were gone. I was relieved. At least, I wouldn't have to lie to him again.

I poured myself a bowl of cereal and flopped down onto the sofa, exhausted. With a click of the remote, I had instant company: Barbara Blake.

> **"SFTV is reporting live from the scene of another grisly drive-by between warring street gangs, Oaktown Boys and Satan's Syndicate. Since early December, violent crime in the Bay Area has exploded, with a forty percent increase in homicides. Most are believed to be related to recreational use of Onyx. The death toll keeps climbing with three teenagers caught in the gangs' crossfire tonight. Mandatory military checkpoints and a 10 p.m. curfew have done little to quell the brutality.**

**The violence in San Francisco has spurred increased use of Emovere in other large cities like Los Angeles and New York, prompting government officials to consider requiring the use of EAM monitors. Responding to the public's growing panic, Chief of Police Caesar Gonzalez announced the arrest of two additional suspects linked to disgraced Drug Czar Augustus Porter. Gonzalez called these men "instrumental" in illegally obtaining and distributing Emovere and Eupho. Porter, missing since November, is believed to be responsible for burglarizing several Zenigenic storage facilities, using his public office to traffic EAMs, and introducing Onyx to the streets of Oakland. In other news, workers are finishing repairs on the Bay Bridge, set to reopen—"**

Another click sent Barbara back into a dark and soundless oblivion. I headed for my room.

"C'mon, Artos." He galloped ahead of me and onto the bed, where he circled his favorite spot and nested inside it. With my head overfull of secrets that needed spilling, I opened my journal.

*January 14, 2043,*

*It's been 75 days since Quin left for L.A., but who's counting? And 61 since I made a deal with the devil. I'm not sure which is worse.*

*Speak of that devil, I saw him again today. He's not himself—a good thing, right? But he's no good to me like this. Do psychopaths get depressed? Because that's what it seems like. Maybe he's just hoping I'll feel sorry for him, which I do . . . a little. I haven't even really pushed him about telling me what he knows—yet.*

*Suffered through another Elana/Edison-arranged date tonight. Epic failure. I try to stop thinking about Quin—I really do—but this not-thinking-about-him thing makes me think about him even more. Pathetic, I know, since I practically sent him away. The worst is the not knowing. What is he doing, thinking, feeling? I guess I gave up my right to know, but I never expected this—not one word from him.*

Lifting pen from paper, I sighed. Quin's complete silence rubbed my heart raw. For the past month, he'd been ignoring Mr. Van Sant's calls.

I tucked my journal into the nightstand drawer alongside my mother's poetry book, unopened for weeks now. Feeling the pit in my stomach, I took it out and turned to the dog-eared page. Closing my eyes—*I couldn't look*—I snatched Quin's old notes, a fistful. I balled them in my hand, squeezing so tight my fingers hurt. Part of me wished for the magic to make them disappear. I imagined opening my hand and watching tiny, white doves take flight from my palm. Instead there was only a crumpled wad of paper.

## CHAPTER FOUR

# UNLIKELY HERO

I OPENED MY EYES to terror. A man sat at the foot of my bed. He faced the wall, unmoving. His shoulders were broad, his posture rigid and nearly transfixed. *I know him.* I said his name aloud—*Augustus*—but he didn't answer. An awful sound slithered out of him—a hiss. His golden-brown skin began to pulse as his long, soft-bellied body stretched slowly to the floor. His unnatural curve slowly disappeared inch by inch from view. Then suddenly, like the strike of a whip, his tail writhed and he was gone. A silent scream rattled in my throat.

I woke to the electronic hiss of my cell phone vibrating against the nightstand. Still suspended in nightmare, my heart was beating fast. Artos was curled near my feet, nose buried in his tail, completely unaware. I reached for my phone with lightning speed, pulling my hand back to safety under the covers. My father had texted me.

*2:34 a.m. Are you awake?*

*2:35 a.m. Turn on the news.*

*2:36 a.m. Call me.*

A cold dread crept through me. Beneath the blanket, I shivered. It was 2:40 a.m. As I padded barefoot to the living room, I dialed my father's number.

"Lex." He sounded relieved. "I've been trying to reach you." I clicked on the television while I paced in front of the sofa. Artos watched me with curiosity from the bedroom door.

"What happened?" I stared at the screen with anticipation.

"Are you watching?" I couldn't answer, couldn't even move. *Quin.* The sight of his face knocked the wind from me. Through the camera's eye, he looked older, harder somehow. Stubble shadowed his jaw. His mouth was set—firm, fierce. His hair was mussed from the wind. Behind him, Zenigenic's headquarters towered like a beacon into the sky, so tall that the top of the building was hidden from view. An oversized metal *Z* was anchored into the concrete at its entrance, replacing the statue of Jackson Steele, Xander's father, which was vandalized in the riots after the McAllister verdict. Police officers traveled in packs around it, herding bystanders to the periphery. Barbara Blake, microphone at the ready, was watching it all unfold.

"Lex?"

"I'm here."

*ASSASSINATION ATTEMPT ON ZENIGENIC CEO THWARTED BY UNLIKELY HERO* scrolled at the bottom of the screen. "Did Quin . . . ?" The words got lost on their way to my mouth. "Try to kill . . . Xander?" He wasn't in handcuffs, but I still felt the heat from his words when I told him and Mr. Van Sant about my encounter with the tattooed man just before the verdict. "I knew it," he'd said. His voice simmered, only part of its steam meant for me.

"Just the opposite," my father answered, disbelieving. "He *saved* him."

Barbara Blake turned toward Quin, jabbing at his face with the microphone.

"Mr. McAllister, can you tell us what happened tonight?"

Not taking my eyes from Quin, I sat down on the sofa. "Dad, I'll call you back."

## CHAPTER FIVE

# STRANGER THINGS

WHEN MY FATHER OPENED the front door three hours later, I was stuck in that same spot. My eyes felt like sandpaper, sleep tugging at their lids. Still, I couldn't stop watching. SFTV replayed the interview again and again until I knew Quin's words as if I had spoken them myself.

"I was taking a walk to clear my head." Quin gestured over his shoulder to Zenigenic's headquarters, as he explained the incident to Barbara. "I noticed the lights were on in the lobby. I thought that was strange, since it was so late. Then, out of nowhere, there's this guy in a mask running up to the building. He had a gun. That's when I saw Mr. Steele coming down the stairs alone."

"Then what happened?" Barbara asked.

Quin shrugged. "I guess I did what anybody would do."

Wide-eyed, Barbara countered, "I'm not sure just anybody would tackle an armed gunman. Mr. Steele has called you a hero."

"I'm no hero. I was in the right place at the right time. That's all."

"You are a humble young man, Mr. McAllister." She seemed a lot more convinced by Quin's story than I was. But then, maybe not. "However. . .your father's attorney, Nicholas Van Sant, has been quite vocal about his belief that Zenigenic played a role in framing your father for murder."

"Is that a question, Ms. Blake?" Quin's eyes flashed to the camera, mischievous. In my imagination, they connected only with mine.

"Just an observation," Barbara answered. "It is ironic, to say the least—you rescuing Xander Steele."

"Stranger things have happened." Quin smiled a little.

Barbara turned her face away from him toward the camera. "They certainly have, Mr. McAllister. They certainly have. This is Barbara Blake, reporting live from San—"

The television went silent, muted by my father. "Dad!"

"Yes?" My father raised his eyebrows at my protest. "I'm guessing you've already memorized the entire broadcast." He collapsed onto the sofa with a deep sigh. His eyes looked as tired as mine.

Ignoring his sarcasm, I asked, "Have you heard anything?" I stopped myself from adding, *about Quin.*

"They've released the name of the suspect. Peter Radley."

"Radley," I repeated, trying to place the name. On just a few hours' sleep, thinking felt strenuous.

"Sound familiar?" My father handed me his computer tablet. "Press *play*," he instructed. "I think you might've seen this before." He was right. On the screen, George McAllister addressed a crowd of anti-EAM activists.

*"I wish that I could say that my life was the only one impacted by the government's greed, but I am not alone. Tonight, you will hear from Mr. Peter Radley, a Guardian Force survivor like my son, and—Emma, come on up here—Ms. Emma Markum."*

I hit *stop*, before the camera panned to Emma. I had heard those words before. "So he's a former Guardian?"

My father nodded. "And a member of the New Resistance."

"Who knows Quin."

"It seems likely."

"Is that it?" I asked, desperate for more.

"That's all they're telling us right now. What about you?" He looked toward my phone on the coffee table, its screen dark, lifeless.

A flame of anger—*how could he not call me?*—licked through my exhaustion. "If you're asking if I've heard from Quin, the answer is no."

## CHAPTER SIX

# SLIVERS

LEAVING MY FATHER drifting in and out of sleep on the sofa—with a contented Artos as a pillow for his arm—I slunk away to the bathroom. I pulled my hair into a clumsy ponytail and stared at my face in the mirror. The corners of my eyes were a pinkish red. *Awful*, I muttered to myself, a word that seemed to sum up everything. I scooped two handfuls of cool water and splashed it on my face.

"Lex, your phone!" Water dripping from my chin, I was already in mid-stride using the collar of my shirt as a makeshift towel. I reached for the phone as it buzzed with urgency.

"Oh." My voice flattened. "It's a text from Max. He heard. He's coming over." My father nodded, pretending not to notice my disappointment. He was awake now and scrolling through a social media website on his laptop.

"Hey, take a look at this," he said, patting the seat next to him. "It's Peter Radley." A master of distraction, my father turned the computer screen toward me, revealing a young man's face. He didn't look like much of an assassin or even a former Guardian. His skin was the color of plaster, his cheeks plump and splotchy.

"Only fifteen friends." My father tapped his finger to Peter's profile stats. I wasn't surprised. He looked like the kind of boy who was used to being picked on or worse . . . ignored.

My father clicked on a recent post dated January 10, 2043.

*Demons inside of me. Howling. This night, every night, always the same. I murder them in my sleep. Watch their bodies convulse and writhe. Cut them into slivers and swallow them. Demons inside of me again.*

"Well that's intense," I said, watching my father mouth the last sentence to himself.

"Pretty disturbing, I'd say."

I shrugged. "I don't know, Dad. It sounds like typical teenage-boy angst to me."

My father chuckled. "Is that your official diagnosis, Doctor?"

My smirk faded as I pointed to Peter's last post, a captioned picture from January 13. "Now *that's* disturbing," I said. In the photo, he wore his military uniform, its buttons straining around his belly. The Guardian Force logo was obliterated with a line of red tape. He held his cell phone in one hand, aiming its lens at his bathroom mirror, where the mark of the New Resistance was drawn in red. In the other, he cradled a gun. His face was blank, his mouth a thin dash. Beneath it, he had typed two words: *It's time.*

"Looks like an open-and-shut case to me," my dad concluded. "The guy was clearly a little off kilter."

"He probably has Ryker and the Guardian Force to thank for—"

Stopping mid-sentence, I watched my father's finger trail down the list of Peter's friends. Third from the top was Sebastian Croft.

## CHAPTER SEVEN

# BULLETPROOF

MAX DIDN'T BOTHER KNOCKING. "Have you heard from Quin?" he asked, shutting the door behind him. Still dumbfounded, my father and I sat side by side, studying the computer screen. I shook my head.

"You two look like you've seen a ghost or something," Max said, positioning himself behind us to get a better look.

"Or something." I followed his eyes until they reached String's face and opened wide. He steadied himself against the chair.

"Is that? Is this?" He stumbled over the answers to his questions before he could finish them. "Whoa."

"Did you know Peter Radley?" my father asked.

Max nodded. "He was recruited by the Guardian Force just before I got the ax. I didn't really know him that well. But he was at that rally in the fall, the one String forced me to go to. I talked to him for about ten seconds. He seemed . . . off."

"What do you mean?" My father was already typing. Max's words—*he seemed off*—materialized on the screen.

"It's hard to describe. He reminded me of my mom, the way she gets when she's trying to convince me that she's still clean, but it's obvious she's not. I figured he had probably relapsed and just didn't want to admit it."

"Did you ask him about it?"

Max laughed at my father's question. "That would've been the pot meeting the kettle. I wasn't exactly the model of sobriety myself."

"And String? Did they talk? Did he ever mention Radley to you?"

Max exhaled and slunk down onto the sofa next to me. "Dad, cool it with the inquisition."

Looking a little guilty, my father shrugged, but kept typing.

"Never," Max answered. "How long have they been *friends*?"

"Looks like they connected on this site about two weeks ago."

"Two weeks." Max said no more. It had been two weeks since their last breakup—and two weeks since Max returned home to his family, his mother supposedly off Eupho again.

My cell phone buzzed again, prompting my father to look up from the computer screen. "It's from Elana," I said. Her text was five familiar words with an answer that stung.

*Have you heard from Quin?*

As I typed my standard reply, Artos' ears perked. He stood and trotted toward the door, eyeing it with interest. Then a knock. "I'll get it, Dad." I peered through the peephole. On the other side, biting her lip, was an unexpected face.

I turned to Max. "Emma," I mouthed, my stomach twisting with the turn of the knob.

We stood there stalemating—each of us waiting for the other to speak first. The tip of her nose was blush pink. I could tell she had been crying. "Hi," she finally said, breaking the silence. Her voice, fragile at first, gained strength as she continued. "Is Quin here?"

"No."

"Oh." My answer seemed to startle her. "Well I need to talk to you." She looked over my shoulder into the living room. Max and my father stared back at her. "Alone." As much as I wanted to send her away, I couldn't. Whatever she had to say, I knew it was about Quin. "It's about Qu—"

"I know," I interrupted. "Come in." I directed a what-is-she-doing-here glance at Max and my father and ushered Emma inside.

"Hey, Artos," she said, rubbing the top of his head. He greeted her with a lick to the hand. *Traitor.*

"We can talk in here." I pointed to my bedroom. The clop of Emma's boots followed behind me. She took off her jacket and sat at my desk chair. It was strange seeing her—glowing blonde hair, black braid, perfect bow lips—backdropped by *my* things. On her neck, there was a freshly inked tattoo. "Is that new?"

She pulled back her hair, revealing it to me. The dark cursive writing traced a path from her earlobe to her clavicle. Thankfully, it didn't read *Quin*. "Bulletproof," she said, grinning.

I smiled back at her. "Clever."

"It was Quin's idea."

Suddenly, like the pin-pop of a balloon, my smile disappeared. I glared at her. "Why are you here?"

"Believe me, if there was any other place for me to go for help, I would be there right now."

"Help? Do you really expect me to help you?" As I spoke, Emma appraised my desk. She picked up one of my trophies and held it up to the light.

"First place, senior science fair." Her voice was singsong, mocking. She grabbed a group of my award ribbons, rattling them off in rapid succession. "Citizenship award. Perfect attendance. Most likely to succeed." Her contempt was tangible. "No wonder Quin broke up with you. You're such a goody-goody. I'm sure he was bored out of his mind."

I resisted the overwhelming urge to yank her braid until she screamed. "Did you really come here to insult me?"

With a careless flick of her wrist, she tossed my ribbons back on the desk and rose from the chair. We stood face to face. Hand on her hip, she replied, "I came here because I thought you should know that Quin has—" She lowered her eyes. "There's no other way to say it—he's lost it. Completely."

"What do you mean?" I knew what she meant.

"Xander. I'm assuming you've heard."

I nodded.

"Quin left me in L.A. three days ago. He didn't even tell me he was going. Just disappeared. He and his dad had this big fight—or at least that's what he said—before he left. Next thing you know, he's saving Xander from a bullet and then this." She held out her cell phone. In my mind, it was a hot coal. I reached for it, but I didn't want to. I knew it would burn.

There were several days' worth of texts, ranging from demanding to disappointed—all from Emma to *Q*. Then there was this:

*Emma: Where are you?*

*Emma: Please, tell me. Please.*

*Emma: I know we're not "together," but still, I thought you cared.*

*Q: You're the one who begged to come to L.A. I told you a long time ago not to get involved with me. Lose my number. Forget you ever met me.*

When I looked up at her, Emma was catching tears on her cheeks with the back of her hand. "It doesn't sound like Quin, right?" Her voice sounded desperate. "What do you think, Lex?"

I took a breath, steeling myself, willing away the words *together* and *involved*. I shrugged. "Maybe you're not as bulletproof as you thought."

## CHAPTER EIGHT

# MEAN

FROM THE DOORWAY, I watched Emma leave. She had a way of walking—a strut, really—that was undeniable, even now. Her hair sashayed behind her with a bounce that seemed both effortless and intentional. With one graceful swing of her leg, she was seated on her motorcycle. She gave a halfhearted wave as she circled the cul-de-sac and drove out of my sight.

Max and my father sat on the sofa, engaged in pretend chitchat. I waited for their questions.

"Well?" I asked finally when neither spoke.

My father grinned. "Well, what?" He turned to Max. "Did we miss something?"

With a straight face, Max shrugged. "I didn't see anything."

I glared at them. "Whatever." They both laughed. I flopped onto the chair nearest them, sighing. "Emma thinks Quin's gone off the deep end."

"A reasonable assumption, I suppose," my father said. I was grateful when he added, "For someone who doesn't know him that well."

"I'm not sure," I admitted, replaying Quin's harsh words to Emma. "I'm beginning to wonder how well I know him anymore. His text sounded—" *Mean*. The ring of my father's cell phone interrupted me.

"I've got to get this," he said, phone in hand, heading toward the kitchen. "It's Langley, my assignment editor." He answered in his professional voice. "Bill Knightley, *Eyes on the Bay*."

"So what else did Emma say?" Max asked, with my father out of earshot.

I rolled my eyes. "Here's a replay of the highlights. There's a new tattoo on her neck. She's flabbergasted I didn't kill Quin with my utter dullness. Apparently he left her in L.A. They weren't *together*, but might've been *involved*, whatever that means. And she hasn't heard from him since."

"O—kaayyy." Max drew out his voice, awaiting my reaction.

"Oh yeah, one more thing. Quin told her that he had a fight with his dad right before he left."

Max cocked his head to the side, perplexed. "That's odd."

I nodded. "But not as odd as Quin popping up out of nowhere and saving Xander."

"Or String knowing the guy taking the shot." Max's smile didn't hide his melancholy. "Do you think String and Radley were . . . dating?" He said the word carefully, as if its edges were razor sharp. "He said we could see other people."

"I seriously doubt it." *In fact, I hadn't even considered such a mundane explanation.* "He doesn't exactly seem like String's type." I combed my hand through my hair in an exaggerated preen.

Max half smiled, then sighed. "We really need to talk to Quin."

"Hold that thought," my father said. With one hand, he looped his press pass around his neck while the other shoveled his laptop in its briefcase. "Xander's giving a press conference at Zenigenic in forty-five minutes. Who's coming with me?"

## CHAPTER NINE

# HOOPLA

"HEY, LEX, LOOK!" Max pointed to a row of mahogany-framed portraits lining the lobby wall at Zenigenic. "It's your mom." I nodded, melancholy with memory.

The last time I was inside this lobby, I was thirteen years old and watching my mother receive the Z Innovator Award and a standing ovation for her contributions to the development of Emovere. That evening, my mother radiated. It seemed the whole room was in an orbit of awe—myself included—spinning around her. But looking back, her disenchantment was just a fingernail's scratch below the surface. At the night's end, we all stood on the roof of the building, eyes to the sky, watching the company-sponsored fireworks. My mother whispered, "All this hoopla for a drug. It seems silly, doesn't it?" I didn't know why, but my stomach hurt when she said it. She resigned a few weeks later.

My father patted my arm as we walked along the periphery of a crowd of reporters. "Are you okay?"

"Fine," I said, one foot still in the past. "It's just been a long time."

"Will you tell me about it later—if you want to?"

Sometimes it was overwhelming. There were entire books of my life that my father had never opened.

"Of course," I reassured him. Just outside the lobby, a large group of protestors was gathering. I could hear their chanting even through the soundproof glass. "Steele must go! No more drugs!"

Max nudged me with his elbow. "Is that Quin?"

My heart revved. "Where?" I stood on tiptoe and followed Max's finger to the stage. Standing just behind Xander's spokeswoman, Gina Tan, was Quin. He was shoulder to shoulder with Zenigenic security, his black suit jacket and stony expression camouflaging him among them. Now that he was so close, it was hard to be still. It was silly, but I imagined shouting his name, pushing through the crowd, throwing my arms around him. Since Quin left, I daydreamed this moment many times. But this reunion—confusing, detached, and very public—wasn't what I had pictured.

"He seems . . . official," Max whispered.

"Good morning." Xander addressed the crowd. Like Quin, he wore a black suit, his demeanor just as dispassionate. When he spoke again, his face softened, but his eyes were steel. "I'm grateful to see so many of you here today. In fact, I'm grateful just to be here. As all of you know by now, early this morning, there was an attempt on my life just outside of this building. In the past few hours, Zenigenic has learned the suspect, Peter Radley, suffers from serious mental health issues, which we believe may have motivated his actions. We also suspect he may have been under the influence of Onyx at the time of the attack. Zenigenic has graciously agreed to fund his psychiatric treatment in lieu of criminal proceedings."

I watched Quin as I listened. His gaze shifted, subtle but deliberate, scanning the room row by row.

"I also want to publicly acknowledge Quin McAllister, a true hero." Xander gestured toward Quin with a buoyant grin. Quin stopped scanning the room—his search ended. He looked right at me, then away. "It's no secret we haven't always been on the same side, but I'm hopeful that's about to change. This young man is the reason I'm standing here today. Thank you, Quin." Cameras flashed as Quin gave a cursory nod to the crowd. His smile never reached his eyes.

"While I have you all gathered here today, I want to take this opportunity to share my vision of a revitalized Zenigenic. This great company has lived in the shadow of Emovere for far too long. In the coming days, we plan to release a new emotion-altering drug, just as powerful as its predecessors with absolutely no side effects. It goes without saying that we will continue to support the ban on Emovere, Agitor, Euphoractamine, and Onyx. We have also started a charitable fund for all those recently impacted by EAM-related violence in our community."

I glanced sidelong at my father. His eyes were wide. "A new drug," he mouthed. I couldn't help but think of Dr. Donnelly. A few weeks after the trial ended, his body was discovered in Muir Woods, his death ruled a suicide. By that time, Stanford already had appointed a replacement professor. Not that it mattered now—classes were on permanent hiatus per government orders.

"I'll allow a few questions," Xander announced. There was a startled silence made awkward by the muted chanting of the New Resistance. The old Xander never took questions. Then a barrage of voices pounded the stage.

"Tell us about the new drug, Mr. Steele."

"Did you know Peter Radley?"

"What is Zenigenic doing to help get Onyx off the streets?"

"No side effects?"

"Was Radley working alone?"

Xander smirked, biting at the last question. "Well that's an easy one. I'm not a betting man, but I'd stake a small fortune on the fact that our disgraced drug czar was involved. There was a reported sighting of him in the area last week. Rest assured, the authorities are looking into it." The mere mention of Augustus unnerved me. *What if he was involved?* As haggard and dejected as Augustus appeared, my dream-self tugged at me, reminding me that he was still the same old snake underneath.

"Quin, what does your father think of your heroics? And Zenigenic's new drug?"

"Do you still believe Zenigenic framed him for murder?"

Quin offered no response. That was expected. His wall—stone or matchsticks—was always as strong as he needed it to be.

Xander raised his hand to quiet the crowd. "Mr. McAllister will not be providing a statement today. This will conclude my remarks. I look forward to seeing you all again soon."

Signaling to Gina, Xander descended the stage. Following him was a swarm of black suits, his security detail. I found the tattooed man, Clive Valkov, strutting at the back of the group. Thanks to the investigative efforts of Mr. Van Sant and my father, he was no longer nameless. A step behind him was Quin.

As they passed us, Max called out to him, but the lobby was so loud that his voice fell away, swallowed by all the others. And yet, Quin turned toward the sound. There was no sign of recognition—his feet never stopped moving—only a look, a look that seemed to say something (but what?) and nothing at the same time.

## CHAPTER TEN

# THE UNBEARABLE PARTS

"YOU'RE AWFULLY QUIET," my father observed. Max chattered nonstop—a welcome distraction—until we dropped him off at home. In his absence, the silence sat like a ghost between my dad and me. "Are you thinking about Quin?" he asked.

"A little." The truth was that seeing Quin had left me with far more questions than answers. "But mostly about Mom."

My father patted my knee. "Do you want to talk about it?" I did, and I didn't. Talking about her kept her memory latched to me, a comforting shadow. But along with it came everything else . . . the unbearable parts. It was a hopeless contradiction.

"Why did she wait so long to leave Zenigenic—until they forced her out? She was obviously unhappy."

My father offered an understanding smile. "Your mother wasn't a quitter. And Emovere was her life's work. She wanted to see it through. As infuriating as it was then, I get it now."

"But, Dad, she knew." I let myself be mad at her. Of everything I felt for my mother, anger was the simplest. "She knew Emovere was dangerous. She knew about the side effects. She even knew Zenigenic never destroyed that initial formula. Why did it take her so long to confront them?"

He sighed. "Honey, I wish I had the answers for you. What can I say? Your mother was a complex woman. She was a riddle I never solved."

I hadn't cried in months, but I felt the tears coming. "It's so unfair. She created all of this. It was her fault you left . . ." I knew I was irrational, but

I didn't care. "Her fault Quin's dad murdered his mom, her fault she died. She just left us here to pick up the pieces." I turned away from my father, toward the window. My hot, ragged breath fogged the glass. "Sometimes, I just . . ."

"Lex." My father's voice was gentle, intended to calm whatever was brewing. Even so, I had to say it. Somehow the words escaped from a locked box deep inside me—and once released, they wouldn't be denied.

"Sometimes, I hate her."

Pulling the car to a slow stop on the side of the freeway, my father reached for me. He was tentative at first, but when I felt his arms around me, I couldn't hold it in any longer. "It's okay," he said. "It's okay." He repeated those words again and again until I realized they were meant for both of us.

## CHAPTER ELEVEN

# A STRAY

XANDER'S PRESS CONFERENCE was the featured story on SFTV that night and the next morning, the attempt on his life nearly overshadowed by the speculation surrounding Quin's heroics and the announcement of a forthcoming new drug.

"Maybe it'll cure arrogance," my father suggested. He looked up from his computer, a faint smile toying at the corners of his mouth. "A humility pill."

I played along. We both needed to laugh. "*Humble*oxotine, perhaps? At least we know he's not sampling *that* product."

Chuckling with me, my father said, "It was pretty bold of him to blame all of this on Augustus. The guy could be dead for all we know, right?"

"Right." This lying thing was getting easier—too easy. My father's words left me with an overwhelming need to see Augustus. "I think I'll take Artos for a run," I suggested. "It's been a long time." Since our near brush with death in December, Artos and I hadn't ventured past our block.

My father frowned. "Is it safe?" We both knew the answer. "Just keep your eyes open. And take your cell phone." Within a few minutes, Artos was leashed, and we were out the door.

Sparked by a mishmash of emotions, I set a fast, Quin-like pace. It felt good to run—to pump my arms fast, feel my legs burn, suck in the cold air. Whoever said you can't outrun your problems was right, but you can tire them out a little. By the time we reached the marina, my head was mostly quiet, blown clear by the needful pull and push of my breath.

I slowed to a purposeful stride, tightening the slack on Artos' leash until we were walking side by side. Artos' nose was fixed to the ground, leading the way. When we neared the boat, his sniffing grew frantic, desperate. Thinking of their first and last encounter—Augustus' pant leg in a vise grip between Artos' canines—I whispered to him. "Artos, stay." His eyes reluctant, Artos lowered his haunches to the ground and watched me as I climbed aboard.

Every time I came here it was always the same. Memories. Anticipation. Dread. A curious mixture that turned my stomach with every step. I took a breath and opened the cabin door.

"Augustus?"

Inside it smelled of shaving cream and pimento. My father's borrowed shirts, usually folded near the bed, were missing.

"Are you . . . here?" The only answer came from the boat's steady creaking as it rocked on the waves. Outside, Artos whined.

The cabinets were emptied. Antibiotics, food, water—all gone. I peered inside the small bathroom. On the side of the sink was a half-emptied bottle of water and a razor. A few hairs from Augustus' beard lined the drain like a scattered trail of ants.

"Don't play games with me," I threatened. The sound of my own small voice—pretending to be brave—frightened me. I flung open the corner closet and pawed my way through a curtain of musty clothing until I could see the wall inside. The space was barely big enough for a few blankets, much less a man Augustus' size. Still, I half expected him to be there, coiled in wait, blinking up at me with his dead eyes.

Artos barked and I jumped, hitting my elbow against the wall. "Ow!" I started to laugh at myself until I heard voices approaching, faint at first, then louder.

A man spoke. "Hey, it's a dog."

"Looks friendly enough," another man answered. "Seems to like you."

"He's just a stray. Leave him alone." There was no mistaking the third voice. Quin. It was so familiar—like a song I couldn't stop singing—yet, different too.

"Doesn't seem like a stray. He's got a leash." The voices were close now, too close. And my thoughts were racing. I crouched down low, peeking up through one of the cabin's windows. I couldn't see anything. I crawled toward the far window, hoping for a clearer view.

"I thought you wanted me to show you where I saw him last." Quin again. *Was he talking about Augustus?* "You're wasting time with that stupid dog." My own head a muddled muck, I could only imagine what Quin must be thinking.

"Fine," the first man answered. "Didn't you say it was this boat?" As he spoke, the man came into my view. Two things made me shudder. He was pointing at *my* houseboat—and he was Clive Valkov.

* * *

I tried not to panic. *Tried.* I scurried back to the closet. There were no other options. I pushed my back to the bare wall and pulled the door shut. Tucking my knees in close against my chest, I concealed myself behind the clothing inside. I was a ghost, an invisible person. I made my breathing quiet.

"Not that one," Quin protested from outside. "The next one over."

Valkov answered. "Yeah? Well you said this one—*this* boat when we got here."

"Well, I changed my mind." *Really, Quin? That's the best you can come up with?* "Have it your way then. You guys get that one, and I'll take a look in here." *Now you're thinking.*

"Nah." Valkov was on the deck, right outside the boat. His voice was gravelly, nearly a growl. "Mr. Steele may trust you, but I don't." As he spoke, I heard Artos scratching at the door. "Our furry friend seems awfully interested in this one. Don't cha, boy? We'll check both. Together."

It was inevitable now. Fear sat heavy on my chest, its hand at my throat, squeezing. Footsteps surrounded me, their echoes impossible to locate. Next came the methodical open and shut, open and shut of the cabinet doors. Then—even worse—silence. I imagined Valkov squinting, beady-eyed . . . considering the bathroom sink with disgust . . . stalking toward my hiding place with dark intention. "Someone's been here," he said.

Horrified, I watched the slow turn of the closet's knob. The whoosh of my own heartbeat in my ears drowned all other sounds. I was as still as a rabbit hidden in tall grass.

"Got something in there?"

"Nothing." Quin seemed to look through me. "Just a bunch of old clothes." Maybe I was invisible. But then he reached his hand toward me, finding my knee in the pitch black and giving it a gentle squeeze. That secret touch, tough and tender, was everything I loved about Quin. His fingertips electric, my skin tingled even in their absence. For the first time in a long time, I didn't feel so alone.

After concealing me in darkness again, Quin told the others, "Whoever was here is gone now."

## CHAPTER TWELVE

# JUST A SQUIRREL

WITH THE SHUTTING of the cabin door, the pall of fear lifted a little, and I breathed deep—as deep as I could in that airless tomb. I wriggled from underneath a raincoat, repositioned myself, and stretched my legs. The closet was too small to straighten them.

"Mr. Steele will want to know about all this." Valkov's voice—faint, but forceful—startled me. I pressed my ear to the wall, listening. "And the dog? Should we take him? Maybe he belongs to Augustus." *No!* I didn't move, but I was screaming inside. The thought of him leading Artos away was unbearable.

"Augustus never had a dog," Quin reasoned.

"McAllister's right about that," the second man agreed. "That guy was opposed to most living things—including me. I can't believe I worked for him as long as I did."

*He worked for Augustus?* Surprisingly, Augustus had spoken the truth for once. He'd said that most of his men were poached by Xander shortly after he fled. "Loyalty only runs as deep as your boss's pocketbook," he'd advised between bites of pimento. At the time, I thought it was a ploy for sympathy. But his stealthy escape from the boat left me wondering if Augustus was truly on his own.

From outside, Valkov spoke again. This time his voice was patronizing, sickeningly sweet. "C'mon, doggie. Here, doggie. Valkie won't hurt you." Judging by the bite in Artos' bark, I wasn't the only one not buying it.

"Get out of here, dog!" Quin shouted. Any trace of guilt, he covered with sheer power. "Go on! Go home!" Artos' yelp—knowing he couldn't possibly understand—wrenched my heart.

I heard nothing else for a long time. Finally, I closed my eyes and started counting. At five hundred, I put my hand on the knob and turned, half expecting Valkov's severed snake tattoo to greet me on the other side. There was no one.

I stood—my knees cricking and cracking from being cramped for so long—and took a look around me. The razor and the half-empty water bottle were gone. And a quick glance out the window made me realize, so was Artos. Over two hours had passed since I left home. I dialed my father's number.

"Lex! Where are you? Are you okay?" *To lie or not to lie.* It wasn't even a question. Once you start keeping secrets, they grow like moss in the dark space inside of you, taking on a separate life and multiplying without meaning to. It became hard—impossible—to stop. I wondered if my mom felt that way too, keeping my dad's letters from me for so long.

"I'm fine, Dad. But Artos got away from me. I think he might've run home." I blurted the story out with no effort.

"Where are you?" he asked again.

"On my way." I started jogging. "I'll be there soon."

"Okay. I'll keep an eye out for Artos. It's not like him to run off. Did something happen?"

I increased my pace. "No." *The houseboat, Augustus, Quin, Valkov, the closet*—the entire scene replayed in an instant. "Just a squirrel."

## CHAPTER THIRTEEN

# EXCLUSIVE

I WAS COMFORTED by the sight of Artos' leash hanging on its hook in the entryway. Just like Quin told him to, he went home.

"Dad?" At the sound of my voice, Artos padded into the hallway, offering a canine grin. I bent down toward him and rubbed his head. "Our secret, okay?" I whispered. My father's voice traveled from his office.

"Yes, I understand . . . exclusive." His tone was equal parts excitement and confusion.

"I know what it means. And I want to do it—but are you sure he requested me?" He paused for a moment, then said, "Okay, I'll be there."

"Lex?" My father opened the door. "There you are," he said, relieved. He gestured toward Artos, trailing a nose-length behind me. "I found this guy out on the porch, leash still on. No squirrel, of course." We both smiled, and for a moment, I almost believed my own lie.

"I have news," he said.

"Good or bad?" His voice hinted at both.

"I'm not sure yet. That was Langley on the phone. I've been assigned an exclusive interview, a special request by Xander Steele."

"To interview him?"

My father shook his head. "No. Quin."

His answer knocked the wind from me. "Quin?" I put a hand against the doorframe to steady myself. "When?"

"Tonight."

"Where?"

"In the courtyard outside Zenigenic. They want the piece to look conversational."

"Why you?" I asked, finally. That was the real question. *What was Xander plotting?* I waited for my father's clever comeback, a corny joke, a sarcastic quip. Instead he answered, "I have absolutely no idea."

## CHAPTER FOURTEEN

# B-LIST

I WATCHED FROM THE BACK of the *Eyes on the Bay* news van as my father's face was puffed, powdered, and prodded into camera-ready submission. A permissible stowaway, I promised Langley I would sit quietly and stay out of the way. Translation—*don't talk to Quin.*

I could tell my father was nervous. He fidgeted with his hair until it was combed and spritzed back into place. He fidgeted again, another spray. Just like my father, the scene was being carefully prepared. Two metallic benches appeared near the oversized *Z* with lush plants strategically interspersed between them. A rope and stanchions secured the perimeter—with plenty of Zenigenic security on hand to enforce its boundaries. Outside the ropes, a small crowd began to assemble, clamoring for a better look.

I chuckled to myself as a few giggling, rosy-cheeked girls pushed their way to the front. One held a heart-shaped sign that read, *Marry me, Quin!* But not everyone was so welcoming. The mark of the New Resistance decorated another sign, *TRAITOR*, spelled out in thick black letters underneath. The stone-faced man who carried it considered the girls with sheer disdain as they bumped up against him, laughing. The juxtaposition was jarring, and it made me wonder. *How had all of them already made up their minds about Quin, when I was still as confused as ever?*

Someone in the crowd drew my father's attention. He stopped flipping through his note cards and turned toward the sea of faces. Without even a courtesy glance to security, Mr. Van Sant lifted the rope and ducked underneath it. Edison followed behind him, slightly less certain. I couldn't hear him speaking, but Mr. Van Sant's mouth looked angry. My father's head dropped in deference. I cracked the door of the van.

"This is ridiculous!" Mr. Van Sant barked. "Completely unacceptable, Knightley."

My father cowered, but held his ground. "I'm sorry. I don't understand."

"You don't understand? Well let me enlighten you. This interview—your interview—could undermine any chance of a successful appeal for my client. Are you okay with that?" As he huffed, Mr. Van Sant's face turned from pink to an indignant purple.

"What do you mean?" My father was flustered by Mr. Van Sant's attack. "I'm not planning to ask any questions about George McAllister."

Mr. Van Sant threw his head back in sardonic amusement. "Do you think your plan matters to anyone? Trust me, there's a plan here, and it's not yours."

Two Zenigenic security guards approached Mr. Van Sant from behind, placing their hands on his forearms. "Sir! Sir, you can't be here. You need to go back behind the ropes." He shrugged them off with disgust, then began walking away. "Think about it, Knightley!" he called back over his shoulder. Looking apologetic, Edison mumbled something to my father. He nodded and patted Edison's shoulder.

"Pssst." One of the guards swiveled his head in my direction, trying to locate the sound. I shut the door and waited. "Pssst." I tried again. "Edison."

"Lex!" He slinked away from the crowd, backpedaling slowly toward the van.

"Get in," I instructed. Edison climbed inside, taking a seat next to me. "What's going on? Why was your father so upset?"

Edison groaned, loosening his tie. "I told him not to blame your dad, but he's convinced Quin is about to do something stupid."

"Like what?"

He shrugged. "You know Quin hasn't returned his calls in weeks. And a few days ago, my dad talked to George. He said they had an argument."

"That's what Emma said too."

Wide-eyed, Edison turned toward me. "Emma? You mean blonde, tattooed, motorcycle-riding, Quin-obsessed Emma? Since when do you talk to her?"

I laughed. "Since she showed up at my house yesterday. It's a long story."

He smirked. "I'll bet."

"Seriously, though . . . Quin would never—" I stopped myself. The past two days were undeniable evidence I couldn't be sure anymore what Quin would and wouldn't do. "I just can't imagine him saying anything that would hurt his dad."

Edison smiled. "Those were Elana's exact words. She wanted to come, but her mom wouldn't let her."

Outside the van, the crowd started to buzz. The girls in the front row screamed in unison, "Quin! We love you!"—but their voices were quickly drowned by another chant, "Traitor! Traitor! Traitor!"

Next to me, Edison shook his head in disbelief. "Ms. Knightley, I think your favorite B-list celebrity has arrived."

## CHAPTER FIFTEEN

# PAWN

A BLACK CAR with tinted windows pulled alongside the Zenigenic entrance. As the back door opened, Edison and I spoke at once.

"What the—?"

"Wow." For a moment, I felt like one of those silly girls in the front row. I could imagine them whispering, "He's so hot," before melting into screams and giggles.

"Is this an interview or an audition?" Edison deadpanned. Xander at his side, Quin waved to the crowd, unsmiling. Then he shook my father's hand as if he was a stranger, before taking his assigned position on one of the benches. I knew Edison was joking, but in a way, he was right. Quin seemed like an actor playing himself. All his rough edges concealed by a tailored gray suit and a superficial shine. Like a polished stone, he was smooth—and somehow, far less interesting. When he removed his dark sunglasses, tucking them inside his jacket, I was relieved. His eyes were uncertain.

I flipped the green switch on the van's control panel, and the screen came alive. Langley was still primping my dad, her mouse-like hands straightening his tie. "We go live in one minute," she said, her small voice audible through the nearby microphone. Behind her, security scurried to quiet the crowd.

Considering Quin with concern, my father asked him, "Are you sure about this?"

Quin didn't answer. He simply nodded. I scanned the crowd once more, finding Emma at the outskirts, standing on tiptoe for a better view. Nudging Edison, I pointed to her. "Guess you're not the only fan," he teased.

"Forty-five seconds," Langley warned. As she spoke, Xander sidled up to her, flashing a wicked grin. He handed her a stack of note cards, much like the ones in my father's hand. "What's this?" she asked, annoyed.

"These are the only questions Mr. McAllister will be answering today."

"Excuse me?" My father stood and faced Xander. "That was never our agreement."

"You want the interview, right?" Disregarding my father, Xander addressed Langley. "Or shall I contact Barbara Blake?" He held up his cell phone and began dialing.

Langley stopped Xander's fingers with a forceful hand on his wrist. "We want the interview."

"I thought so."

Langley passed the cards to my father. He flipped through them in disgust. "Sorry, Bill," she said. "There's no time to negotiate now. We can't lose this."

Edison and I locked eyes. "I don't know how he does it," he said. "And it really irks me sometimes. But I'm telling you, my dad is always right."

I watched Quin's face for signs of life, but he stared blankly at his hands folded on his lap, seemingly oblivious to the tension around him. It was hard to believe that, just a few hours ago, those hands were touching my knee. Looking from pretend Quin to my father, my stomach flip-flopped again. Zenigenic knew how to sell a product, and Quin was certainly packaged for sale. *But, what were they selling? And why was Quin playing the pawn?*

"In ten, nine, eight, seven, six, five, four, three, two. Cue Bill. Go Bill."

# CHAPTER SIXTEEN

# LIVE TV

"GOOD EVENING AND WELCOME to a special edition of *Eyes on the Bay*, your trusted source for Internet news. I'm Bill Knightley. Joining us for an exclusive interview tonight is Mr. Quin McAllister. Many of you will recognize Mr. McAllister as the exceptional young man who, in the early morning hours of January 15, saved the life of Zenigenic CEO, Xander Steele. Quin, it is a pleasure to have you on the show."

"Thank you. I'm happy to be here." Those were his words, but his tone was joyless.

My father glanced at the Zenigenic-approved note cards. "First, Quin, I think we're all dying—no pun intended—to know exactly what happened that evening."

Quin's laughter seemed canned, hollow. "I have to admit I was upset that night. As your viewers probably know, my dad is in prison in Los Angeles." My father nodded, but he seemed as surprised as I was at Quin's directness. "I haven't talked about it much—I'm sort of a private person—but my dad and I had a fight." Quin paused. *Was this on the note cards?* Xander was standing just off set. He appeared unconcerned.

"This fight . . . " My father began. "What was it about?"

Quin breathed audibly, fuzzing the microphone. Whatever was coming, there was no going back. "His innocence."

"Are you sure we should be talking about this, Quin?" *Definitely not on the note cards.* Xander's eyes narrowed in Langley's direction. She shrugged. As she mouthed to Xander, I read her lips, "Live TV."

"I want to talk about it," Quin answered. "For a long time, I believed my father was innocent. I blamed Zenigenic for Shelly's death. I blamed Zenigenic for a lot of things. But the truth is—what I now believe—my father is a murderer. That's who he was, is, and always will be. Zenigenic and Xander Steele are not responsible for his actions."

I felt like I might throw up. Next to me, Edison clutched my arm. "What is he doing?" he whispered. I couldn't answer.

My father's face drained of its color, but he held it together, thanks to Xander's note cards. "Well that's certainly an unexpected turn of events, Quin. You've had your own experience with EAMs as a member of the Guardian Force. How do you feel about Zenigenic's recent announcement regarding the production of a new drug?"

Quin smiled. His eyes didn't. "I'm excited. Really excited. Mr. Steele has shared some of the early research with me and assured me this new drug will have none of the unpleasant side effects of Emovere, Agitor, or Euphoractamine." *Unpleasant?* "In fact, Mr. Steele has been generous enough to offer me a position as a spokesperson and advisor for the new EAM campaign."

Edison gasped. "It's not real," I insisted. "It's an act. It has to be."

"I don't know, Lex. It seems pretty real. Besides, Quin's not much of an actor." He was right about that.

Flipping to the next card, my father asked, "What about Onyx? Certainly you've heard about the devastation Onyx has caused in the Bay Area. Just yesterday, there were three more gang shootings believed to be linked to this dangerous EAM."

"I've heard the reports. I think it's a tragedy that one of our trusted leaders, Augustus Porter, introduced this deadly substance to our streets. I can only hope he'll be behind bars with my dad, where he belongs."

My heart sunk, anchored by the weight—the cold unfairness—of Quin's words. "Emma was right," I told Edison. "He's totally lost it."

As I watched my father watching Quin, I knew he was making a decision. I hoped he wouldn't regret it. "Quin, as uncomfortable as it is, I have to ask. Is someone forcing you to say these things? Are you being paid off by Mr. Steele?"

Xander was storming toward Langley, signaling—hand across throat—to end the interview.

"Absolutely not," Quin replied. "Mr. Knightley, I think we both know you have your own ax to grind with Zenigenic. Maybe it's interfering with your objectivity."

Stonewalled by the response, the flawless deflection of his new protégé, Xander stopped walking. My father was equally stunned. "Thank you, Mr. McAllister. I appreciate your time this evening. *Eyes on the Bay* wishes you success in all your endeavors, and we will continue to follow your story. This is Bill Knightley, signing off for *Eyes on the Bay*. Good night."

## CHAPTER SEVENTEEN

# HERO ACT

"HOLY FREAKIN' COW!" I heard Edison react, but I was already out the van door, barreling toward Quin.

"What is wrong with you?" I shouted at him. Open-mouthed, he just stared at me.

"I told you to stay in the van," Langley snapped. "Bill, control your daughter."

"Lex, go back to the van." My father tried to usher me away.

"No, Dad. Not until I talk to Quin."

Quin looked at Xander, then back at me. "I don't have anything to say to you, Lex. Listen to your dad. Go back to the van."

"How could you do that to him?" I demanded, gesturing to my father. "After everything he did for you." I was so angry I could hardly think.

From behind me, Edison grabbed my arm. "C'mon, Lex. He's not worth it. He never was."

"Stay out of it, Eddie!" Quin yelled.

Edison stomped forward until he was standing chest to chest with Quin. "Or what?"

Their eyes locked in standoff—that is, until Valkov emerged from the line of security barricading the crowd. "Or you'll have to answer to me," he snuffed, his beady yellow-brown eyes laser-focused on his prey. Without any effort, he shoved Edison, knocking him to the ground.

"Gentlemen, please," Xander stepped in between them. "Let's remember where we are." I turned toward the crowd. They were captivated. Quin's adoring fans and his detractors were filming it all on their cell phones. The tiny screens shone like bright eyes watching us. Worst of all, Emma was looking at me with pity.

"That wasn't necessary," Quin chided Valkov as he extended his hand to Edison.

"I don't need your help, McAllister." Edison climbed to his feet and brushed himself off. "Whatever you've got going here, don't make me a part of your hero act."

Quin looked at me, and for a moment—*one thousand one, and it was gone*—his eyes softened. I waited for him to address me, but he didn't. Instead he spoke to Edison. "It's not an act. It's as real as the first time I knocked you out," he boasted. "Remember that, right? Pretty real."

"Whatever." Edison rolled his eyes.

"Lex." My father said my name like a command, his instruction clear.

"Fine," I said. "I'll go back to the van." Edison followed behind me. When I looked back—*how could I not?*— only the back of Quin's head was visible, the rest of him shielded by a pack of Zenigenic security. As the crowd cheered and jeered him, they whisked him inside the building.

# CHAPTER EIGHTEEN

# PLAYING EDDIE

BACK AT THE VAN, standing just out of view, were two surprise visitors. "Elana! Max! What are you doing here?"

Without answering me, Elana wrapped her arms around Edison. "We saw the whole thing. Are you okay?" she asked him.

Edison cradled her face between his hands and kissed her. "Better now, Red. But I thought you couldn't come."

"I decided I don't need my mom's permission. I'm not a little girl anymore." She winked at Edison. "Besides, I couldn't let Max go alone."

"What a jerk!" Max said distracted, still looking toward the Zenigenic entrance where Quin had disappeared. "The last time I saw him act like that I punched him in the jaw."

Elana and I exchanged a knowing look. "He's bluffing though, right?" She looked to me for a response.

I shrugged. As usual, my heart gave one answer, my mind another.

"Now you see what I mean." A familiar voice approached us from the crowd. Like the others, Emma considered me with expectation. I knew she was waiting for me to speak, to solve the unsolvable riddle of Quin. I said nothing.

"Well?" she demanded.

"What do you want me to say?"

She sneered at me, likely preparing some clever comeback. Then she sighed. "I care about him too, you know."

I nodded. "I think we're all just as confused as you are."

"Speak for yourself," Edison said, grinning. "I'm not confused. Am I the only one paying attention around here?"

We all turned toward him with inquiring eyes. One hand on her hip and an exacting expression, Elana spoke for us. "Explain, please."

Edison scanned our surroundings with caution. Most of the crowd had dispersed, leaving just a few stragglers to sort out the night's chaos. The two girls, heart-shaped sign in tow, stood a hopeful watch at the ropes, monitoring Zenigenic's door with fervent interest. My father, his brow furrowed, was talking to Langley as the cameramen dismantled their equipment. I hoped he wouldn't be too upset with me.

"Not out here," Edison concluded. "Get in." He held open the van's door and we piled in. Except for Emma. She stood alone, staring in at us—waiting for an invitation.

"Are you coming or not?" I asked her.

"Uh, yeah, I guess, if you're okay with it." I waved her inside.

Edison pulled the door shut behind her. "The first time Quin and I got in a fight my girlfriend, Chloe, was there." He glanced sheepishly at Elana. "I was such an idiot back then. I thought she liked him better. She was always bringing him food and feeling sorry for him. That night, I said something to Quin, something about his mom." Contrite, he met my eyes. "I didn't know. Anyway, Quin hit me really hard. I realized right then I didn't want to fight him, not in front of Chloe. So I just laid there—pretending he had knocked me out. It wasn't real."

"Are you sure Quin remembers all that?" Emma asked.

We all laughed. "Quin would never let me live that down. He called it *playing Eddie*, like playing possum."

"So if it's not real, then what?" Emma asked. "Where does that leave us?"

I sighed, wondering the same thing. But Edison grinned. "For right now, I think it leaves us sitting in this cold, smelly news van while Quin splits champagne and caviar with Xander Steele."

## CHAPTER NINETEEN

# INTUITION

THIRTY MINUTES LATER, my father sat beside me in that same smelly news van. Langley was at the wheel. Since we'd left Zenigenic, he'd said three words to me, "Scoot over, please." Langley, on the other hand, had plenty to say—about me ("What were you thinking?"), about Xander ("What a pompous twerp!"), but mostly about the 200,000 views my father's interview already garnered on their Internet-cable station. Somehow my father seemed less than thrilled.

"Can't shut you two up back there," Langley joked, taking a long swig of coffee. I saw her hazel eyes in the rearview mirror as she pretended to fiddle with her bangs. "Bill, why don't you take the rest of the night off? You deserve it." For at least the tenth time, my father flipped through Xander's notecards, then rested the stack on his thigh. I reached for them, curious about the questions he hadn't asked—but he snatched them away, frowning at me.

"Dad? Are you mad at me?" I asked.

He stared straight ahead. "We'll talk about it at home."

"Because I was just defending—"

"At. Home. Lex."

Langley cleared her throat. "I don't want to break up this party, but I just got a text from the station. There's been another gang shooting in Chinatown, multiple fatalities, probably Onyx-related. Do you mind if we . . . ?"

"It's fine," my father said flatly. Without looking at me, he added, "This time stay—"

"I know, I know. Stay in the van."

"Hold on," Langley advised before making a hairpin turn down Grant Avenue and flooring the accelerator, the green-roofed gates of Chinatown up ahead. We screeched to a stop near a police cruiser. Langley grabbed her handheld camera and started running. I saw the outline of two bodies lying in the street—one covered with a white sheet, the other attended by medical personnel. My father issued one last warning with his eyes before trotting toward them.

I covered my ears to block out the wailing sirens and peered out the back window up Grant Street, where the street lamps were casting halos of light on the sidewalk. It was nearing 8 p.m., just two hours until the curfew, but it was already deserted. Now that I was alone, the entire day stretched out behind me, scene by scene, each begging to be revisited. But I chose to focus on one . . . Quin's hand on my knee. Even more than Edison's story, Quin's touch—like an emotional shorthand—comforted me. The message, simple: It's me, Quin.

In the distance, I saw a figure—a man walking. He stayed just to the edge of the light, obscured by shadow. The closer he came, the more certain I was. I knew him . . . his lanky stride, his spiked hair. A block away from the van, he veered left. It was definitely String. I'd recognize that hair anywhere. Since their breakup, he had told Max he was *hangin'*—String's word—at the beach in Santa Cruz for a while, trying to earn a little money. I didn't tell Max, but I suspected *hangin'* was code for something illegal, immoral, or both. *What was he doing here? And did it have anything to do with Radley? Or that picture of George McAllister that Max found inside his backpack?* Within me, I felt pulled—the gentle tug of intuition—to follow.

Through the front window, I found my father interviewing witnesses, the light from the camera spotlighting the worries on his face. Leaving now would be wrong. Leaving now would be dangerous. But to stay—I watched as String disappeared from my sight—I just couldn't. I sent a quick text to my dad. Another lie, of course.

8:10 p.m. Getting late, curfew time. Got a ride home with Elana and Max just in case. See you in the morning.

I opened the console where Langley kept her gun—or as she liked to call it, her confidential informant. I tucked it into my waistband, pulled the hood of my sweatshirt over my head, and cracked the van door. *Act natural*, I told myself as one of the police officers stalked toward me. "Hey, you!" I froze, but he headed right past, not even noticing me. I crossed the street, ducked into the shadows, and started walking.

## CHAPTER TWENTY

# LONG SHOT

JUST AS I LOCATED String's Mohawk, he turned onto Montgomery Street and into the Financial District. Though most of the businesses reopened within the past year, a few remained frozen in time, their doors chained or boarded, marked with Resistance graffiti from before the city's evacuation. At this time of night, with the curfew looming, everyone was somewhere else. Aside from the faraway rumblings of car engines and the occasional, unnerving crack of gunfire, it was quiet. I stayed several blocks behind String, afraid he might hear the padding of my sneakers behind him. But he seemed focused on whatever or whoever lay ahead. *Was he following someone too?*

Further up ahead, breaking through the fog, was Coit Tower. Like many of the city's landmarks, restoring it wasn't a priority. I hadn't been back since my escape from Resistance headquarters, but Quin had. The last time he went, it was cordoned off with hazard tape, thick plywood blocking the door. Parts of the base had started to crumble away, leaving the structure vulnerable to collapse in an earthquake. When Quin told me, I was secretly relieved. I wanted it to be ours and no one else's.

String paused—his first moment of hesitation—at the bottom of the Filbert Stairs, the steep climb that led through the trees and right to the tower. Concealing myself behind a dumpster, I watched and waited. His head swiveled left, then right, then left again, searching. He retraced his steps and peered down the nearby alleyway, then returned to the stairs, where he sat down. He removed his cell phone from his pocket. Surrounded by silence, the smooth timbre of his voice chilled me.

"Hey man, I lost him."

"Um, sort of near Coit Tower."

"You can tell him that he's a lot harder to tail than his dad."

"Fine."

"Should I wait?"

"Okay. Later." String directed one last intent gaze up the stairs before he reversed course back down the hill. I watched his shadow get smaller and smaller until there was only sidewalk.

*Now what?* I whispered to myself. I sat on the curb and took out my cell phone. In the corner of the screen, the tiny battery flashed red. *Great.* As I texted Elana, a raccoon trotted past me, heading for the dumpster. He climbed its edge and disappeared inside.

*8:40 p.m. Are you still here in SF?*

*Elana: Back at home. Why?*

*8:41 p.m. Long story . . . but I need someone to pick me up by Coit Tower.*

*Elana: I wish I could help. My mom's watching me like a hawk since I left without telling her. Try Edison . . . and be careful!*

Another raccoon tumbled headfirst into the bin. I listened to the sounds of their scavenging, trying to ignore the persistent warning from my phone. *Battery low.* I composed another text, this time to Edison.

*8:45 p.m. Any chance you could come and get me?*

At 8:50 p.m., there was still no response. I wasn't surprised. Elana always complained Edison was a bad texter. "Is that even a thing?" Edison asked me once. At the time, I laughed with him, but now, I had to agree—*bad texter.*

By the time the third raccoon began his plundering, my screen had dimmed—my battery critically low—and I was running out of options. Max's mom would never let him take their car into the city, especially with the curfew looming. And my dad was probably gone by now. Just the thought of his face, his disappointment tangible, twisted my stomach in an impossible knot of guilt. I settled back onto the sidewalk, all but resigned to my fate. It was going to be a long night . . . unless. I scrolled do-or-die through my phone until I landed on my last hope. To say the least, she was a long shot.

## CHAPTER TWENTY-ONE

# CLEAN

EMMA TOSSED ME A HELMET and patted the seat behind her. Her mouth was moving, her words drowned by the throaty growl of her idling motorcycle. Hesitant, I stepped toward her—still surprised she agreed to come at all—and buckled the helmet tight under my chin. " . . . getting on or not? We don't have all night."

"Are you sure it's safe?" I asked, instantly cursing myself. *There I go again. Boring Lex.*

Emma rolled her eyes at me as expected. "Safer than sleeping out here." Then she revved the motor, laughing when I jumped. "It's 9:40. We gotta go." She tapped her watch.

"Coming," I said. Securing Langley's gun inside my waistband, I tried to imitate the graceful leg swing Emma had perfected. Mine was not so effortless.

"Are you alright back there?" Emma snickered as I scooted into place. The bike purred beneath me, a momentarily contented beast.

"I'm fine."

"Hold on tight—I like to drive fast." *Shocking.* I locked my arms around the soft leather of her jacket, squeezing until I felt the knobs of her rib cage. "Not *that* tight, Knightley. I still need to breathe."

The first part of the ride was the worst and the best. Engine roaring, we careened straight downhill, Emma's blonde tendrils blowing back in my face. At the bottom, she let out a loud whoop. I stayed quiet. But inside, I was secretly thrilled. It was a little bit like flying—with a deranged pilot at the helm. We took a hard turn to the right, and the weight of the whole world leaned with us. With ease, Emma steadied the bike, commanding it forward, a marvel for someone so small.

"How was that?" she asked, her voice breathy with exhilaration.

"Fine."

"Fine?" She was incredulous. "Seriously?"

I smiled to myself. "Okay, it was awesome," I admitted. "Terrifying, but awesome."

Within ten minutes, we whizzed by the first sign for the Golden Gate Bridge. *MILITARY CHECKPOINT AHEAD, CURFEW IN EFFECT: PREPARE TO STOP.* The bridge itself was invisible, cloaked behind a dense layer of fog. Emma's watch read 9:50.

"Do you think we'll make it?" I yelled into the wind.

She answered with a forceful turn of the throttle, sending us past the tollbooths in a blur. It seemed we were alone on the bridge, a white cloak shrouding the highway. Though I couldn't see them, I knew at its end, waiting, were the watchful, red eyes of the checkpoint. "Slow down," I cautioned as we approached, even as Emma went faster and faster, speeding into an opaque oblivion.

In the fog, everything around us was formless, unseen—until it wasn't. Light poles appeared alongside us, as if from nowhere. A gull swooped in from another world. A man materialized, hand raised, cautioning us with his palm.

"Stop!"

Emma squeezed the brakes hard—the bike screeching and skidding to a halt inches from his boots. The soldier's mouth remained set in an unforgiving line. "This is a mandatory checkpoint. Are you aware of the speed limit?" It was the sort of question that had no right answer. His partner hung behind him, waiting for instruction. "Get over here, Greenhorn."

"Yes, sir—uh, Commander." The soldier followed orders, shuffling over toward us.

"Sorry," I muttered to them, offering an apologetic smile. Unaffected, Emma removed her helmet, shaking out her hair. "We were—" I began.

"Don't bother explaining. I need both of you to step off the motorcycle. We're going to have to test you."

"Test us for what?" Emma asked.

With a nudge from his partner, the greenhorn handed her a laminated card with a list of banned EAMs. "Have either of you used any of the drugs on this list?"

"It's in your best interest to fess up now," the commander added.

"Of course not," Emma said.

"Fine. Have it your way." The commander shook his head in disdain. "Your reckless behavior would strongly suggest otherwise."

I protested with a lie. "Someone was chasing us."

"Oh really?"

"He followed us out of the city," I added, waiting for Emma to back me up. She said nothing.

"You were running for your lives?" His voice was flat, unconvinced. He put his hand above his eyes, peering out from under it, as if he was looking out through the fog to the horizon. "And where is this mysterious culprit?" When neither of us responded, he reached inside his pocket and withdrew a small plastic applicator, then handed it to the greenhorn. "Who's first?"

"I'll go," I volunteered, extending my arm toward the young soldier. He swiped the applicator across my wrist several times, then looked at Emma's forearm with expectation. Wrinkling her forehead in annoyance, she rolled up her jacket sleeve.

"Guardian Force," he observed stoically, considering her tattoo. Emma gave him a blank face. On his forearm was a matching mark, but its borders were red and swollen, as if newly inked.

"When did you serve?" I asked him, trying not to stare. It was becoming nearly impossible to believe the Guardian Force was really disbanded.

"I just—"

"Greenhorn! Zip it!" The commander sidled over to him, placing a heavy hand on his shoulder. Unlike his inexperienced partner, his Guardian Force tattoo was well worn—there was a thick, circular scar in its center, similar to the one on my side. "Do your job," he hissed, his breath like steam in the cold air. Then with a sardonic smile, he addressed Emma. "Pretty tough to quit Emovere, huh?"

Scowling at his forearm, she shot back. "You would know." I swallowed a gasp. The young soldier watched Emma from the corners of his eyes, as if she was a sleeping tiger. Nonplussed, the commander stepped toward her. He leaned down until his face was inches from hers.

"What's your name?" Emma stared straight ahead—eyes to the middle of his chest. "Your name," he demanded. Her jaw tensed, but she made no sound. *Stalemate.*

The greenhorn consulted the applicators in his hands. Mine was a bright shade of green. He nodded at me. "Clean."

"Does that mean we can go?" I asked, rushing to put my helmet on. The cool blade of dread pressed to the back of my neck was too persistent to ignore. My question remained unanswered. Both the commander and the soldier stared at the second applicator as it turned from white to pink, then to a vibrant red—the kind of red that meant *stop*, the kind of red that meant *danger*, the kind of red that meant Emma was most definitely *not* clean.

## CHAPTER TWENTY-TWO

# START'ER UP

"YOUNG LADY, you are under arrest." The commander was smug, that red strip a mere formality, confirmation of what he seemed to know all along. *How could I have missed it?* "Put your hands behind your back," he told Emma.

In the space between us, Emma's fingertips twitched like live wires. I held my breath, waiting for whatever was coming. The commander shoved the greenhorn toward her. "Cuff her." His eyes trained on Emma, the soldier took a methodical step forward, then another. Her move, when it finally came, was sudden, unexpected, charged like a spark of lightning. She grabbed at my waistband. The gun!

"No!" I yelled at her as I reached for it too—and so did the greenhorn. But our hands only clutched air. Then I felt the barrel pressed against my temple, the heat of Emma's body behind my back. I gulped. Warm, bitter bile rose up into the back of my throat.

"Don't move." Emma's voice was ice at my ear, smooth and biting cold. "If you move, I'll kill her." *Her. Me.* "I'm going to get on my bike and ride away." I imagined she was looking up at the commander with indifference—matching his deliberate stare. The greenhorn was less focused, his gaze traveling from Emma to the commander and back again. "And you're going to let me," she said. "You're both going to forget you ever saw us." *Us?*

Emma jabbed at me with the gun, nudging me toward her motorcycle. "Get on. You're driving." It wasn't a question, so I swallowed my words—*I've never driven a motorcycle before*—and mounted the bike. She followed alongside me, the gun's barrel never far from my head.

"Think about what you're doing," the commander cautioned. "You won't get away."

"Start'er up," Emma instructed, completely oblivious to his threat. *Must be Emovere*, I thought. *It would certainly explain a lot.*

I considered the mechanical beast in front of me. *How hard could it be?* I turned the key in the ignition. Silence. *Apparently, harder than I thought.*

"Ugh," Emma groaned in frustration. Keeping the gun pressed firmly to my skull, she pointed to a button near the handlebars. "The ignition switch—you have to press it." Following her lead, I brought the engine rumbling to life, its motoric heartbeat reverberating through me. Emma nodded, satisfied.

"Put your weapons on the ground and kick them to me," she directed. Both men complied, sending their guns scuttling toward her feet. "Now turn around. Slowly." Like a music box figurine, the commander began a slow spin until his broad shoulders faced us, but the greenhorn's feet stayed firmly planted. Only one of his hands was visible. It made me nervous. "Move," Emma said blandly, unconcerned.

The soldier's face was serene. "Alright, alright," he agreed, his voice equally as calm. His flat tone and dead eyes made me wonder if I was the only *clean* one around here. With a lightning-fast step, he lunged for Emma and stabbed a liquid-filled syringe into her leg. She barely noticed, hardly flinched. As he tried to depress the plunger, she kicked him in the stomach, sending him flying into the commander. Both of them toppled like felled trees. By the time they scrambled to their knees and the commander retrieved his lost weapon, Emma was on the back of the bike screeching at me. "Go! Go! Go!"

Panic flooded me, leaving my hands and feet as heavy as lead. "I don't know how!" I screamed back at her, instantly breathless with the effort of my hysteria.

The commander stumbled toward us, regaining his balance. He aimed the barrel at Emma, its lethal black eye trained on her chest. "Drop the gun or I'll—"

Emma fired.

Silenced, the commander crumpled to the ground. The center of his uniform began to darken.

She didn't even look at me—just pushed me off the bike and pulled the still-full syringe from her thigh, discarding us both on the highway. While I sat there, shell-shocked, the greenhorn discharged shot after shot into the drifting white clouds until his gun was empty. The bike's steady snarl mocked him long after Emma disappeared into the fog.

## CHAPTER TWENTY-THREE

# GONE

"IS HE DEAD?" I asked. The greenhorn didn't answer. He was hunched over the commander's body, pressing his fist, wet and red, against the wound on his chest. A soft gurgling came from the commander's mouth. I thought of Elliot, the unnatural arch of his body on the library floor, the first death I'd seen (caused) in real life. Somehow, I felt responsible for this one too. After all, I'd assembled the pieces—Langley's gun, Emma, the race to outrun the curfew—and set them in motion. I watched the commander's chest, waiting for the constant rise and fall, but it was stiff, still.

I heard the rumble of a vehicle in the distance. The greenhorn stood, wiping his hands across his uniform. He turned back toward the bridge—where the bridge should've been. The massive structure once again had vanished in the fog. Gone. Just like Emma.

Finally, he looked at me. He already seemed older, hardened. "Who was that girl?" he demanded. "Where is she going?"

"I don't know," I mumbled. At least part of that was true. When he glared back at me with obvious disbelief, I felt grateful to hear the roar of the approaching engine. It wasn't a police car or an ambulance as I'd expected, but a military jeep that barreled out from the fog, pulling to a stop just short of the checkpoint. Four soldiers emerged from inside it. After a hushed conversation with the greenhorn, they surrounded the commander's body, cocooned him in black plastic, and carried him away, sliding the corpse into the back of the jeep.

One of the soldiers—a tall, dark-skinned woman with thick, black eyebrows—scoured the scene, collecting and bagging a spent shell casing and our discarded EAM test strips. She walked through the commander's blood without pause, leaving a trail of macabre footprints behind her as she approached the greenhorn.

"Where is it?" she asked him. Though her voice was almost robotic, she managed to sound threatening. It was a relief she didn't acknowledge my presence.

"It's here. Somewhere." He gestured around him. "I saw her throw it before she drove away."

She considered him with contempt. "What were you thinking letting her leave like that?" I pretended not to hear her.

The greenhorn opened his mouth to respond, but stopped and turned to me instead. "You have it, don't you?" He stalked toward me and grabbed my wrist, pulling me up from the ground.

"What are you talking about?"

"You know what." Leading me by my forearm, he shoved me against the jeep, his hands pulling and prodding at my jacket pockets.

"Get off me!" I shrugged out of his clutches in a huff.

"Stand down, Greenhorn." The female soldier stepped in between us. Her face seemed to soften with a promise of understanding, but I didn't trust it. "Young lady, we are looking for something *very* important." She spoke to me like a child. "It's essential that we get it back. It looks like a needle, the kind a doctor would use to give you a shot."

I nodded at her, playing along. "I saw it," I told her. "The girl . . . she rode off with it still stuck in her leg." The woman scowled at the greenhorn.

"She's lying," he said.

"Go ahead. Search me." I reached into my jacket pockets, pulled them inside out, then spread my arms wide.

As the greenhorn eyed me eagerly, a methodical voice from their walkie-talkies broke the silence. "Incoming vehicle with civilians. Looks like a news van. *Eyes on the Bay*." Dad! I knew he would be disappointed in me, but the thought of him was an undeniable comfort.

The female soldier shook her head disapprovingly at the greenhorn and walked toward him. She didn't seem nervous, but her pace was quick. Before she began her staccato march to the jeep, she passed him a plastic container with several cylindrical slots. I pretended not to see her, but I knew exactly what it was. Quin had called it a field pack.

From the door, she tossed him a camouflage raincoat to cover his bloodstained uniform. "Put this on. And get back to work." As the jeep accelerated, heading in Emma's direction, she leaned out the window. "We'll find her. Just make sure this one gets home safely." I heard the greenhorn mutter to himself, but he said nothing to me. He assumed his position, guarding the checkpoint like a concrete pillar, his face just as stony as the rest of him.

My feelings were a strange contradiction—uneasy, but elated—like I'd been standing just out of the path of a tornado, opening my eyes to see the world flattened on either side of me. *What just happened?* Letting out a long, slow breath, I tucked my pockets back into my jacket, composed myself, and waited.

First came the yellow glow from the headlights, like twin halos submerged in the clouds. When the nose of the *Eyes on the Bay* news van broke through the last layer of whiteness, I was grateful to see only my father inside. "That's my dad," I told the soldier. "He can give me a ride."

My father blinked a few times at the sight of me, but kept his what-must've-been utter shock muffled. As the soldier approached the van's open window, he flashed his press pass, one of the few credentials allowed an exemption to the curfew.

"Good evening, sir." There was nothing pleasant about the greenhorn's pleasantries. "Do you know this young lady?"

"She's my daughter." My father raised his eyebrows at me. "Is she in some sort of trouble?"

The soldier didn't answer. He signaled me toward the van with a quick nod. "Coming," I called out to him. I wanted to run, but I forced myself to fast walk instead.

"Are we free to go?" my father asked when I was buckled into the passenger seat. I finally removed Emma's helmet from my head and tucked it between my feet.

"Make sure I don't see you again," the soldier warned me. "Or your friend."

"She's not my friend." I stared straight ahead. If eyes were windows, I didn't want him looking inside mine. "And you won't."

My stern-faced father quietly seethed until all we could see of the checkpoint were its tiny flashing red lights. "Alexandra Grace Knightley, I don't even know where to start with you. What happened back there? I thought you were getting a ride with your friends. And—"

I stopped him. "Dad, I know you're angry."

"Angry? Angry?" His voice grew louder with repetition. "That's putting it mildly."

"Okay, furious then. But you can yell at me later. There's something I have to show you first." I slipped my fingers inside the lining of the motorcycle helmet, carefully palming its contents. I opened my hand and displayed the syringe—still filled with clear liquid—to my father.

"What is it?"

"I'm not sure. But I think it's important." I pointed to the base of the plunger. It was marked with a small metallic *Z*.

## CHAPTER TWENTY-FOUR

# PEACE OFFERING

MY FATHER SAT ACROSS from me at the kitchen table, the syringe encased in a plastic bag between us. It was like a bomb rigged for explosion. Since Emma fled into the fog, time had run together, night blurring into day, into night again. Outside, it was nearly dark. The promise of sleep tugged at my eyelids as I watched my father's head droop—down, down, down—then snap back up again. He slept right through a text from Elana asking if I'd made it home alright. *Sort of,* I answered. *Will explain later.*

"Are you still mad at me?" I finally said aloud. My father's head in mid-droop, he didn't answer. "Dad?"

"Huh? Is she here?"

I shook my head. "Not yet. It's at least a six-hour drive from L.A." I glanced at my watch. "Soon though."

"Was I sleeping?" He wiped a spot of drool from the corner of his mouth.

"A little." I pointed to the cup of coffee on the table, long since cooled. "I made that for you." *A peace offering.* I was encouraged when he smiled a little.

"Have you been online yet?" he asked.

I nodded. "I've been checking all day. There's nothing. Like it never happened."

"And the interview?"

My stomach flip-flopped, thinking of my exchange with Quin. "Almost a million views. They're calling Xander a marketing genius."

"Hmph. I could think of a few other things to call him."

I chuckled. "Dad, I know I've already said it a hundred times, but—"

"I know." His tone was harsh. "You're sorry." *Still mad, apparently.* "I've just never seen you act so reckless. First the interview, then the bridge. Then, you confess that you've teamed up with Augustus!" He made the name sound vulgar. Even so, it was a relief not to have that secret anymore. "I always thought you were more like me, rational, with a good head on your shoulders, but this . . . " He finished the sentence with a disappointed shake of his head.

I rolled my eyes, rankled by what he didn't say. "I know I disappointed you, but I'm not perfect. And I'm not Mom. You don't know everything about me. You missed a lot—remember?" His jaw hardened, but he said nothing, leaving an irritated silence buzzing between us.

Ten minutes later, the slam of a car door abruptly ended his brooding. I jumped to my feet. "She's here," I announced. My father was already out the door. I hung back in the foyer, suddenly anxious, but Carrie's wave to me from the driveway compelled me outside.

"Lex! Bill!" Her cheeks flushed when she smiled, but there was no mistaking the melancholy in her eyes. She wiped tears from under her wire-rimmed glasses and sighed. "It's been too long." *A year and a half to be exact.* The last time I saw Carrie she was newly hired as a consultant for the government-sponsored Guardian Force Rehabilitation Program, designed to help the recruits displaced after our assault on Alcatraz. Since then, all my texts went unanswered. It felt strange seeing her here at my house again. Familiar and strange, a ghost from a past life. She looked exactly the same though—mousy brown hair, petite frame, kind eyes. I was the one who had changed.

When I hugged her, I thought only of my mother. For a moment, the weight of memory pressed hard and heavy against my chest, squeezing me with the sudden ferocity I still hadn't grown accustomed to. "I'm so glad you're here," I managed to say.

"Me too. I can't believe you found me."

I pulled away from her, finding my breath again. "Blame the nosy reporter." I gestured to my father with an ironic smile. It had taken all of his persuasive powers to convince Carrie to make the drive. *They're using a new drug*—a scientist to her core, that's what finally got her. But even then, she hung up, still uncertain, only to call back an hour later and give her reluctant promise.

"Ahem." My father straightened up tall and pulled his shoulders back. "Journalist," he corrected. "Ms. Donovan, it's nice to see you again. Thank you for coming all this way."

Carrie shrugged. "Of course. I must admit our discussion left me intrigued." She lowered her voice. "Intrigued but nervous. I've been trying to stay as far away from EAMs as possible since..." Her eyes scanned the empty, shadowed street.

"Maybe we should talk inside," I suggested.

"Good idea," she agreed. As we followed my father into the house, Carrie put an arm around my shoulder and whispered. "You look so . . ." *Tired. Confused. Overwhelmed.* "Grown up," she whispered. "Your mother would be proud."

* * *

The syringe was empty now—what was left of its contents in a glass vial pressed between Carrie's careful fingers. We sat next to her on adjacent stools at the long table in the garage, all my mother's lab equipment humming with purpose again.

"What do you think?" my father asked. "Is it Onyx?" He hovered over her shoulder, impatient as a schoolboy.

"Umm . . ." Carried turned the vial over and over again in her hand, sending the clear liquid rushing back and forth. "I don't know what it is, but I can tell you what it's not." My father and I both nodded eagerly. "It's not Onyx. It's not Emovere, and it's not Agitor."

"Eupho?" I asked.

She shook her head. "No, but it's not entirely dissimilar. Euphoractamine contains a high dose of phenylethylamine, a chemical that enhances dopamine production. There are traces of that in here, but there's also something else." Carrie pointed to a beaker containing a small sample of the unknown substance she had analyzed. "I'll need to do more tests, but it has the properties of oxytocin."

My father raised his eyebrows. "Oxy-who?"

Carrie and I both snickered. "C'mon, Dad. You've heard of it. The love hormone."

His blank face reddened slightly. "Clearly, I'm not the scientist in the family."

"Lex is right. But oxytocin isn't just about love. It promotes relaxation and trust—and inhibits aggressive behaviors."

"That makes sense," I said. "Emma definitely needed a good dose of that." In my head, I saw the commander stagger, clutch at his chest, then fall. All morning, I couldn't stop seeing it.

"Emma?" Carrie asked.

I nodded. "She's the one we told you about, the girl on the bridge."

"Emma Markum," my father offered. "You may have heard of her. She was in the news a few months ago during the McAllister trial." *McAllister trial.* To me, the words were jarring and cruel, like ripping up a favorite photograph. But my father sounded detached. Maybe it was the journalist in him.

Carrie returned the vial to a small rack on the table. Drumming her fingers against its surface, she twisted her mouth uncomfortably, as if the words inside it were stinging ants. "Emma Markum," she finally repeated, her fingers now silent. "I know Emma Markum. She's the reason I quit the rehab program. She's the reason I've been in hiding."

## CHAPTER TWENTY-FIVE

# DAMAGED

MY FATHER AND I stayed still, waiting for her to continue. Next to me, Carrie's wavering was almost tangible. "I'm not sure I should tell you anything more," she said, giving my father a weak smile. "Am I off the record here?"

"Of course."

Carrie removed a folder from her bag and pushed it toward us. "I wanted you to see this." Inside was a stack of printed computer screen shots. The bottom of every page was marked *United States Government, Guardian Force Rehabilitation Program* and stamped with their not-so-subtle logo, a phoenix.

"What are these?" I asked.

Carrie leafed through the folder and withdrew a single page. "Evidence," she answered.

"Of what?" I studied the page carefully, with my father reading along. It was titled: *Recovery Analysis.*

Carrie pointed to the first column, where hundreds of names were circled in red. "These are the recruits I evaluated six months post-Alcatraz. The government asked me to determine the extent to which their brains recovered from EAMs." She traced her finger down, then stopped at Legacy 413. *Red circle.* "This is Emma." She scanned the page and tapped another name, Greenhorn 387. "And this is Peter Radley." *Another red circle.*

"Why are their names marked?" my father asked. Carrie frowned at his question. Whatever the reason, I knew it wasn't good.

"The red circle indicates an incomplete recovery. Essentially, a damaged brain." My stomach churned at the familiarity of her words, the day she showed me Elliot's brain, the shrunken mass of coils irreversibly damaged by Emovere.

"Is it permanent?" I could guess at the answer, but I wanted to hear her say it.

"Probably. We administered repeated trials of Resilire, but your mother always knew it wouldn't work on everyone."

"You said Emma was the reason you quit."

"Mm-hmm." The reluctance in her voice convinced me that she had shared this with no one else.

"Why?" I asked.

Carrie paged through the file and handed me a letter dated December 28, 2041. Her signature was at the bottom. "It was happening again," she said. "And I couldn't stop it."

"It? What do you mean?" Carrie said nothing, so I looked to her letter for my answer.

*Dear General Maze,*

> *As we discussed, I have grave concerns about your recommendation for Legacy 413. Returning to military service in any capacity would be a serious risk to her and the public. Legacy 413 has not responded favorably to psychopharmacological treatment. Even with the highest doses of Resilire, the changes observed in her brain, specifically a diminished frontal lobe and supramarginal gyrus, have persisted.*
>
> *At this time, she remains particularly susceptible to EAM dependence. She is more likely to engage in risk-taking behavior, to display minimal empathy and concern for others, and to be at increased risk for violence. Legacy 413 shares my concerns and has asked to be dismissed from further consideration.*

"So Emma wanted out?" Carrie gave a solemn nod. I tried to ignore the pesky worm of sympathy that was already busy burrowing its way into my heart.

"Out of what exactly?" my father asked.

"I can't say for sure, but Emma told me that she was approached about joining a special military unit, one where the damage to her brain wouldn't matter—and could even be an asset. Emma wasn't the only one they wanted."

I pointed to the red-circled Greenhorn 387. "Radley?"

"Yes and all the others. All the damaged ones. Against our recommendation, most of them left rehab early to join after they were recruited."

When I looked at my father—his eyes wide with an amalgam of fear and outrage—I saw everything I felt. "It sounds a lot like . . ." I couldn't say it, but my father could.

"The Guardian Force."

Carrie didn't say yes or no. She didn't have to.

"And Emma? What happened with her?" I asked.

Still quiet, Carrie hung her head. "I thought I was doing the right thing," she lamented. "But now . . ."

I patted her arm. "I'm sure you did the best you could. You couldn't have known what would happen."

Carrie produced another paper from her bag, her letter of resignation, dated January 1, 2042. In it, there was no mention of her concerns, only her admission she had acted inappropriately with a recruit, Legacy 413. "It was written for me," she explained. "I was forced out. And I've been running from them ever since." I had convinced myself that Carrie didn't want to be found, that she wanted to forget me, my mother, and everything that happened here. But somehow, hearing the truth was even worse. I could feel my father twitching on the stool next to me, desperate to ask the question, so I did it for him.

"What did you do?"

She answered fast, expelling it all with one breath. "I helped Emma escape."

## CHAPTER TWENTY-SIX

# VISITOR

THE NEXT MORNING, we were back in the lab with Carrie rehashing the story of Emma's escape, as she labored over my mother's equipment. The sound of a motor idling outside the garage interrupted us. Kneeling on a stool, I peeked through one of the tiny windows.

"It's String." There was blatant dread in my voice. My father groaned. After revealing the latest of String's suspicious behavior, I knew his trust was wearing thin, nearly threadbare. Mine had unraveled long ago.

"String?" Carrie murmured, confused.

"Max's ex."

She tried to conceal her surprise with a flattened, "Oh."

"Among other things," my father added. "What do you think he wants?"

I shrugged. With String, it was anybody's guess. Shifting uncomfortably on her stool, Carrie's stare was fixed on the door. "Don't worry. I'll get rid of him." I slipped outside, hoping it would be that easy.

"Got company?" String asked, gesturing to Carrie's vehicle parked in the driveway. He was leaning against the side of another car—his, apparently—a sleek black sedan that practically screamed he was up to no good. Familiar dark sunglasses masked his eyes.

"Is that stolen?" I countered, sidestepping his question.

"Borrowed." One corner of his mouth turned up in an ironic half smile.

"My dad's friend from the station came over. They're working on a story together."

"Working?" String chuckled. "I thought your dad would be running the show after his performance with Quin."

"You saw it?"

"Who didn't? Your ex-boyfriend is quite the celebrity." He perched his sunglasses atop his head, revealing himself—only the parts he wanted me to see. The rest he kept hidden, like his Internet-friend, Peter Radley. "Speaking of ex-boyfriends, have you seen Maximillian?"

"Not since the other day. He's not staying here anymore. You know that." He nodded, disappointed. "Besides, he said you were in Santa Cruz." I studied his newly unveiled eyes for any sign of an impending lie.

"I was." Didn't even blink. "Came back yesterday."

"What were you doing there?" I asked, pushing my luck.

He held out his milky white arms. "Perfecting my tan. Can't you tell?"

I rolled my eyes at him. "I should probably head back inside. I'll let you know if I hear from Max."

His shoulders slumped like a scolded puppy, but his eyes were mischievous. "I guess I no longer warrant an invite inside Fort Knightley. Are you hiding Quin in there?"

I tried not to show it—I knew I was blushing—but his question caught me off guard. With String's spotlight on me, a sharp realization cut through my discomfort. He wasn't here looking for Max. "Why do you care?" I asked, my voice harsher than I intended.

He shrugged, then gave my arm a playful punch. "Easy there, killer. I was just teasing." And for a moment, I almost believed him. "See ya later, Lex." As he opened the door and crouched down low to swing his lanky legs inside, his sunglasses fell from their perch and landed at my feet.

I retrieved them from the ground, brushing them off with my T-shirt. "I hope you didn't scratch your man-of-mystery glasses. That would be a real tragedy." He grinned, taking the glasses and returning them to his face.

He preened a little, then took a quick glance in the mirror. "Lucky for me, my image remains intact." As the window began its push-buttoned ascent, I spied his other hand on the passenger seat, palm down on his jacket, covering a white label. It was the kind of *HELLO, MY NAME IS* badge my mother always detested wearing at every conference she attended. I couldn't really see it through his fingers. Lucky for me—I silently mocked String—I didn't need to. I knew exactly where it was from.

* * *

The first and only time I visited Green Briar Recovery Center was with my mother, their newest and most famous, part-time counselor. Over a year had passed since the bombs exploded in Chicago, then New York, Boston, Los Angeles, Miami, and Dallas. Most of the patients at Green Briar were injured in the L.A. bombings or addicted to Emovere—or both.

After I visited and vowed never to return, the name irked me, nettling at me every time my mother said it aloud. *Recovery Center.* Green Briar wasn't the kind of place where anybody recovered. You went there because somebody decided you were beyond recovery. Your pieces were irretrievably broken. When I saw the row of tiny printed redwood trees under String's finger, I recognized them instantly.

While I drove, my father continued reading Zenigenic's latest press release, his computer in his lap, cell phone in hand. "'*We are not at liberty to disclose the location of his treatment, but rest assured, Peter Radley is receiving the best care possible.*' That's a quote from Xander's spokeswoman, Gina Tan."

*Best care possible.* I rolled my eyes.

"You really think he's at Green Briar?" my father asked. At my insistence, we were on our way there, none of us quite sure who or what we would find.

"Maybe. It might explain why String had a visitor's pass."

"Green Briar," Carrie repeated, almost to herself. "I've been trying to figure out why that name sounded so familiar. Wasn't that little boy taken there? The one who—?"

"Yes." I cut her off mid-sentence. If I let her finish, I knew I would have to tell them I was there that day. And it was enough to live it once.

I quickly changed the subject. "What was Radley like?" I asked, eyeing Carrie in the rearview mirror. In a mere forty-eight hours, SFTV had discovered his twisted poem on social media, analyzed it, and immortalized it.

"Angry." Her eyes seemed far away, but she answered instantly, as if she was already thinking it. "But I didn't know him that well. He was assigned to another specialist. We were told he was one of the first Guardian Force recruits to receive Onyx. He'd been taking it for at least six months when he entered rehab. Truthfully, at the time, I expected worse."

"Do you know when he left?"

Carrie shook her head. "I didn't hear anything until Quin's dad was arrested. That's when I saw the video of Peter speaking at one of those rallies. And Emma too. I was shocked." *That makes two of us.* "I wanted to contact you," she said, squeezing my shoulder. "I was worried about you—and Quin. But I couldn't. I was so afraid they were still looking for me." Her voice was a choked whisper. "Still am."

"It's okay," I assured her. Carrie hadn't pressed about me and Quin. She approached everything like a scientist—precise, exacting, patient. I liked that about her.

"We're here," I told them, slowing the car to a crawl. The entrance to Green Briar was just at the edge of Muir Woods, where the ancient redwoods extended themselves in a perpetual reach toward the sky. The sign was the same—a sleek stone that was intended to camouflage but somehow looked out of place. Just as I had on my first and only visit, Carrie read the inscription aloud:

*Like a tree, our branches break, and we grow strong again.*

"Sounds promising," she said with a smirk.

"Uh-oh." My father pointed to another sign just beyond the entrance. *No media allowed.* "I'd say they wouldn't recognize me, but after that interview last night . . . "

I laughed. "I think you said goodbye to your anonymity, Dad."

Nervous, Carrie cleared her throat. "I-I can't go in. Of course, he'd recognize me, and—"

I kept driving past, then pulled the car off the road, pinecones crackling under the wheels. "I'll go alone."

## CHAPTER TWENTY-SEVEN

# CAGED

THE SMELL OF GREEN BRIAR—bleach and pine needles—knocked me back. Certain places, no matter how dull or how ordinary on the outside, are bewitched. They're portals to the past. Just one step inside, within the snap of a finger, you're transported back in time. As I closed the door behind me, I felt myself slowly becoming the girl that I was. Then. Before. No matter how much time stretched beyond it, my mother's death was an indelible line of demarcation.

"May I help you?" The young woman behind the desk addressed me without looking up from her computer tablet. I suppressed a gasp when I saw Quin's face on the screen. She was watching a video of the interview.

"I'm here to visit a patient." I hovered at the edge, then dove head first. "Peter Radley."

She flinched a little, then pressed pause and directed her eyes toward me. "Sorry. I shouldn't be watching that." Glancing down, she snickered at me conspiratorially, on the screen a frozen close-up of Quin. "I just wish a guy like that would save my life."

I smiled back at her. "I know exactly what you mean, Julie." She looked befuddled as I pointed to her name tag.

Chuckling at herself, she asked, "So who did you say you were here to see?"

There was no going back now. "Peter Radley."

I watched her face flush and her eyes blink, blink, and blink again. She gave a small, almost indiscernible shake of her head and swallowed hard. "We don't have any patients by that name."

"Right." Of course, it wouldn't be that easy, but at least she was a really bad liar. "Do you usually have visitors sign in?"

She gestured toward the tablet on her desk. "It's all computerized."

"Could I take a look?"

With a tap of her finger, Quin's handsome face disappeared, a far less exciting spreadsheet in its place. "This is from the last few days," she said. I scanned the thirty or so names one by one until I found it.

*9:00 a.m. Max Powers*

"Were you here this morning?" I asked her.

She nodded. " Since 8. Why?"

"I was just wondering if you remembered my friend, Max. He was here around 9 today." I watched her face carefully, hoping she was as harmless as she seemed.

Her eyes brightened, and I was relieved. "Uh, you mean tall, dark, and gorgeous Max with the great hair?" She pantomimed String's slick Mohawk perfectly. "He's quite the charmer."

I gritted my teeth, grinning through my uneasiness. "He certainly is."

"We don't usually have anybody that young here for the tour." She gestured to a group of adults huddled in the far corner. They weren't speaking. A few pretended to consider the portrait of Green Briar's founder looming large on the wall behind them. The others traded vacant stares. "It starts in five minutes, if you're interested," she added.

I shrugged, not wanting to seem too eager. "Sure."

Julie reached into the desk drawer and produced a visitor's pass. In the white space beneath the row of tiny printed redwood trees, I wrote a name: *Emma Markum.*

* * *

"Welcome to Green Briar." Hamilton, our middle-aged tour guide, offered a thin, condescending smile, ushering us like a troop of wayward ducklings down the first long hallway toward the elevator. "As I'm sure you all know, Green Briar is *the* premiere treatment center specializing in emotion-altering medication dependence. We offer several state-of-the-art programs designed to assist in overcoming the effects of Euphoractamine, Emovere, Agitor, and even . . . " He lowered his voice to a dramatic whisper. "Onyx." The woman next to me gasped. She muffled her shock with a hand to her mouth, but Hamilton frowned at her anyway. Her name tag read *Jeannie.*

"We'll be visiting the third floor," Hamilton advised us as we crammed inside. "It's where most of the action takes place. The treatment and evaluation rooms are there, and I'll show you an empty model of a patient's living quarters. Right now, most of our patients are housed on the tenth floor, so don't expect to see many of them out and about." *Tenth floor.* I filed that information away for later. As we traipsed out of the elevator, two by two, Jeannie nudged me.

"Who are you here for?" she asked. I disguised my annoyance with a polite smile.

"A friend," I murmured, hoping she wouldn't press for more.

"My daughter's about your age." *Leave me alone.* "She's why I'm here. Well, her and Emovere." I nodded, avoiding eye contact. I had purposefully fallen behind the rest of the group, hoping to slip back to the elevator, and I didn't need company.

With a sidelong glance through the small windows, I surveyed the treatment rooms as we passed. All empty with a circle of chairs at the center. "Keep up, please," Hamilton scolded. I momentarily increased my pace, but as soon as the rest of the group rounded the corner, I stopped. So did Jeannie.

"Wonder what that's for." She pointed to a metal cage secured to the wall with large iron bolts.

I shook off a memory: my panicked mother slamming one just like it shut and locking it, with a boy—*the boy*—inside. When the police brought him here, she'd told me to wait for her in her office. I wished I'd listened. "It's called a therapeutic module," I answered.

Leery, Jeannie ran her hand along the links. The soft *clink* was the only sound in the eerie quiet. The boy had touched them too, but not like that. He'd grabbed them with the ferocious desperation of a rabid animal. "Do they put people inside it?" Jeannie asked.

"Sometimes." Emerging from the hallway, Hamilton cleared his throat with intention, and we both jumped. "Sorry," I said. "We're coming."

He stared back at me hard. Then, putting an arm around Jeannie, he guided her back to the group. "Don't worry. Those are only used in extreme circumstances." He glanced over his shoulder and narrowed his eyes at me.

"Like what?" Jeannie asked.

Hamilton twittered nervously. I watched him flounder in silence, wishing I could speak for him. I wouldn't give her my mother's answer. "Therapeutic modules are used for containment," she'd said. The truth was the cages were for the uncontainable. Like the boy. The one my mother put there on the day the government finally banned Emovere.

"Therapeutic modules are for containment." Hamilton was obviously well versed in Green Briar dialect. "They're for the safety of our patients and staff." Behind his back, I rolled my eyes.

"But they look like . . . cages." Jeannie offered the word cautiously.

Exasperated, Hamilton groaned, as if she had personally offended him. "We don't call them that here. Cages are for animals." Jeannie looked down at her feet, scolded.

Up ahead of us, the group was crowded just outside an open doorway. "All of our patients have their own room, much like this one," Hamilton explained. I stood on tiptoe to get a view of the sparse quarters—a twin-sized bed, a small desk, and a single chair. "We find simple living conditions promote success. With EAM addicts, it's best to reduce stimulation."

A well-dressed man near the front tapped Hamilton's shoulder. "How long does it take?" he asked. "Before they get better?" All of their faces stilled, hopeful, hanging on his answer. I felt sorry for them.

"I wish I could tell you." Hamilton looked sympathetically at the group as their expressions deflated. "But it varies significantly from patient to patient. I'm going to leave that to one of our top-notch doctors." He shut the door, then pointed to the left, down another long hallway. A tall, gray-haired woman in a white coat stood at the end. "Speaking of which, let's meet Dr. Henley. She'll be able to help with any questions you have about the course of treatment." Led by Jeannie and the well-dressed man, the group hurried toward her. I imagined how she must feel—at once, both powerful and inadequate, just like my mother.

When I watched my mother talk to the boy that day—his ten-year-old eyes a piercing, gun-metal blue—I saw for the first time just how vulnerable she was. That she didn't have all the answers everyone thought she did, that Emovere was something she'd unleashed on the world and couldn't take back. After the boy had exhausted himself shaking the cage, he finally spoke to her.

"Can I go home?" His voice more timid than I'd expected, the Emovere wearing off by then. I was surprised by that. They'd said he injected the entire vial he found hidden in his parents' bedroom.

"No. You have to stay here." My mother said nothing more. I'd wondered who would tell him and how. He didn't have a home to go back to.

"Allow me to introduce my esteemed colleague, Dr. Elizabeth Henley. She was formerly employed by Zenigenic and has been working here with us for the past two years as our EAM expert." Hamilton's obnoxious pronouncement jarred me back to the present.

With all eyes on Dr. Henley, I slipped away, skirting back down the corridor and onto the elevator. *Ten*, I whispered to myself. When the elevator doors parted, I moved with purpose, checking the small name tags affixed to each door: Rouse, Peterson, Marshall, Smith. *No, no, no, no again.* I glanced over my shoulder, imagining Hamilton standing there shaking his head at me. But there was no one, so I soldiered on. Room after room, name after name, all *no.*

Then at the third room from the end . . . *yes.*

## CHAPTER TWENTY-EIGHT

# OBLIVION

THE CHAIR WAS THE FIRST THING I saw. Its wooden back to me, the chair faced the curtained window. The room was a deep gray, the color of loneliness.

"Peter?" My voice sounded strange to me. "Is anybody here?" I took another step inside and quieted my breathing. I could see him now, slumped forward in the chair, head in his hands. His reddish-brown hair was matted to his head. He wore a white T-shirt and khaki pants, the standard uniform for Green Briar then and now.

"Are you here to kill me?" He sat up straight, his arms as stiff as rods next to him. There were long, red marks down the length of them.

"No." He didn't seem as relieved as I expected. "What happened to your arms?" I asked.

"Agitor withdrawal." He spoke through gritted teeth rubbing the abrasions with his fingernails. "Can't. Stop. Scratching." A line of blood appeared on each arm. I couldn't stand it. I took another step forward and reached my hand toward him.

"Don't." I pulled away at the finality of his tone.

"I want to help you," I offered, not even sure that was possible.

"You can't. No one can." He reached toward his lap out of my view. When his hand returned to the armrest, his fist was a tight ball. He opened his fingers slowly the way a bud blooms. Resting on his palm, a small vial and a syringe. "I failed."

"What do you mean?" He uncapped the needle and plunged it into the bottle, drawing the clear liquid inside. "What is that? Who gave it to you?

"I wasn't supposed to get caught. That wasn't part of the mission."

"What mission? Tell me what happened."

"What happened . . ." His laugh scraped my soul. It was like the desperate cry of an animal. "Sebastian told me someone would try to convince me to talk. You know what happens if I talk."

At the mention of String, I had to remind myself to breathe. "You can't trust Sebastian. Please let me—" He pressed the point of the needle against his skin until it slipped beneath the milky whiteness.

"Sebastian is my only friend. That's why he brought me this. To make it easier."

Peter stood on wobbly legs and pulled back the curtains, revealing an expanse of blue sky. With one hand, he shielded his face from the light. A tight knot twisted in my stomach. Peter grabbed the chair and hurled it through the window—then leaned forward, stuck his head into the crisp winter air, and closed his eyes. He seemed suddenly calm. My knot loosened a little, until an alarm began screaming relentlessly.

"Dead men don't talk." I compelled myself to move, but it was too late. He swung one leg over the jagged-glassed windowsill, then the other. The last thing I saw was Peter's shock of reddish hair as he dropped—without a sound—into oblivion.

## CHAPTER TWENTY-NINE

# LONG GONE

AS MY HEART throbbed in my throat, the elevator began its labored crawl downward toward the first floor. I pushed away Peter's last words, focusing instead on the small, numbered buttons that stood between me and anywhere else but here.

*Please don't stop. Please don't stop. Please don't stop.*

At the final *ding*, I took a quick breath and steadied myself against the rail, waiting for the doors to part to chaos. I felt wooden—lifeless and hollow. Green Briar's first floor reappeared slowly, an inch at a time. But once revealed, it wasn't at all what I expected, and I shuddered. While Peter's freefall sent my entire world spinning off its axis, everyone else was oblivious. A uniformed security guard pushed past me, muttering under his breath. "Probably another false alarm." Blank-faced, I nodded.

With her eyes reaffixed to her computer tablet, Julie barely noticed when I willed my legs past her and out the door.

"Hey!" she called after me. "You forgot to sign out."

For the second time in my life, I was running from Green Briar with my mother's voice in my head.

"Emovere was never intended for a growing brain." She was sitting at her desk facing me, clutching the boy's file in her lap. Her eyes were hard, but her hands shook a little as she spoke. A few minutes after my mother had left him, the boy collapsed inside the cage and was comatose.

"Who was it intended for, Mom? All these people here, they all have problems because of it. Why can't you just accept that?" My words were pointed. Poison arrows, they catapulted toward her before I could redirect them.

My mother was quiet, and I was overcome by an immediate swell of regret. I knew she already blamed herself. I opened my mouth to tell her that, but she smacked the file down against the desk, preempting my apology. It felt like a slap to the face. "Don't you think I know that? Don't you think I wish I could do it all differently?" She stood up, her fists clenched at her side. "Not a day goes by that I don't have regrets, but I did it all for you."

"For me?" I felt the sear of indignation at the back of my throat. *She was blaming me?* "Are you saying this is *my* fault?" I wriggled away as she reached for me. "Wow, Mom. Wow. A ten-year-old boy shoots up with his dad's Emovere and burns down a whole block, killing his whole family in the process, and it's my fault." I knew I was being unreasonable, that wasn't what she meant—*what did she mean?*—but I bolted from her office anyway, punctuating my escape with a slam of the door.

It seemed we were both running. Me and the girl that I was. My breath was coming in staccato gasps that I could barely control, but I kept running. My legs burned, then went numb, but I kept running. At the sign—where I'd let my mother catch up to me five years ago—I stopped, half expecting to find my old self there. But she was long gone, and I was alone.

* * *

I felt an arm around my shoulder. "Lex, are you okay? What happened?" I opened my mouth to answer, but I couldn't. Not yet. Still, Carrie's voice was a comfort. At least I wasn't alone anymore. Her hand on my back, she guided me to the car.

My father had repositioned himself in the driver's seat. As we approached, his eyes took me in and revealed his worry all at once. I collapsed into the front seat, suddenly exhausted. "Radley's dead." I let the words fill the space around us. They were the suffocating kind, words that demanded more words, but I wasn't ready to offer any. The wail of an ambulance, blaring around the corner, gave a voice to the bedlam inside of me. I watched in the side mirror as the ambulance made a hurried turn to Green Briar. I didn't even know I was crying until I tasted the warm brine of my tears. I rested my head against the seat and let them fall.

## CHAPTER THIRTY

# THREATS AND PROMISES

WE WERE ALMOST home before I spoke. I could feel my father watching me, waiting for something. *Anything*. I listened to Carrie's breathing, shallow at first, then deep and even. I matched my breaths to hers. "I think he took Emovere first," I finally said, breaking the spell of silence. "Then he jumped."

My father's eyes opened wide, but he withheld his questions, allowing me to continue. Once I started talking, I couldn't stop. The words tumbled out—the whole story—as if it was essential to exorcise them. We sat in the driveway with the motor running until I finished.

"Did he say who sent him on this mission?" my dad asked after I stopped speaking and turned to him.

I shook my head, then shrugged. "The New Resistance? I don't know." I unfastened my seat belt, opened the door, and slogged toward the house with Carrie behind me. My father jettisoned ahead, already typing furiously on his computer tablet.

"It sounds like this String fellow could shed some light on that," Carrie suggested.

My father stopped walking and spoke over his shoulder. "If we have to count on String's help, we're in big trouble." We exchanged a knowing look. Peter Radley trusted String. Counted on him. Look where that got him.

* * *

That night I found a red-eyed Carrie in my mother's lab, hunched over a folder. On the counter nearby was one of the boxes marked *Dishes*. "What are you looking at?" I asked.

She motioned me over without looking up and answered with a question of her own. "Can't sleep either?"

"Not really." Carried nodded, unsurprised. Over her shoulder, I read the name on the file: *Inmate 413 Everett Markum*. Emma's father. Carrie was holding a newspaper article, tracing the headline with her finger. *San Francisco Ex-Con Massacres Family, Leaves Nine-Year-Old Daughter As Sole Survivor.*

"Did Emma tell you about her dad?" I asked.

Carrie sighed. "She didn't have to. Once they agreed to participate in the rehab program, they were assigned a specialist like me. We received their Guardian Force files and were required to learn everything about them." *Everything*. That ambitious word repeated itself in my head. I doubted anyone knew everything about Emma.

"Well, maybe not everything," Carrie amended. "But I knew enough. I should've guessed she would do something like this." Her guilt was palpable.

"What do you mean? How could you have known?"

"The Prophecy Program for starters."

I stifled a gasp. "You knew about Prophecy?"

She nodded. "Only after I started working with a few of the Legacies." I didn't let on, but I was relieved my mother hadn't told her. It would have felt like another betrayal. "This probably won't surprise you, but Ryker knew all along. They made special efforts to recruit Legacies at risk for the gene. Emma told me they followed her for months before she agreed to enlist." I squirmed in my seat, thinking of Quin and how the Guardian recruiting officers searched for him before Edison turned him over.

Carrie read my mind. "I'm sure they pursued Quin as well."

"So you think Emma was genetically predisposed to kill someone?" I wasn't entirely sure I wanted an answer.

And Carrie didn't seem eager to give one. "Yes and no." She paged to the tab marked *Criminal History*, line after line—several pages worth—of Everett Markum's misdeeds. I scanned the page along with her. Robbery, assault, resisting arrest, domestic violence. *Murder.* "Emma was impulsive and reckless like her father, but she wasn't callous. Not without Emovere and Onyx anyway. Her records from the Guardian Force showed that. Her empathy scores prior to recruitment were above average." I resisted the urge to scoff.

Carrie flipped through the rest of the file to the back. A Markum family photograph was affixed with tape to the folder. It had yellowed a little around its edges. In it, Emma was immediately recognizable. She was sitting on her mother's lap, directing a playful smile at the camera. "Emma warned me," Carrie said. "She told me she would never go back. No matter what."

I remembered how Emma reacted when the commander asked for her name. At the time, I assumed she was being her usual uncooperative self. "Were they still looking for her?"

Carrie shrugged. "There were so many more like her. It was me they wanted—for starting it all. But, Emma was a leader too. After she left, others followed."

"Do you think Radley was one of them?"

"Maybe, but I was long gone by that time." Carrie's eyes were somewhere else again. When I touched her shoulder, it startled her. "Did you know the rehabilitation program was partially funded by Zenigenic?" she asked.

My stomach lurched. "I thought it was sponsored by the government."

Carrie cackled. Her laughter was unhinged, equal parts fear and irony. "Is there any difference?" Since the government's cover-up of its involvement with General Ryker, I had asked myself the same question. The answer—it should have been obvious by now—was still unsettling. Suddenly, Carrie's eyes were teary. "I'm sorry," she said. "I know I sound bitter . . . and paranoid."

"Did they threaten you?"

Carrie swallowed hard. "I wouldn't call them threats. More like promises. They made it clear what would happen to my family if I didn't resign."

"Your family?" As soon as I spoke the words, I saw my mother's face, and my thoughts started spinning. "That little boy you mentioned earlier, the one at Green Briar . . . "

Carrie nodded at me. "I remembered his name," she said. "Logan Arrington. The boy responsible for the ban on Emovere, right?"

"Right. Logan." Saying his name aloud felt dangerous, as if it had the power to transport me back there. "I was there with my mom when they brought him in. She told me something that day I only just remembered—that she did this all for me. Do you think . . . ?" I couldn't finish. I wanted it to be true—my mother unselfishly toiling away at Zenigenic as long as she had to, not to quell her ambition, but to protect me. I also wanted it to be untrue. How could she set all of this—Emovere, Onyx, her death—on my shoulders?

Carrie put her arm around me. "I know your mom would've moved heaven and earth to keep you safe."

"Did she ever say anything to you?" I held my breath.

"No. Nothing." *Of course not.*

* * *

*It's not real.* I tried to say the words aloud but no sound came from my mouth. My mother was kneeling at my bedside. Her eyes were closed. *Why won't she look at me?* Shame coursed through my body as thick as blood.

"Mom?" My voice was a croak, but at least I heard it. She did too. Her eyes opened, and she raised her head. Twin tears tracked her cheeks, but she stayed silent. Around her neck was a rope. Underneath it, her skin was red and raw. I followed its coarse braid to the hand that held it. The grip was fierce, unforgiving. I peered into the thicket of shadows desperate to see the face.

"Doctor, isn't this what you wanted?" The hand gave a forceful jerk and my mother winced as the rope cut deeper into her neck. *That voice.* It came from the darkest corner of the darkest room on the darkest day of my soul. "Or would you rather I destroy the very thing that you gave birth to?" *Ryker.* I recoiled at his words. They were familiar, slimy with his disgust for me, for my mother.

"Lex, you have to wake up now." My mother's voice was just like I remembered it.

From his hiding place in the shadows, I felt Ryker reach for me with intention. His fingers wound around my arm, tight and tighter still.

"Lex, wake up."

Suddenly, he was close, way too close, but I was afraid to look. *It's not real.* I willed my head to turn toward him and met the electric blue of Xander's eyes. "Your mother works for me now. She always has." I coiled my fist into a tight ball and punched him in the face.

## CHAPTER THIRTY-ONE

# FUGITIVE STATUS

I'LL ADMIT IT. Ever since I first met her, strutting around Edison's house like she owned it, I've always wanted to punch Emma. So I was more than a little disappointed I didn't get to see her expression when my knuckles collided with her perfect nose. Luckily, I woke up in time to witness the aftermath.

"Ow!" Emma doubled over, clutching her face a few feet from the lab table, where Carrie and I had fallen asleep. "I'm bleeding." She pulled her hand from her nose and displayed the evidence to Carrie. Her palm was a shocking shade of red. Clutched beneath her fingers was a key.

"What are you doing here?" I demanded, sitting upright. I was suddenly but completely awake. "Is that our spare key?"

"Why did you hit me?" she countered. Before I could respond, she turned to Carrie. "Why are *you* here?"

Carrie's eyes darted between us, uncertain where to land. "Lex and I know each other. We met when I worked for the Resistance."

"Of course, you did." Emma rolled her eyes. "Does she know?"

Carrie nodded.

"Great." Evidently, fugitive status had done little to improve her attitude.

I stood up, and Emma reflexively stepped back. I almost laughed. She was afraid of me. "I was dreaming. I thought you were Xander." I walked to the door and opened it, ready to usher her out. "But I'm glad I did. You can't be here. They're looking for you."

She smirked. "Don't you mean us?"

"What are you talking about?" Accusatory, I practically spit the words out at her, but my stomach took a nosedive.

"See for yourself," she said. "It's all over the news."

I was reeling inside, but I wasn't about to let Emma stay in my house any longer, not after what she had done. "Leave. Now." I motioned toward the door. "And I'll need that key back." She wiped it on her jeans, leaving a swipe trail of her blood across her thigh. "How did you find it anyway?" I asked. The key was expertly hidden by Quin, what seemed like forever ago, beneath a loose board on our porch.

Emma raised her eyes to mine. "Do you really want to know?" I cocked my eyebrows, waiting. "Quin told me where to find it."

My fist begged to hit her again. "I don't believe you."

"He said you'd say that and to tell you that he hid it there himself." My heart suspended in my chest—stuck, stuck, stuck—like a fly in amber. I barely registered Emma's next few sentences. " . . . didn't have anywhere else to go . . . cornered him . . . alone outside Zenigenic . . . said you'd help me . . . " The worst part was I couldn't send her away now. Quin was counting on me.

We marched in silence, single file back to the house. Inside, my father was awake. So was Artos. They were planted side by side on the sofa, my dad staring intently at the television, so focused he didn't even hear us come in.

Artos perked his head, sending my father on a desperate search for the remote, trying to delay the inevitable. "I already know. They're looking for me."

"How do you—?" His face blanched as his eyes registered Emma. "I'm calling the police." He reached for his cell phone. Its screen was flashing: *10 missed calls*. Probably all from Langley.

"Dad, think about what you're saying." I joined him on the couch. "The police aren't even looking for Emma, remember? Besides, Quin told her to come here." Frustrated, he returned his phone to the coffee table—where it sat still blinking—as a stone-faced Barbara Blake revealed my fate. "Well, you can't stay," he added as an unconvincing afterthought.

> **"Tonight, I am reporting live just outside the gates of the Green Briar Recovery Center with breaking news. Only hours ago, we were informed that 19-year-old Peter Radley sustained fatal injuries after falling from his tenth-story window. Authorities have confirmed he was under the influence of Emovere at the time. Though the death appears to be a suicide, investigators have been reluctant to rule out foul play. They are searching for a person of interest, Emma Markum, who visited Green Briar around the time of Mr. Radley's death."**

"Funny," Emma said. "I don't remember being there." As we exchanged a mutual glare, I saw myself on the screen. I was running.

> **"Video surveillance captured Ms. Markum fleeing the facility just before Mr. Radley's body was discovered. At this time, she is not a suspect in a crime, but is encouraged to turn herself in to police for questioning. As many of you are aware, Emma Markum is no stranger to tragedy. In 2032, her mother, stepfather, and older sister were fatally shot by her father. She was the only survivor."**

I lowered my head into my hands and took a deep breath. "What are we going to do?" I asked without looking up. "It's only a matter of time before they enlarge that image and plaster my face everywhere."

Emma laughed to herself. "You didn't seem to have a problem plastering my name everywhere."

I turned to look at her, matching her sardonic smile. She was right, but still, she hadn't even mentioned—much less tried to explain—what happened with the commander. "I guess after seeing you shoot someone, I didn't think you were really that concerned about your image." As I expected, Emma had no reply.

My father's phone buzzed against the table. "Langley again," he said, after a quick glance.

"You should answer it," I told him. "It'll look suspicious if you don't."

"I agree," Carrie seconded. "Right now, nobody knows it's Lex they're looking for." *Right now.* My brain stuck on those words as my father put the phone to his ear and a finger to his lips to silence us while he did damage control with Langley.

He offered a lame excuse. "I guess I must've fallen asleep. Yes, I heard. I'll be there in twenty minutes." After he hung up, he groaned. "Well, guess who's been assigned to investigate Emma's connection to Radley?"

"Maybe I should just turn myself in, answer their questions. How bad could it be?"

"No!" Carrie and my father answered in chorus. Even Emma shook her head.

Carrie sat in the chair across from us. "Until we know how Radley fits into this, I think it's safe to assume we should trust no one." I couldn't help but stare at Emma. She was watching Barbara Blake drone on about Green Briar's treatment success rate. *How could Carrie trust her?*

"I don't trust you," I blurted out, pointing my finger at Emma. "I want to know why you were using Emovere." Next to me, my father was nodding his encouragement so I kept going, even as she opened her mouth to reply. "Why did you kill that soldier? Did you even tell Quin what you did?"

Emma winced. "He's dead?"

"You shot him in the chest. What did you expect?"

She crumpled onto the sofa next to me, a pained look on her face, as if I had punched her again. It was the closest she'd ever looked to crying. "I didn't mean to kill him, but he recognized me. I know he did. He was one of the recruiting officers who tried to enlist me from rehab. And I couldn't go back. I just couldn't." Her eyes pleaded with Carrie's. "He was going to take me back—back to the Guardian Force."

"How do you know?" my father asked.

Emma looked only at me when she answered. "Because I wasn't using Emovere. Or Onyx. Or anything. I was clean."

## CHAPTER THIRTY-TWO

# DAMAGED GOODS

"DAD, YOU FORGOT THIS," I said, handing him his press pass at the door.

Embarrassed, he shook his head. "I'm not thinking straight. Are you okay with me leaving you alone?"

"It's fine." I gestured over my shoulder to Carrie and Emma. "And I'm *not* alone."

"Okay." The worry lines in his forehead hinted he wasn't completely satisfied. "But I probably won't be back until tomorrow."

"I'll call you if we need anything. I promise." He squeezed my shoulder and headed down the sidewalk, looking back every few steps. Inside, Carrie and Emma were at the kitchen table staring awkwardly at one another. "Hungry?" I asked them. It was almost morning—still dark—but close enough for breakfast.

"Not really." Carrie answered for both of them.

Plodding through their heavy silence, I prepared a bowl of cereal for myself and sat down. There was only one question I wanted to ask. *How was Quin?* But I wasn't ready to ask it. Instead I scrolled through my missed calls and text messages as Emma snuck covert glances at Carrie, opening then shutting her mouth. Apparently, I wasn't the only one censoring herself.

Edison's response arrived earlier that night, a mere 48 hours or so late. *Just now reading your text. Sorry! Bad texter, remember?*

There were three missed calls—two from Elana and one from Percy—and two text messages from Max. *Did you hear about Radley?* And a few hours later: *And Emma?!? Where are you? Call me!*

I ran my thumbs across the screen, pondering a reply. It seemed impossible to sum up the last day and night in a text. *Where would I even begin?* Emma's positive test for EAMs? Her holding me at gunpoint—then shooting and killing a soldier? Witnessing Radley's suicide? *No, I'd start with Emma's bloody nose.* I half smiled to myself, clicking on Percy's voicemail.

He sounded nervous, his nasally voice a bit squeakier than I remembered. "Hi, Lexi. I mean, Lex. It's Percy—uh, Percy Danforth—I was just calling to tell you I had a great time with you the other night. Um . . . so, yeah. I'd love to hang out again. If you want to, of course. No pressure, though. Just give me a call. Or text . . . or email . . . well you know what to do." *Lousy timing, Percy. Really lousy timing.* I laughed without meaning to.

"What's so funny?" Emma asked, scowling at me.

"Nothing." I placed my phone on the table and met her eyes. I was ready to start asking questions. "So how well did you know Peter Radley?"

Emma looked at Carrie with uncertainty. "It's okay," Carrie assured her. "I showed Lex and her father the Recovery Analysis results for you and Peter."

"Is that supposed to make me feel better?" Emma asked, her face reddening. Then with no answer from Carrie, she looked at me. "So Carrie told you I'm damaged goods, huh?" She snickered, but it seemed pretend. That nettling worm of sympathy dug its way a little deeper.

"You don't know that for sure," I said. "Besides, it's not your fault. Those drugs should've never been created in the first place." I wondered if my mother would've agreed with me.

The irony wasn't lost on Emma. "That's pretty rich coming from Victoria Knightley's daughter."

I shrugged. "I loved my mom, but I didn't always agree with her." Emma grumbled a little under her breath, but she didn't argue.

"I didn't really know Peter at all until we got to rehab. He was always writing me weird poetry. I guess he sort of had a crush on me." *Of course he did.* I remembered Edison's description of Guardian Force Emma batting her eyelashes. "After our final test results came back, we were recruited for a special mission. That's what they called it."

"Mission?" I raised my eyebrows at the word. "What did they tell you about it?"

"Not much. You didn't learn the details unless you enlisted, but they made it very clear that our scrambled brains wouldn't be a problem." She paused to look at Carrie. "I never told you this part. They said we could keep taking Emovere and Agitor—even Onyx—if we wanted to." If Carrie was surprised, she didn't show it.

"Did Peter leave right after you?" Carrie asked.

"I'm not sure. I didn't see him again until I went to an anti-EAM rally. That's where I met Quin and Mr. McAllister."

"Didn't you ask him what happened?" I wondered. Emma frowned at me, as if the answer was obvious. She gave a labored sigh.

"Of course, but he was different. Quieter. Withdrawn. A loner. I just gave up after a while."

I asked the only question I had left. "And Quin? Did he say anything else last night?"

"About?" Emma's tone was coy.

"Never mind."

I put my bowl in the sink and headed for the sanctuary of my bedroom. I flopped down on the bed, watching as Artos nudged the door open with his nose, padded inside, and squeezed himself into the small space next to me. "How do you always know when I need you?" I whispered to him. I ran my hand down the length of his fur again and again, until we both closed our eyes.

* * *

It seemed only seconds later Artos' whining woke me—but outside my window, it was still twilight. Emma was standing over me, her hand hovering above my arm. "You've got to stop doing that," I said. "Unless you *want* to get punched again."

She smiled. "Well . . . it would give me an excuse to hit you back."

"Touché."

Suddenly serious, Emma lowered her voice. "There's something I didn't tell you." She looked down at her feet. "I didn't think you'd want Carrie or your dad to know." I sat up, pushing Artos from the bed and frowned at her. “Alright, alright. I wasn’t sure I was going to tell you at all. Ever. But, Quin told me to ask you to meet him.”

“When?” *Ugh.* I sounded annoyingly eager.

“Tonight just after the curfew.”

I took a breath and calmed my voice. “Where?”

She shrugged. “He didn’t tell me. He said you’d know where.”

I nodded. “Anything else?”

She shook her head. “There was no time. One of Xander’s guys came around the corner—that mean-looking one who pushed Edison—and I had to make a run for it.”

“Valkov,” I muttered. “Did he see you?”

She laughed. “He chased me. I heard Quin tell him I was just a fan, you know, wanting to meet him after the interview, maybe get a picture or an autograph.”

It was impossible not to laugh. “Sounds believable.”

She rolled her eyes. “This coming from the president of the Quin McAllister fan club.”

“That’s Madame President to you,” I said, and we both giggled.

Mid-laugh, Emma paused at the door. “I’m sorry I left you at the checkpoint,” she said. “I didn’t want to, but—”

“I know,” I interrupted. “I guess it’s time I learn how to drive a motorcycle.” I gave her a wink.

## CHAPTER THIRTY-THREE

# A LITTLE KINDER

"ARE YOU SURE you can handle this?" Emma asked me, running her hand along the length of her cherry red motorcycle fender. It purred steadily beneath me, on the verge of a roar. "She's my baby. I need you to bring her back in one piece."

"They say a student is only as good as the teacher," I teased.

A cocky smile played on her lips. "Well then, I guess I have nothing to worry about." Emma was right. She was a surprisingly good teacher—showing me the ins and outs of riding in a couple of hours. Still, I was nervous. The bike seemed to have a life of its own, a pounding heartbeat that was much quicker and much more reckless than mine.

"What should I tell Carrie?" she asked. "She'll be awake soon."

"Tell her the truth. I'm sure she'll understand."

"And your dad?" Emma raised her eyebrows. "What if he comes back before you?"

I shrugged. There was no right answer. "Same. Maybe just soften it a little—if you can."

"Soft, it is," she said, with a nod of her head. "By the way, do you know where you're going?" Her voice turned up at the end with an uncertain lilt. I knew she was curious. I didn't answer, just revved the engine a little and grinned.

She offered a reluctant half smile. "Alright, alright. I get it. You win." For a moment, she seemed wistful, and I wondered if she was thinking about Quin. "You're still a goody-goody. You know that, right?"

Just like she taught me, I squeezed the clutch and put the bike into first gear. I felt my pulse accelerate, matching the motor's rumble as I made a circle around her. "But I'm a goody-goody who can ride."

* * *

Elana was waiting for me on the bottom step of Mr. Van Sant's porch, her face illuminated by a halo of light from the street lamp. As I brought the bike to a shaky stop in the driveway, dragging my feet against the pavement, I watched her eyes narrow then widen. Her jaw dropped.

"Lex?" She hesitated before taking a step toward me.

"It's me."

"I didn't know you could . . ." I could feel her staring over my shoulder as she hugged me. "Is that Emma's bike?"

"It's a really long story. We should go inside." I started up the staircase, but she grabbed my arm, pulling me back. Her face was clouded with worry.

"Did you go through the checkpoint?"

"Of course." Despite my near collision with a traffic cone, I sailed through unseen. Emma had swiped a license plate and swapped it with her own just in case the soldiers were still looking for her bike. As it was, no one seemed to notice.

"Why? What's wrong?"

"Have you seen the news? SFTV has been showing that video all day. They're looking for you. And Emma." She paused. "I mean, they think you're Emma."

"How could you tell it was me?" She stood motionless, her face blank. Fear began to creep up around me like a twisted vine anchoring me to the ground. "Elana?"

"I wasn't sure at first," she finally answered. "I thought I recognized your jacket." She took a deep breath. "You haven't seen it, have you?"

"Seen what?" I croaked, feeling strangled.

"About an hour ago, they started showing your face. Up close. It's grainy, and they're still calling you Emma, but . . ."

I swallowed hard, then nodded. I knew it would happen, but not this soon.

"Why were you at Green Briar? Why were you run—"

"Hey, Red," Edison poked his head out from behind the door and gave me a sly grin. "At least let her come in before you interrogate her."

"Sorry," Elana said, ushering me up the stairs. "I am in desperate need of an update."

I squeezed her shoulder as we went inside. "It's okay. I've been dying to talk to you too." I knew exactly where to start. I snickered a little. "I punched Emma in the face."

Elana guffawed. "Oh my—"

From the foyer, Edison shushed us, then pointed. I followed his finger into the living room, where his father sat perched on the edge of the sofa, his broad, suited shoulders leaning forward, as if he was preparing for takeoff. "He doesn't like to be disturbed when he's watching the news," Edison whispered. "It's his quiet time."

"Son, stop spouting off and get in here!" Mr. Van Sant didn't turn around, but his voice descended like the head of a misguided hammer, fracturing quiet time with one blow. Edison flinched. Meeting Elana's gaze, we both snickered. It was a relief to laugh with her, but it didn't last. My eyes settled on the over-sized television screen. Just behind the ever-composed Barbara Blake was my face. Blurry, almost indiscernible, but mine nonetheless.

"Ms. Knightley, may I have a word with you?" Mr. Van Sant finally stood and faced me. His tie was loosened at the neck, his shirt untucked. Disheveled, he was no less intimidating.

"Uh, um, yes." Edison nudged me forward, and I forced my feet to move, stumbling a little.

"Sit down." I sat, of course. Mr. Van Sant loomed next to me, his large hand clawing the arm of the chair. "What were you doing at Green Briar?" His tone was calm but forceful. And for an agonizing moment, I imagined being on the witness stand opposite him—*The* Nicholas Van Sant. *He's on my side,* I reminded myself.

"My father and I went there to see Radley." I didn't mention Carrie. I wanted to protect her as long as I could.

"Why?"

"A hunch," I offered weakly.

"A hunch?" Mr. Van Sant paced away, then made a rapid turn back in my direction. Elana watched me over Edison's shoulder, both so silent, so still, I wondered if they were breathing.

"A hunch *and* Sebastian Croft." Mr. Van Sant cocked one eyebrow. "He showed up at my house yesterday asking questions—with a visitor's badge from Green Briar he didn't want me to see. He knew Radley. They were *friends*." I made air quotes with my fingers. "On the Internet."

Edison's mouth opened a little, and Elana gasped, but Mr. Van Sant was nonplussed. "I see. And you signed in as Emma Markum?" I could feel my cheeks reddening.

"Yes."

Unable to stay quiet any longer, Edison blurted, "Did you see Radley? Did you talk to him?" I waited for his father to scold him for interrupting, but Mr. Van Sant appeared far more interested in my answer than in correcting his son's subpar etiquette.

"I saw him jump." I looked down at my hands folded in my lap, but I could only see Radley's arms, red and raw from scratching. I closed my eyes and opened them again, hoping to reset my memory.

Mr. Van Sant said nothing. He returned to the sofa across from me and ran a tense hand through his hair. When he finally spoke, there was urgency in his voice. "Did he say anything? Anything at all?"

"Not much," I told him. "He said he'd failed at his mission by getting caught, and he thought I was there to kill him. He used something String brought him. Emovere, I guess. He had a vial with a syringe."

"Did he mention Steele?"

"No." I couldn't shake the feeling Mr. Van Sant knew something I didn't. "Why?"

"I think you're in danger." I felt the hairs on my neck raise. It wasn't his words but the way he said them that sent a shot of ice through my veins. "I have a contact at the police station. Steele's pressuring them to find this Emma Markum—" He gestured toward the television. My picture was gone, replaced by an image of Peter Radley dressed in his Guardian Force garb. "—to find *you*."

"But that doesn't make sense," I said, arguing against the tightening knot in the pit of my stomach. "I thought Xander would be relieved to see Radley gone."

A concerned Edison joined his father on the sofa. For the first time, I noticed a matching furrow between their eyebrows. "Xander believes

Radley told you something. That's what we suspect," Edison explained. "Maybe something incriminating."

I scoured my memory, replaying Radley's words, inspecting each one for traces of Xander. Finally, I shrugged. "He said String told him someone would come to force him to talk, but he didn't mention—" *Xander.* Before his name left my mouth, I saw him, a headline running beneath his powder-white face. *Zenigenic To Make Major Announcement.* "Turn it up," I said, directing Mr. Van Sant to the remote. Barbara Blake was reporting.

> **"In an exclusive interview, Mr. Steele informed SFTV that he was very excited to announce the release of Zenegenic's new emotion-altering drug, Docil-E. Mr. Steele stated that the drug will likely be approved by the government for public use in the coming weeks. Though he remained relatively tight-lipped about this new EAM, Mr. Steele hinted Docil-E would support the common good. He said, "Our company is extremely proud of Docil-E. We believe this product will go a long way to making the world a little kinder."**

Mr. Van Sant muted the television and turned to me. "Now I'm really worried." Edison nodded gravely as Elana and I looked on, confused.

"Xander Steele is up to something," Edison explained.

"You're right, Son. That man doesn't do *kind.*"

## CHAPTER THIRTY-FOUR

# FIRST QUESTION

I TURNED UP the collar of my jacket to shield my face from the biting wind—its cold, desperate fingers whipped and tousled my hair. It was just after 9, leaving me roughly an hour to walk the two miles from Pacific Heights to Coit Tower. I set a brisk pace, just in case. *Just in case*—the words Edison said to me before I left. *In case of what?* I didn't want to answer my own question, but it burned in the back of my brain.

Elana had tried to convince me to stay. "Lex, I'm not so sure this is a good idea. Can you really trust Emma? What if she lied to you? Set you up?"

I couldn't reassure her. I had the same doubts. "I'll be okay. I promise."

Edison reached into his waistband and held out a gun. "Take it," he instructed. "Just in case."

I could feel the weighty metal of it pressed to my skin as I walked, passing block after block of houses, each indistinguishable from the last. With the curfew nearing, most were lit from within, their occupants hidden away, safe. Like I wished I could be.

I stopped again to look behind me. The empty street extended into the darkness, and I imagined Valkov's yellow-brown eyes stalking me from beyond where I could see. There was a gnawing in my bones, a crawling in my skin, an unshakeable feeling I was being watched. It wasn't until I reached the stairs and the familiar dumpster with its raccoon family that it hit me. String had been following Quin. He followed him here. To Coit Tower. And along with that came another, darker thought—*what if he's following me?*

In the distance, I heard the rapid drumbeat of footsteps. I crouched behind the dumpster and quieted my breathing. The sound drew nearer, filling the silence—louder and louder—until it stopped right in front of me. A young man I didn't recognize stared ahead. His eyes were panicked, darting with desperation. Then he ran. Seconds later, I saw them, wearing black bandanas around their mouths just like they had on that cold December afternoon: Satan's Syndicate, one of the Bay Area's most violent street gangs. And that was *before* Onyx.

They traveled in a pack, huddled and fast, stalking their prey. I waited until they were out of sight, waited for the gunshot I knew would come. Expecting it, I flinched anyway—feeling grateful, then ashamed—as I stepped from behind the dumpster.

I edged around the base of Coit Tower toward the entrance, holding the gun Edison gave me close to my side. The door was pulled shut, the boards that once secured it propped against the concrete wall. Stepping over a wad of discarded *KEEP OUT* tape, I gave the door a gentle push with my foot, then ducked out of sight, its gentle creaking the only reply. I inched forward until I could feel an icy draft escaping from within. Past the doorway, the blackness seemed to pulse with life, even if *it*—whatever *it* was—remained just out my sight. I stepped inside.

In an instant, everything happened. So fast, it was impossible to sequence the pieces, but there was no mistaking what came first: the smell of pimento. A hand covered my mouth, then an arm twisted mine until I felt my shoulder wrench, loosening the gun from my grasp. I bit down hard, both relieved and horrified at the taste of blood.

"Ow!" A howl of pain—familiar somehow, though at first I couldn't place it—and the vise grip around me tightened.

Then a realization. "Quin?" Like an incantation, when I said his name, I was free again. Stupefied, I turned to face my captor. From the darkness, a flashlight's click revealed his face.

"Lex?" He wasn't celebrity Quin anymore. He looked like himself again—blue jeans, T-shirt, my favorite leather jacket. He shined the light on my arm. It was hanging loose and throbbing at my side. "Are you okay? Did I hurt you?"

I shrugged, wincing as I moved. I glanced at Quin's finger. It was bleeding a little. "I should ask you the same question."

He wiped his finger against his jeans, then examined it in the flashlight's glow. A half-moon of teeth marks dotted both sides. "I'll live."

Now that we were face to face and finally alone, all my words—the speeches I practiced, the questions I collected—every single one of them escaped me. Quin, too, seemed stumped by our reunion.

"I guess you got my message," he said finally as I retrieved the gun from where it had fallen. "What happened with Emma? And why were you at Green Briar?"

"It's a long story. And you're famous now. I'm not sure if you really have time for it."

Quin sighed. "I deserve that."

"Yeah, you do." I frowned at him. "I think I'm entitled to ask the first question."

"Okay," he agreed. "It's a deal. There's just one thing I have to do."

"Make it quick." I half expected him to turn off the flashlight and disappear again. But Quin stepped toward me and pulled me close to him, his breath soft and even in my ear. Surprised, I stiffened. The last time I was this close to him was the day of the verdict, a lifetime ago. It wasn't until I felt him start to pull away—the cold space widening between us—that I understood I was waiting for this.

"Or not so quick," I whispered against his neck, hugging him tighter, inhaling the scent that disappeared from his T-shirt long ago. When he finally released me, we exchanged shy smiles.

Quin pointed to me. "Lex. First question. Go."

"Do you have Augustus?"

His eyes widened in momentary astonishment. Then his poker face returned. "Yes."

"Where?" I scoured the narrow stairwell.

Grinning, Quin shook his head. "Uh-uh. It's my turn now." I rolled my eyes but didn't protest. "How did you know?" he asked.

"Easy," I bragged, wrinkling my nose. "Pimento."

Quin pointed to a room just inside the tower and answered my second question. "He's handcuffed in there." I stared at the small wooden door and listened to the profound silence. Not the way I'd imagined an ensnared Augustus would sound.

"Are you sure?"

He nodded, gesturing me over as he cracked the door. Augustus was secured to the railing, head hung down. Since I saw him last, he was thinner. His twig-like wrists seemed as brittle as pencil lead—his pothole cheeks, dark and sunken in. At the noise, he looked up, his eyes brightening. "Hello, Lex. It's so nice to see you." I lurched back at the sound of his voice, as if I was bitten. He never called me Lex, always Ms. Knightley or Alexandra. And his tone . . . it was soft, kind. Docile.

I raised my eyebrows at Quin.

"I'll explain later," he said as he ushered me out. Still in disbelief, I glanced over my shoulder. Augustus gave me a vacant smile and a childlike wave. "Bye-bye."

"What's wrong with him? How long has he been here?"

"Since just after Xander's press conference. C'mon." He took my hand and pulled me toward the stairs, but I resisted. I swallowed the question on the tip of my tongue. *Can I trust you?* My heart answered the way it usually did, but I couldn't trust it either—not when it came to Quin.

"Where are we going?" We had been whispering until now, and my voice came out louder than I'd expected. In here, it echoed.

Alarmed, Quin spun toward me. He put his finger to his lips. "Where do you think?" he mouthed.

I shook my head and spoke out loud again. "Not until you tell me what's going on."

Quin grabbed my arm, securing me in front of him, my back to his chest. My breath hitched, heart jolting into my throat. With his hand over my mouth, he pressed his lips to my ear, and for a moment, I couldn't tell whether I was terrified or exhilarated. "Lex, I'm being followed."

I tried to speak. "Mmmnoh."

*By String. I know.*

"Mmmnoh," I said again into his palm.

He eased his grip, and I relaxed against him. "It's safer up there. We can see what's coming." He paused, his breath marking time against my cheek. "Can I let you go now?"

I nodded. I was glad he couldn't see my face. *Exhilarated. Definitely exhilarated.*

## CHAPTER THIRTY-FIVE

# DÉJÀ VU

"I'M HAVING SERIOUS déjà vu right now," Quin teased as he opened the door to the observation deck. I followed behind him, tiptoeing over the boards he used to secure it.

I giggled. "You mean we've been here before?"

"Well, it *was* pretty forgettable." He opened his arms wide and threw his head back, looking straight up at the sky. There was only a sliver of moon. The sky was velvet, a thousand stars winking at us through ancient eyes.

"The view or the company?" I asked.

He pretended to ponder my question, and I elbowed him playfully in the side. It felt strange—good, but strange—to joke with Quin. His laughter trailed off, his face solemn, and I wondered if he felt the same. I left him standing there, walked to the ledge, and looked out at the city. At first glance, it seemed just as deserted as the last time I saw it from up here. Quin pointed to a trail of slow-moving headlights snaking down a nearby street. At the front of the convoy was a police car flanked by a military jeep.

"Patrols," he said.

I nodded, shivering, not just from the cold. "Seems familiar."

"Too familiar."

The longer I looked at the city, the more I saw. Behind night's curtain, shadows moved with dark purpose. The more I saw, the more I heard. *Was that a scream? Another gunshot?* I had a flash of the Syndicate, rifle in hand, blindly firing out the window as Artos and I took cover.

The doomed man's eyes as he ran from certain death. Since the curfew's inception, not one night passed without violence. And this night was no exception. That was Onyx, and it was out there. But so was Valkov, and I wasn't sure which was worse. I watched the distant caravan of lights press on without pause. Quin was right—it felt safe up here.

I sat down against the wall, pulling my knees to my chest, shielding myself from the buffeting wind. Quin sat next to me. "So you have questions."

"A lot of them."

"I have answers."

There were so many blanks I needed to fill, I wasn't sure where to start. "What's wrong with Augustus?"

Quin reached into his pocket and opened his hand to me. In it was a small vial of liquid, the trademark *Z* etched on its label. "Docil-E," he said. "Xander's new product. I've been dosing him every eight hours." He glanced at his watch. "He's due for another one pretty soon."

"What does it do exactly?"

His brow furrowed, pensive. "That depends who you ask."

"Well, I'm asking you."

"Compliance. Obedience. Submission." I immediately thought of Emma, the syringe protruding from her leg. Carrie's analysis of the unknown substance made complete sense now.

"They tried to give it to Emma," I told him. "That night on the bridge." Quin seemed more disturbed than surprised. "And if I asked Xander? What would he say about it?"

"It's a miracle drug. Ends violence. Promotes kindness. It even cures Augustus." I let myself laugh, but I felt unsettled. Edison was right. Xander was up to something.

"Is that how you got him here?"

"Sort of. When I came back from L.A., I headed to the boat. It seemed like a logical place to stay, at least for a day or two." He narrowed his eyes at me. "Imagine my surprise when I saw Augustus sunning himself on the deck. I figured he wasn't there by accident. Anyway, I wasn't sure what to do at first. Then the thing with Xander happened, and I realized Augustus might make a good bargaining chip. So I went back to the boat. It took a little convincing . . ." Quin held up the vial. "But he came around."

"How did you get past the checkpoint?"

"Easy," he mimicked my word. "I put him in the trunk of my brand new sports car." When I didn't ask, he added, "My thank you gift from Xander."

Quin waited for my reaction, but I was stoic, thinking. "Then why did you bring Xander's men to the boat? You knew Augustus was gone."

"Exactly," Quin said. "I thought Xander would trust me if he thought I was trying to help him find Augustus. Of course, I didn't expect to have visitors."

"Neither did I."

"By the way, why was Augustus on our houseboat?" Quin asked. "Of all places?"

"Ours, huh? I didn't think there was an *ours* anymore."

"You know what I mean," he said. "Besides, that was what you wanted." *True*, I thought, but looking at Quin, it was nearly impossible to remember why.

"I had to keep him somewhere," I told him. "We made a deal. I help him stay out of prison, and he helps me prove Xander and Valkov framed your dad."

"So *now* you care about my dad?" I scrutinized Quin's face in the dim light. He looked everywhere but at me. "Now you believe him?"

"Quin, you know that already." He just stared straight ahead until I couldn't take it anymore. I pressed my fingertips against his jaw, forcing his eyes to mine. "Do *you?*" I demanded. "Do *you* still believe him? Or is what you said in that ridiculous interview the truth?"

Quin took my hand from his face, holding it for a moment, before returning it to me. "What do you think?"

Exasperated, I exhaled audibly. "I'm not sure. Obviously. Or I wouldn't be asking the question."

He chuckled to himself. "I guess I'm a better actor than you thought."

I groaned. "Remind me to give you your Oscar."

Grinning mischievously, Quin took a half bow. "I'd like to thank the Academy, and—"

"Speaking of acting," I interrupted. "I'm dying to know how you ended up saving the life of your mortal enemy."

"It's genius, right? I only wish I could take credit for the idea. My dad and I decided I should come back here, tail Xander for a while and hope he'd slip up. So we came up with the story about an argument between us. That night, I followed Xander to Zenigenic. I was waiting for him to leave, when I saw Radley. I guess it was just right place, right time, you know? The perfect chance to get on the inside. But I gotta say, I never expected it to work this well."

Listening to him, a wisp of unease fluttered through me. "A little too well . . . " I tried to put my finger on it. "Why is String tracking you?"

"I'm not sure," he admitted. "But I'm guessing it must have something to do with that picture of my dad Max found. Do you think he's still working for Augustus?"

"Maybe." *Anything was possible when it came to Augustus.* "But he knew Radley. He was there right before he jumped. He gave him Emovere."

Quin's mouth twisted, perplexed. "Weird."

"Very." I kept hearing String's voice, smooth as honey, the night he lost Quin outside the tower. "I think he might've been following your dad too."

"My dad? Why?"

"Well, the picture, of course, and something I overheard him say. He said you were harder to tail than—"

Suddenly, Quin turned toward me, his expression earnest, and I stopped talking. "Lex, I have to say something." I nodded, barely breathing. "I'm sorry. About that awful interview with your dad, but not just that. I never meant to lie to you or keep you in the dark. I only wanted to protect you. That's all I've ever wanted."

"I keep telling you not to do that." I expected him to look away, but he didn't. I broke first. My eyes traveled to his hands. They were planted firmly on his knees, unmoving. I found myself wishing he would touch me.

He shrugged. "Old habits die hard, remember?"

And I did remember. Old habits, some habits, don't die at all.

## CHAPTER THIRTY-SIX

# BLUE AND RED

"WAKE UP." It was Quin's voice, and he was afraid.

I tried to find the thread to trace it back to the last thing I remembered, but I couldn't get further than a dream—Quin's arms locked around me, his face nuzzling my hair. *I love you, Lex.* It must've been a dream because when I opened my eyes, he was standing over me. And he was frantic.

"Get up!" He grabbed my forearm and pulled me to my feet so fast I felt light-headed. "The police are here." Brain buzzing, I ran to the ledge and looked down just as Quin yanked me back. But not before I saw them. The base of Coit Tower flashed blue and red, blue and red.

I sank down to my haunches and buried my face in my hands. *Breathe, Lex.* "How long have they been there?" I asked, finally looking up.

Quin shook his head, disgusted with himself. "I don't know. We fell asleep." He paced to the wall and back again. "This is my fault. I shouldn't have asked you to come here."

"Don't panic." My words were meant for both of us. "We can't even be sure they know we're—"

"Alexandra Knightley." The megaphoned voice traveled up from below us, finding and claiming me with its shrill insistence. "This is the police. Come out with your hands up." In spite of my racing heart, I half smiled at the irony.

"You were saying . . . " Quin deadpanned. I met his eyes and shrugged.

"Guess they finally figured out I'm not Emma." He nodded, then hung his head. "Quin, it's not the end of the world." I walked to where he stood. "I'll just turn myself in. They only want to question me, and I haven't done anything wrong."

Before I finished, he was already protesting. "I can't let you do that. Do you really trust the police? The military? Xander has them all in his back pocket, you know."

The voice came again. It was emotionless, almost mechanical, but simultaneously menacing. "Alexandra Knightley. This is your last warning. You have two minutes to surrender or we're coming in."

"Xander doesn't care about me," I argued. "I'm not a threat to him." Both Quin and I knew that wasn't completely true. There was the issue of Radley's last words, whatever Xander believed they were. And I'd seen Valkov's tattoo. But that was months ago, and I was still here, still breathing. As far as I could tell, Valkov wasn't even really hiding it.

Quin was quiet. He took my hand. "You're a Knightley. You'll always be a threat to him."

"Fine," I agreed. "And that's exactly why you can't blow your cover now. You said it yourself, you're on the inside. Besides, if I don't go down now, they're coming in. They'll find us anyway. And Augustus."

"Augustus!" Quin's eyes opened wide. Disbelieving, he stared at his watch. It was 4 a.m. "I forgot! I was supposed to dose him hours ago."

"Are you sure it wears off that quickly?"

"I guess we'll find out." Quin shrugged, nonchalant, but his eyes were dark with worry.

"I'm sorry I messed it up for you. If I hadn't come here—"

Quin gritted his teeth in frustration, then wrapped me in his arms. There was no space between us, and I could feel the wild beat of his heart caged in his chest. He took a breath and exhaled my name. "Lex." That's when I remembered—the last thing I told him, before we fell asleep.

"Emma taught me to ride a motorcycle," I had mumbled, barely awake.

And his answer, soft with sleep. "Sexy Lexi."

* * *

The stairwell was so cold, I gasped. The shock of it cleared my mind like a face full of ice water, but I didn't think. I just moved. Didn't stop moving until I reached the wooden door where Augustus was hidden. Just beyond it, the concrete was awash with flashes of blue and red. Even though I couldn't see them, I felt the eyes. Watching. Waiting. For me. I didn't go toward them. Not yet. I had to look. Just once more.

I turned the knob and peeked inside. A pair of handcuffs hung from the railing, one opened. Beneath them, a spider's web glistened with dew, its eight-legged occupant gone, probably scurrying—like Augustus—somewhere just out of my view. Numb, I shut the door and backed away. I took five leaden steps to the entrance and raised my hands in surrender.

## CHAPTER THIRTY-SEVEN

# STANDARD PROCEDURE

WHEN THE FLASHLIGHT hit my face, I winced with the sudden sting of regret. I squeezed my eyes shut and turned my head from the light.

"Get down on your knees." Momentarily blinded, the voice seemed to come from nowhere and everywhere at the same time. My legs wobbled a little as I lowered myself, hands still raised. "Slow! Slower!"

"Okay," I mumbled, surprised my mouth could even form the word. My knees pressed into the ground, shards of gravel pricking at my skin even through my jeans. I forced myself to take a slow, deep breath to quell the panic that was swelling inside of me. Mid-exhale, the light was gone. I opened my eyes.

"Alexandra Knightley?" The officer didn't wait for my answer. He patted down the length of my body, pocketing my cell phone. I was thankful I'd left Edison's gun with Quin. It would have only made me look guilty of something. And this officer didn't need any more convincing. He cuffed my hands behind my back. Just beyond him, a barricade of military and police personnel assembled, weapons drawn. They blurred into one unmovable dark line.

"Am I under arrest?" I asked, fighting off another wave of panic.

"Standard procedure." Nothing about this felt standard. I waited for him to explain, but he didn't. With a jerk, he pulled me to my feet. Though I knew I was too far away to see Quin, I longed to look up to the tower behind me to feel less alone. But it was a risk I couldn't take. We agreed Quin would stay there until he knew it was safe to come down.

"Is this really necessary?" I held up my hands, the metal already rubbing uncomfortably against my skin.

"Just following orders."

"Whose orders?"

"Walk," he commanded. He grabbed my upper arm and led me down the stairs into the parking lot below, where a group of military vehicles surrounded the perimeter. *All this for me? Why?* My answer came from the shadows. I heard a car door open and shut. It was mundane, but in the stillness, it sounded ominous.

"My men will take it from here." I recognized his voice before I saw his face.

"Of course, Mr. Steele." I went cold. Xander wasn't alone. Valkov marched at his heels, his predator's gaze fixed upon me—intense and excited. The officer extended his hand to Xander, passing him the key to my cuffs, to my freedom. Xander regarded it with indifference—a mere trinket—and transferred it to Valkov. Unlike Xander, he appeared to appreciate its importance. I watched him slip it carefully into his pocket.

"What's going on?" I demanded. My question was ignored, unacknowledged. "I'm not leaving here with him." I turned my face to plead with the officer, but he was already walking away.

One nod from Xander, and Valkov advanced toward me. I was usually drawn to his tattoo—the outward reminder of his inner disfigurement—but a glint of metal on his waistband caught my eye instead. It was the blade of a knife, barely visible, secreted inside a leather sheath. I thought of Shelly. I knew it wasn't *the* knife, of course. Still, I could imagine it gripped tight in his hands, penetrating skin, then muscle, then bone.

"Like what you see?" Valkov grinned at me—wide and hungry—and it was much worse than I could've imagined. When I felt his thick fingers wrap around my arm, my heart quivered like a small animal that knew it was easily chomped and devoured.

I summoned all my courage and sneered back at him. "Don't touch me." I lunged away, pulling my arm out of his grasp. With my hands still cuffed, I lost my balance and stumbled forward. Xander caught me.

"Easy there, Ms. Knightley. I've invested a lot of resources in tracking you down, and I need you in one piece." He ushered me toward a black sedan, where another of his men was holding the door open for me. In another world, it was a politeness, a courtesy. In this one, it was an act of intimidation.

"You're wasting your time. And your resources. Radley didn't tell me anything."

"There will be ample time to discuss that later." Leaning into the car, Xander patted the backseat with a condescending hand.

I tried to stall. "How did you find me?" I asked, not expecting an answer. I scanned my surroundings for an escape route—soldiers everywhere. It was undeniable. I was trapped.

Xander smiled. "Perhaps you should ask Mr. McAllister." I kept my face still, but he seemed to know he had launched a grenade at my epicenter, pin-pulled. I didn't have time to assess the damage. I could hear Valkov's raspy breathing over my shoulder.

"Get in," he growled.

Inside the car, the air was cool and sterile, but with Valkov sitting next to me, I felt suffocated. I scooted as far away from his muscled thighs as I could manage, pressing my body into the door. I turned my back to the door and gently tried the handle. Locked.

"What's the matter?" he teased. "I won't bite." He bared his small, pointy teeth at me, and I grimaced in disgust.

"What're *they* doing here?" Xander was standing outside my window, berating a burly, young soldier. Next to him—biceps straining against his uniform—Xander seemed small and weak. He puffed out his chest in a futile attempt to match the soldier's physique. "I said, *No media*."

"I'm sorry, Mr. Steele. SFTV assured us they wouldn't interfere." Xander stood on loafered tiptoe for a better view. Whatever he saw must've displeased him. His face reddened. With clenched fists, he swiped at the air, shadowboxing. I wondered if—and what—he was using.

"Idiot! That's not SFTV. It's *Eyes on the Bay*. Bill Knightley works for that station." In the wake of Xander's outburst, the soldier appeared unfazed, but a little confused. "Her father!" Xander bellowed. *My father. My father. My father.* I repeated those words to myself like a desperate prayer, my soul on its knees. Still, I wasn't relieved—not with Guardian

Force redux on Xander's side. I was worried. But I wasn't the only one.

"We've gotta go," Xander announced. He signaled to his driver and slid into the passenger seat.

"Right away, Mr. Steele." With the sound of the starting engine came a brutal realization. I was leaving here with Xander.

"Where is my daughter?" My father appeared in front of the sedan, smacking the hood with his palm. His voice was shrill with panic. "Lex? Lex!" He stalked to Xander's window—tinted, of course—pressing his face to the glass to see inside. "Lex!"

"Dad! I'm—" Before I could finish, Valkov's hand was over my mouth. It smelled musty, sour. For the second time that night, I parted my lips, ready to taste blood.

"Lex!" My father rushed the car as the driver slammed the gear into reverse and hit the accelerator, lurching me forward and free of Valkov. The driver screeched to a stop and gathered himself. Through the windshield, I watched in horror as two soldiers pinned my father to the ground. Langley was screaming at them, but we were too far away for me to hear her.

"Go! Go!" Xander urged. As the car screeched past my father, a soldier plunged a needle into his arm.

## CHAPTER THIRTY-EIGHT

# BROADSIDE

THE DRIVER BARRELED DOWN the hill haphazardly, my thoughts racing just as fast.

"What was that? What were they giving him? Docil-E?" Xander didn't look at me. One hand clung to the console, the other was stiff-armed against the dash, trying to maintain his balance. Next to me, Valkov had a tight grip on Xander's seat, anchoring himself in place. With my hands still cuffed, I pinballed right, then left.

*Did Quin do this to me?* That's what I was wondering at the exact moment another car hit us—broadside—and all thinking came to a breakneck stop.

The car folded in on itself like crumpled paper.

Valkov catapulted toward me, his weight stopping my breath.

My shoulder cracked the window. Bones juddered, but I felt no pain.

Then we were spinning. And spinning. And spinning.

Valkov's arm hung unnaturally across my leg. I focused on the familiar—his tattoo. One, two, three, four drops of blood drawn in red. I counted each one before the world went dark.

* * *

"Let's go, Ms. Knightley." Something, someone tapped my cheek. "I'm not going to carry you the whole way."

My head felt so heavy. The smell of gasoline burned my nose. I tried to open my eyes, but shut them again fast when I saw Valkov's bone protruding through his skin like an alien creature hatching from inside him. I gagged a little. There was pressure under my arms. I was moving. Being dragged.

"You owe me for this." I knew that voice.

* * *

I can't say for sure how long I was gone—suspended somewhere between awake and asleep—but when I finally opened my eyes again, I wasn't dreaming. I *knew* I wasn't. The pain in my shoulder was searing, white-hot. Too real to be a dream. Everything else was straight out of an alternate universe. We were driving a police car, where I didn't know. The front end was smashed; the air bags hung loose like deflated balloons.

"You? Saved me?" My voice sounded strange, groggy. I suddenly realized my hands were free, but moving them—*moving at all*—hurt.

"I wouldn't think of it like that." Augustus turned to look at me, revealing patchy discoloration—*burns?*—on his cheeks and forehead. "I felt it was in my best interest to maintain our business relationship." He assessed his face in the rearview mirror, gently touching his irritated skin. "And frankly, I would rather face death or disfigurement than watch Xander Steele get anything or *anyone* he wants."

"So you crashed into his car? Is he dead? Is Valkov?"

Augustus chuckled. The airbag strike to the face had done little to rattle his conscience. "Would you have preferred I stuck around? Called the police? Performed CPR? I did what had to be done."

I wasn't sure what to say. It was hard to think with my shoulder throbbing. And even harder with Augustus sitting inches away from me. "How did you get the cuffs off of me?" I asked finally. His wrists, like mine, were rubbed raw. "And yourself?"

Augustus smirked, pleased with himself. "As you so aptly put it, Ms. Knightley, *a simple thank you will suffice*."

## CHAPTER THIRTY-NINE

# FIVE MILLION REASONS

"THIS IS A REALLY BAD IDEA," I murmured. Augustus was next to me, pressed flat to the wall, well camouflaged by the shadows of early morning. I couldn't even hear him breathing. We'd abandoned the police car several blocks from here and walked—arguing in hushed tones—the rest of the way. I knew our options were limited, but this was unexpected, even for Augustus. He never asked me. He'd already decided where we were going.

"Do it." Two words said aloud, but many more unspoken. In them, everything Augustus was capable of.

I rang the bell, the soft *ding dong* chiming on the other side of the door. I waited for the wail of an alarm to signal our presence, but minutes passed—still as stone—and no one came. "It's too early," I said. "Everyone's asleep."

"Again," he insisted.

Just as I reached my hand out, the door opened. "Lex? Oh my God! We were so worried when we didn't hear—"

When his eyes reached mine, Edison stopped speaking. "I'm not alone," I said.

"Neither am I." He cocked his head in the direction of the living room, where two of his father's security team were partially concealed behind the wall.

As if on cue, Augustus stepped into the doorway, looming over a barefoot, pajama-clad Edison. "You must be Edison Van Sant."

Edison blinked repeatedly, then rubbed his face. "Am I still sleeping? Is this guy for real?" He held out his arm to me. "Pinch me, Lex."

Sneering, Augustus extended two clawed fingers toward Edison. "Allow me."

Wide-eyed, Edison jerked his hand back. "I'm awake. I'm awake."

Augustus shrugged, laughing to himself. Without asking, he sauntered past Edison and into the foyer, pausing to consider the breathtaking print—a Misrach original—of the Golden Gate Bridge, framed in mahogany. "I wouldn't go in there if I were you," Edison warned, just as a gun-toting Barry pinned Augustus against the wall, forearm to throat. His partner, Scooter, positioned himself alongside Augustus, practically snarling.

"Call off your buffoons, please," Augustus wheezed.

Edison lingered, staring at me, bewildered. "What is going on?" he mouthed. "Augustus Porter?" Over his shoulder, I watched Augustus squirm a little as Barry held on tight.

"I can explain inside. Right now, we need a place to hide."

Edison snuck a glance at Augustus. "Let him go." Reluctant, Barry lowered his arm, and Augustus was free again. He rearranged himself, straightening his shoulders and readjusting my father's shirt collar at his neck. He strode by Barry, bumping his arm, then sank into the leather sofa, unfolding his long limbs.

"Sure, make yourself right at home," Edison deadpanned. To me, he whispered, "Have you met my father? I don't think he's going to be too keen on a fugitive lounging on his furniture."

"What if that fugitive had information on Xander—information that might help him win his appeal?"

"I'm listening." Mr. Van Sant was halfway down the staircase. He was a comical juxtaposition, wearing a silk bathrobe, hair askew, aiming his gun at Augustus. "But it better be good." Edison's face mirrored my surprise, but Augustus seemed nonplussed. He didn't even turn his head. If what Augustus hinted at on our way here was true, it was better than good. Yet, a part of me was skeptical. *Why hadn't he revealed it to me before?*

"It is," Augustus assured him. Mr. Van Sant approached cautiously, never taking his eyes—or his gun—off Augustus. He stationed himself in the chair opposite, his security team behind him. The expanse of the living room, vaulted ceilings and all, suddenly seemed much too small for this showdown. Edison and I stayed on the periphery, out of the line of fire.

"Augustus Porter, give me one reason why I shouldn't turn you over to the police right now—" Augustus leaned back and propped his feet on Mr. Van Sant's antique coffee table. His face contorting in disgust, Mr. Van Sant added, "—or shoot you myself."

"Just one reason?" Augustus asked. "I can give you five million."

Mouth agape, Edison nudged me. "Is he talking about what I think he's talking about?"

I nodded. "Tell them," I prompted.

"Patience, Alexandra. Patience." Augustus stared at Mr. Van Sant when he spoke. "I need to know what's in it for me. I need assurances."

"Ha!" Mr. Van Sant scoffed. "I hardly think you're in a position to negotiate."

Augustus' smile was broad. Mind games were his favorite, and he played them better than anyone. "On the contrary, I'm in the best position. I have nothing to lose."

"What do you want then?"

"It's mainly what I *don't* want, Nicholas. Prison. I wasn't meant to be caged." Augustus glared at me. Despite my insistence to the contrary, he still thought I helped Quin kidnap him. "I'm a free bird. Isn't that right, Ms. Knightley?" I rolled my eyes at him. *Yeah, a vulture.*

Mr. Van Sant shook his head. "You know I can't guarantee that. If you're arrested, I'll represent you, but your freedom won't be up to me."

"Represent me?" Augustus was incredulous. "Didn't you hear me?" He raised and flapped his long arms. "Free. Bird."

Edison stepped toward Augustus. "My father's not going to risk his reputation to help you elude capture. Right, Dad?" Mr. Van Sant's silence spoke volumes. "Dad?" He quieted Edison with his hand.

"Before I agree to anything, I need to know how you can help me. If your information is as good as you think it is, I'm sure we can come to some mutually beneficial arrangement." He extended his hand to Augustus and waited.

From behind me, I heard a shriek. Elana was pale-faced, transfixed by Augustus. She must've been sleeping in the guest room downstairs.

"It's okay," I told her. "He's working with us now." She kept staring, speechless.

"Is he?" Mr. Van Sant asked, still offering his hand.

Augustus took it with thinly disguised disdain. "I wouldn't think of it like that."

## CHAPTER FORTY

# TO BE DETERMINED

TEN MINUTES LATER, Elana finally found her voice. A cup of coffee in one hand, she used the other to punch Edison's arm as she sat down between us on the sofa. "I can't believe no one bothered to wake me up."

"Ouch," I teased as she punched me next.

"And I can't believe you were hiding Augustus!"

"So he was your text-happy *boyfriend*?" Edison chimed in.

My cheeks reddened. "I would've told you eventually. I just . . . well, it seemed pretty crazy."

"Or brilliant," Edison offered.

"To be determined, I guess." My eyes traveled up the stairs toward Mr. Van Sant's office. The door was closed. He and Augustus were inside.

"Do you think he's being truthful about that account belonging to Ryker?" Elana asked.

I nodded. "We already suspected as much after Baudin left that clue with the black roses. The real question is, can he prove it?" Mr. Van Sant was hoping Augustus could crack Baudin's coded message.

"And Quin?" she wondered. "Do you think we'll hear from him?" After I'd spit out the story of last night, Elana and Edison were steadfast—Quin would never betray me. He'd never hurt me. But I couldn't free myself from the nasty barbs of Xander's words. I was hooked, a fish on a line. Either Quin was lying to me or he was in more danger than he thought. Both options seemed dire.

"I hope so," I said. "He told me he would find a way to get in touch." I sighed, remembering the way Quin looked in my eyes when he'd said it, just before I walked down those stairs alone. It sounded so different, so much less certain in my own voice. Somehow it was harder to trust Quin now than the first day I'd met him, the day we'd taken that long, dark walk into the BART tunnels. It was knowing that I had so much more than my life—*I had my whole heart*—to lose.

"Then I'm sure he will." Elana squeezed my shoulder.

Edison reached over Elana, grabbing the remote. "SFTV's morning broadcast is about to start. We should see if there's any news about the crash."

"Doubtful," I said, reaching for Edison's phone.

"Anything from Max?" Elana asked. I'd already left him two messages, trying to explain the last couple of days—an impossible task when I didn't even understand it myself.

"No, but I'm going to try my dad again, at home this time." All my prior calls had gone unanswered, straight to voicemail every time.

Five rings and, finally, someone picked up. "Hello?" It was Carrie. She sounded tired.

"Carrie, it's me. Lex."

"Lex!" Silence. "Have you heard from your father?" Her question echoed inside the hollow pit in my stomach.

"No. That's why I was calling. Have you?"

She exhaled. "I've been trying to reach him for hours, ever since Langley texted."

"What did she say?" I didn't really want the answer.

"Uh . . . "

"Just tell me, Carrie. Whatever it is."

It came out fast, in one breath. "He's been taken."

"By who?" In my mind, I saw him—a knee in his back, a needle in his arm, his face pleading not for himself, but for me.

"The military." I already knew, of course, what she left unsaid. What no one seemed to be saying. *The Guardian Force.*

"Stay safe, Lex," Carrie warned before she hung up, cautioning us both.

* * *

When the door opened, Augustus emerged first, sneering. My heart paused until I saw Mr. Van Sant's broad shoulders behind Augustus. Still breathing. He was carrying his laptop.

"Well?" Edison asked. "Any luck?"

Excited, Mr. Van Sant held up his hand to Edison, connecting in a high five. "Eddie, we're back in business." Setting the laptop on the coffee table in front of us, he perched on the edge of the sofa. On the screen was Baudin's cryptic message:

*roSes, are in Bloom oncE again, saMe as bEfore—don't forget to share.*

Underneath, Mr. Van Sant had typed: *January 23, 2043.*

Edison spoke first. "That's it? A date. What does it mean?" He looked expectantly at Augustus.

Augustus' expression was flat—impossible to read. "Surely, I don't have to do all the work around here."

"Listen, you . . . you . . . " Edison approached Augustus, jabbing at him in accusation. His head barely reached Augustus' chin. " . . . you crook. I've heard all about you. You're nothing special. Just a small-time con man. My dad could run circles around you." Augustus acted as if Edison was invisible. I'd seen that before.

"Edison Archibald, sit down." Despite his protestation, there was a proud gleam in Mr. Van Sant's eyes. "It's a substitution cipher, simple if you have the key." He nodded at Augustus. "But Mr. Porter's information is only a jump start. It'll be up to us to do the rest."

"How did you break the code?" I asked Augustus. He said nothing—but held up his middle finger at Edison, chuckling. I gasped. He was wearing a ring with a shiny black stone. I imagined he'd slipped it from Xander's finger after the accident.

Elana chuckled. "Are you kidding? A decoder ring?" I couldn't help but laugh with her, but Augustus wasn't amused.

"Is something funny, Ms. Hamilton?" Her face sobered instantly. She shook her head.

I watched Augustus watching her. He relished in his power, and it made me wonder who was really in control here. "How did you know about the ring?" I asked him.

He tapped his finger against his lip, pretending to think. "How *did* I know about the ring? Let's see . . . oh, yes, I remember. I was about to make a deal—a very lucrative deal, I might add—with General Jamison Ryker, when *someone* got too big for her britches and messed things up for me."

My veins pulsed with fire just looking at him, but I wouldn't give him the satisfaction. "So Ryker told you?"

"Ms. Knightley, did anyone ever tell you the story of curiosity and the cat?" Augustus looked at me with pity. "Poor, poor kitty."

*Two can play this game.* "But satisfaction brought her back." I smiled at him. "If you're lying to us, the deal is off."

With Augustus and me locked in a standoff, neither of us budging, Mr. Van Sant stood up. "January 23," he announced. "Something important happens on January 23."

I took my eyes off Augustus and looked at my watch. "Whatever it is, we have three days—counting today—to figure it out."

## CHAPTER FORTY-ONE

# SLEEPING SNAKE

IN FIFTH-GRADE BIOLOGY, I learned it's almost impossible to tell if a snake is sleeping. Augustus' eyes were closed. His head was drooped lazily against the back of Mr. Van Sant's sofa. His lips were parted, the cave of his mouth slightly open. His fingers twitched. It was unnerving watching him, the feeling he could strike without warning. Knowing better, I leaned in anyway to inspect his face. His beard was returning, a few stubbly patches at a time. Just below his ear was a scar—a dark and jagged line, slightly raised—that extended under the too-tight collar of my father's shirt. I'd never noticed it before. The last time I was this close, I was in his office closet, his fingers coiled around my neck, squeezing.

"What was he like on Docil-E?" Elana whispered. She was observing Augustus too, but not the way I was. To my inquisitive mind, he was a specimen to be examined with neutrality—at least for now. But Elana's face was contorted in equal parts fear and disgust.

"He was . . ." I paused. There was really no word to describe it—his warm, obliging tone, his glassy-eyed smile. "Just imagine the complete opposite of the Augustus you know. That's how he was. He told me he couldn't remember what he said or did, only that he felt sublime."

"Sublime?"

"That was his word."

"Too bad the effects aren't permanent." Next to her, Edison nodded. I couldn't admit it, of course, but I wasn't so sure I agreed. Augustus' predictability, as sly and scheming as he was, brought me comfort. I could see him coming. But like slumbering Augustus, on Docil-E, he was unnatural, the outcome dangerously uncertain. When I turned back to Augustus, his eyes were open, and I felt certain he was never sleeping at all.

"I'm hungry," he announced.

"Don't look at me. My days of pimento sandwich delivery are over." I saw Elana and Edison exchange a glance, but neither questioned me.

"I'm hungry," Augustus said again, this time to Barry, who was stationed across from him.

Barry's jaw tensed. He placed a hand on his weapon. "Do I look like a waiter to you?"

Augustus shrugged, returning Barry's frown with an innocent smile. "You are the hired help, correct?"

"Yeah, hired to put my fist through your face."

"Easy there, you two." Mr. Van Sant returned from his office, rounding the corner just in time. "I need you on the same team right now."

"Hmph." Barry glared at Augustus, but said nothing more. I was relieved, eager for Mr. Van Sant's information on my father.

"Did you find out anything about my dad?"

Mr. Van Sant sighed and sat down next to me. There was pity in his eyes. "Good news or bad news first?" he asked.

"Good," Elana answered for me.

"My law enforcement source confirmed that Mr. Knightley is okay, but . . ." *Here comes the bad.* " . . . he's being held by the military for resisting orders."

"Can they do that?" Edison asked, incredulous.

"Unfortunately, yes. They have jurisdiction during curfew hours." Mr. Van Sant gave me another look, more crestfallen than the last. "I don't think this is about your dad, Lex. It's about you. The police are planning to offer a reward for your arrest."

"Arrest? I thought they just wanted to question me."

"Apparently, Steele changed their minds for them. My source said he's alive—pretty beat up and mad as a hornet—but alive. They both are. Him and Valkov."

Augustus frowned. "How unfortunate."

"So what do we do now?" I asked.

"You're probably not going to like it," Mr. Van Sant admitted. "But it's the only way. We need to deal with this before it becomes unmanageable. You have to turn yourself in for questioning."

I'm positive I stopped breathing. Mr. Van Sant's mouth was moving, but his voice was out-pounded by the bass drum thumping of my heart in my ears. I read his lips. "I'll go with you." I could only nod. "Edison too."

I collapsed back against the sofa. Elana patted my arm. "It'll be okay." *Inhale, exhale*, I reminded myself, watching the rise and fall of my chest until I felt steady again. Mr. Van Sant's words nagged at me, droning over the rest of my thoughts. *Without meaning to, I'd picked a fight with a hornet. A hornet on EAMs.*

Augustus cleared his throat. "Still hungry."

## CHAPTER FORTY-TWO

# AMATEUR

"JUST LET ME DO THE TALKING." Mr. Van Sant's reminder—as if I needed one—came a block from the San Francisco Police Department's headquarters. We had already reviewed his strategy and rehearsed my answers before we left. I would gladly let him speak for me. In fact, I was hoping I wouldn't have to say much at all.

"Pardon me, Mr. Van Sant, but there appears to be some commotion up ahead." I followed Scooter's finger to a mob of protestors. They spilled out into the street, halting traffic. I cracked my window so I could hear their chanting. "No new drugs! No more violence! Clean up our streets!" The crowd was haphazardly moving in the direction of Zenigenic about a half-mile walk from the station.

"Should I let you out here?" Scooter asked.

Mr. Van Sant nodded. "Eddie, keep an eye on Lex, please." Shielding his face with his leather briefcase, Mr. Van Sant headed into the fray. I tagged behind Edison, keeping my eyes on the ground and praying I wouldn't be noticed.

"Mr. Van Sant! Mr. Van Sant!" Her recognition a step late, Barbara Blake nearly tripped in her heels sprinting after Edison's father. "Can we get a statement about Zenigenic's new drug?" She was in pursuit. "The status of George McAllister's appeal?" Still running. "The interview with his son, Quin?" When she finally reached him, she expelled her last question in one exhausted breath. "Bill Knightley's arrest?"

"No comment." The door closed behind him. Barbara paused for a moment, her dejected face reflected in the glass. Then her eyes opened wide with utter thrill. She whipped around toward us as we approached.

"Alexandra Knightley!" The microphone was in my face, its presence as demanding as Barbara herself. "What can you tell us about Peter Radley? Did you know him? Were you there when he died?" Edison stiff-armed Barbara, but it didn't deter her. "What would your mother think of Zenigenic's new drug? Is she responsible for this one too?"

I stopped cold. Since November, when the media obtained the transcript of Dr. Pearson's trial testimony linking Emovere and Onyx, my mother had resumed center stage in the controversy. A few weeks ago *The Real Scoop* had run an exclusive interview with one of her former coworkers at Zenigenic. He insinuated she knew that Onyx, even in its earliest form, would be misused by the Guardian Force.

"C'mon, Lex." Edison stood at the threshold, prompting me.

"Is she?" Barbara Blake demanded. "Is she responsible?" Her eyes were accusing. I returned her stare, harder and hotter, but it was really my mother I was angry with. More and more, she was splitting in two—Dr. Victoria Knightley, ambitious Zenigenic psychiatrist, casting a shadow over my mother. I hated one and desperately loved the other.

*Don't do it, Lex.* "My mother regretted every minute she spent at Zenigenic. She would be disgusted that—"

Edison pulled me inside before I could finish. As the door shut, I caught one last glimpse of Barbara. She was lit with excitement. Beaming, her white teeth signaled victory. I felt sick inside. I was such an amateur.

"Please don't tell your dad." Edison didn't answer, just shook his head disapprovingly. Hard to believe, but San Francisco Police Department's headquarters was more chaotic than the Oakland station where I'd visited George McAllister. Mr. Van Sant had already bypassed a long, disgruntled line and was speaking to an officer at the desk. The man was nodding, his expression deferent.

"What next?" I asked Edison, trying to distract myself.

"We wait." He glanced at me sidelong, amending his instructions. "We stay out of trouble, and we wait."

"Sorry," I murmured. I knew my mistake with Barbara was costly. Alexandra Knightley's statement to the media was probably already being processed and packaged for the next news brief. *Daughter of Victoria Knightley Slams Zenigenic.* That certainly wouldn't win me any points with Xander.

"Comin' through!" The door swung open wide, and two military officers entered, waving their arms to clear a path. Behind them, a row of men, each handcuffed and joined to the other at the waist, filed inside.

"Last night's arrests," Edison whispered. "Mostly curfew violations. They bring them here after they detox." I knew my father wouldn't be there, but I scoured the line anyway, searching for a sign of him. Satan's Syndicate was well represented, at least ten necks tattooed with an unmistakable inverted pentagram. The group was surprisingly subdued. Most held their heads down. None spoke. I had no doubt that, like my father, all these men had been injected with Docil-E.

"Edison," Mr. Van Sant called out over the zigzag of inmates. "They're ready for Alexandra." I stood and waited for the last of them to pass. A tall, scrawny redhead . . . a dark-eyed potbelly . . . a perfectly sculpted, painfully familiar Mohawk.

I jabbed my elbow into Edison's side, and he yelped. "It's String," I hissed, averting my eyes from the line. I wasn't sure where to look so I fixed on their feet until String's boots were several steps ahead of us. I slowly raised my head, then snapped it back down again. He was looking at me—but not just looking. His eyes were issuing a challenge.

"Lex." I heard Edison pleading with me under his breath, but I ignored him. Instead I marched away from him toward String.

"What's a nice girl like you doing in a place like this?" he asked, singsong.

I rolled my eyes. "I would ask you the same, but, well . . . you're not nice, are you?"

String shrugged off my insult. "Whatever you say. You've got it all figured out."

"You killed Peter Radley." The words were out before I could measure their impact.

String blinked, the only movement on the flat landscape of his face. "Peter Radley killed himself."

"You didn't exactly stop him. He told me you gave him that Emovere."

"Funny, I thought you were the person of interest here."

I heard Edison gaining ground behind me, but I wasn't finished yet. "You were following George McAllister. You were following Quin. Maybe you followed me too. Is that how Xander found me?"

String seemed surprised, then incensed by my indictment. "That's a lot of accusations from someone who once said she trusted me." He glanced over his shoulder toward the officer. He was leaning over the desk, back turned to us. "As for the McAllisters, do you really know who you're defending?" I opened my mouth, but he plowed over me in an exaggerated whisper. "I'll tell you who. One twice-convicted murderer and one—"

"Lex!" Edison tugged my arm, but I didn't turn away.

"Let's go, Croft!" The abrupt snarl of a police officer ended the exchange. I watched String's Mohawk disappear behind secured doors, still waiting for him to finish his sentence.

* * *

I took an audible breath, pushing String from my mind. "Let's begin with why you went to Green Briar." *So much for starting with an easy one.* Detective Katherine Brewster—she'd said to call her Katie—smiled at me, as if she already knew the answer. *She probably did.* According to Mr. Van Sant, she was smart and exacting, but fair.

"Go ahead, Alexandra. You have nothing to hide." Mr. Van Sant sat on one side of me, Edison on the other. *A Van Sant sandwich, any criminal's dream.* Except I wasn't a criminal. Just a liar. Lucky for me, my skills at subterfuge were on a definite uptick.

"My dad—he's a journalist—he was hoping to get an interview with Peter Radley."

"I see." She typed a note onto her computer tablet. "So why did you go inside alone?"

"Green Briar doesn't allow media on the premises."

"And you used someone else's name at the front desk . . ."

Before I could answer, Mr. Van Sant held up his hand, stopping me. "Is that a question?" he asked.

The detective rolled her eyes but nodded. "Did you? Did you use an alias?" *Alias.* That sounded bad. I hesitated, glancing at Mr. Van Sant.

"Just tell her the truth."

"Yes," I finally replied. Mr. Van Sant coached me well. *Only answer the question asked of you.*

"Why?"

"I didn't want to give my name—Knightley—because my mother used to work there."

"Who is Emma Markum?"

"A girl I don't like." *I wasn't even sure that was the truth anymore.*

"Did you know she was in the Guardian Force?" That was unexpected. I waited for Mr. Van Sant to interrupt, but he didn't.

"Sort of."

*"Sort of?"*

"How is this relevant?" Mr. Van Sant demanded.

"We're not in court, Nicholas. I decide what's relevant here." I watched Mr. Van Sant for signs of an eruption. No one called him by his first name. Ever.

"She's a young girl, Katherine. She's been through a lot. I'm sure you can appreciate the courage it took for her to show up and answer your questions. Now it was my understanding Peter Radley is the reason we're here, not Emma Markum. Am I wrong on that?"

The detective didn't answer, but asked another question instead. "What happened in the room with Peter?"

I went back there in my mind—his gritted teeth, his rubbed-raw arms, the hollow desolation in his voice—but I couldn't tell her everything. Mr. Van Sant agreed with Quin. Xander had most of the police force in his pocket. "He told me that he failed his mission, and then he jumped."

She opened her eyes wide at me and leaned in. "That's all?"

I shrugged. "I wish I could be more helpful." I sounded earnest, but I doubted she believed me. She was probably accustomed to being deceived.

"Did you notice anything—anything at all—that seemed odd or suspicious? Were there EAMs in the room?"

"It happened so fast, and then I just got scared and ran. I didn't see anything like that."

After typing a few more notes, Detective Brewster gathered her things. Her face was still water—serene, hiding its depths. "Okay,

Alexandra. Give me a minute to finish up my notes, and I'll be back."

With the click of the door, I relaxed. *That wasn't so bad.* I stayed quiet, congratulating myself in silence, knowing there was a camera watching and listening. Meanwhile, Mr. Van Sant was typing furiously. He passed me his computer tablet.

*Something's off. She'd never give in like that about Emma. Be ready.*

I stared at the words, the letters, until they blurred. I tried to be ready, but I wasn't sure how. I squirmed in my seat, tapping my fingers on the table until Edison shushed me with a nudge. Seconds passed, then minutes. I watched them go by on the large clock hung just across from me. Aside from a folding table and four chairs, it was the only thing in the room.

"Sorry that took so long." The detective returned to her seat. "I just have a few more questions. Then I'll let you get back to your life." *Right. My life. Dad in jail. Ex-boyfriend consorting with the enemy. A psychopath as an ally. Let me get back to that.*

"I apologize for asking again, but how well do you know Emma Mar—?"

Mr. Van Sant interrupted her. "My client won't be answering any questions about Ms. Markum."

"Ms. Knightley, would it surprise you to learn she's been staying at your house?" *And there it was. The sucker punch I was supposed to be ready for.*

"Detective Brewster, are you planning to charge my client with a crime? If not, we're done here." Mr. Van Sant stood up. Edison immediately followed. I just sat there, legs leaden, until Mr. Van Sant pulled me to my feet.

The detective sneered at him. "Fine. Have it your way, Nicholas." Her veneer of politeness vanished, she turned to me with obvious disapproval. "After you escaped from military custody this morning, they went looking for you at your house. Emma Markum and Carrie Donovan were arrested there."

I opened my mouth, still unsure what I would say, when Mr. Van Sant yanked me toward the door. "We're done here."

"They're being charged with possession of emotional-altering medication and—"

"Done." Mr. Van Sant repeated. He was already speed walking down the hallway, dragging me alongside him. All I could do was keep up.

## CHAPTER FORTY-THREE:

# BLANK SPACE

Mr. Van Sant was boiling. Red-faced and sweating, he let out a primal yell the moment Scooter rounded the corner from the station. I looked at Edison with alarm.

"Don't worry," he whispered. "He does this all the time."

We rode in silence, the air conditioner blasting Mr. Van Sant's face. Finally, he loosened his tie and spoke. "Well that was a complete disaster."

"Why didn't you tell us Carrie was staying with you?" Edison asked.

I sighed. "I'm sorry. I should have. But she was already so paranoid. After she left the rehab program, she was convinced the government was after her."

"Looks like she might be right," Mr. Van Sant muttered.

Edison tapped his father's shoulder. "What about your source?" he asked. "Do you think he knew about the arrest?"

"Former source," Mr. Van Sant corrected. "And apparently not."

Mr. Van Sant asked Scooter to let us out a block from the house. I felt like a burglar, sneaking in through the fenced back entrance, past the pool and the gardens. Through the picture window, I saw Elana. She was sitting on the sofa, looking up at someone, gesturing wildly with her hands. Even from here, I could see her face was panicked. As we neared the door, the rest of the room came into view. A mildly interested Augustus lounged in Mr. Van Sant's recliner, Barry guarding him hawk-like. Standing over Elana, just as animated, was Max. When we opened the door, all we heard was his frantic voice.

" . . . and then, they just took her away. Emma too. And a whole bunch of boxes from Dr. Knightley's—Lex!" Max ran over to us. His hands were shaking.

"Sit down." Mr. Van Sant guided Max to the sofa, where he reluctantly lowered himself to the edge. "Now take a deep breath and start from the beginning."

I could hear the tremble in Max's breath as he inhaled. "I had a fight with String. That's how it started. Last night, he showed up at my house a couple of hours before the curfew. He was acting funny, asking me a lot of questions about when I saw you last. So I finally confronted him about . . . " Max paused and cut his eyes to Augustus. They opened wide, as if he was just seeing him for the first time. "Uh . . . " His voice quivered. "Does he belong here?"

Mr. Van Sant nodded at Barry. "Take him in the other room."

"With pleasure." With one hand and not much effort, Barry seized Augustus by the arm. Augustus was much taller—but Barry outweighed him by at least fifty pounds of muscle. On the other hand, Augustus' sheer will had a weight of its own. The two of them jostled with each other as they walked toward the kitchen.

"I don't like you keeping secrets," Augustus remarked, pointing with his free hand at Mr. Van Sant. "How can I trust you're a man of your word if I'm shoved out of the room by this—" Barry tightened his grip on Augustus' shoulder, causing him to grimace. "—this heathen every time something important goes down?"

"So then, you've been completely honest with us?" I asked.

"As honest with you, Ms. Knightley, as you've been with me."

"Let's go," Barry snapped, giving Augustus a forceful push through the kitchen door. "You did say you were hungry again, didn't you?"

Max stared after them with utter confusion. "We'll tell you about it later," I reassured him.

Mr. Van Sant touched Max's arm. "Continue."

Another deep breath and Max began where he left off. "I confronted String about everything—Radley and the picture of George McAllister." Now it was Mr. Van Sant who looked dumbfounded. "I found it in his backpack just before the trial ended. I was scared to ask him about it. I wasn't sure what it meant. But yesterday, it just spilled out. I couldn't keep it inside anymore."

"What did he say?" I asked.

Max shook his head. "Nothing. Absolutely nothing. He just left."

"Not even a word?"

"Just that I wouldn't understand." Suddenly, Max's eyes were watery. "I told him I would try, but . . ."

"When did you go to the Knightley's house?" Mr. Van Sant asked, his stern voice yanking Max back from the verge of tears.

"This morning, after I got the text from Edison's phone. I went right over to talk to Lex, but they were already there."

"Who?"

"The military. And Xander."

"Xander Steele?" It was rare that Mr. Van Sant sounded surprised. "Are you certain it was him?"

"Yep. I wasn't sure at first. He looked really bad. His face was bandaged, and he was wearing a sling. But it was definitely him."

Mr. Van Sant raised his eyebrows at me. "I told you. Mad as a hornet."

"So what happened?" I asked, dreading his answer.

"When I got there, the house was already surrounded. The door was busted open. I just hid in the car and watched the whole thing. They brought out Carrie first, then Emma. Loaded them into a jeep and drove away. And I just watched." Max put his head in his hands.

Patting Max's shoulder, Mr. Van Sant tried to reassure him. "Son, you did the right thing. If you showed your face, you would've been arrested too. I guarantee it."

"He's right, Max," Elana added. "You were smart." We all nodded our agreement.

Without raising his head, Max muttered, "There's more." When he looked up again, his eyes found mine. "They took some of your mom's stuff. I couldn't see what exactly, but they loaded a few boxes out of her lab."

My chest felt tight—my heart squeezed and wrung out like a wet dishrag. "What about Artos?" My voice came out as a whisper.

Max shrugged. "I don't know. They were trying to catch him, but he ran off down the street. I called for him before I left—I was afraid to get out of the car—but he didn't come. Sorry, Lex."

"It's okay," I told him. But nothing was okay. I wasn't sure if anything would ever be okay again.

* * *

An hour later, with all our secrets exchanged, Mr. Van Sant allowed Augustus to return to the living room. Still pouting, he dropped down onto the sofa, turned his back to us, and clicked on the television.

"Do you know what I despise most in this world?" he asked. "Boredom." He chuckled to himself. "My mother always said the devil finds work for idle minds." I gave Augustus a skeptical look as Edison and Elana exchanged an eye roll. Augustus had mentioned his mother before—different versions of her—when he was staying on the boat. Sometimes cold and unforgiving, sometimes warm and tender, she seemed to change with his mood. It was impossible to imagine her, easier to believe he'd hatched from a rancid egg.

"I'm sure Barbara Blake will be happy to keep the devil at bay," Edison said, gesturing to the screen where Barbara was finishing her report on last night's violence. *Last night.* It seemed so long ago. It was strange the way bad things expanded, filling every nook of every second, of every minute, of every hour, slowing time to a laborious crawl.

Augustus groaned. "I find Ms. Blake as dull as cardboard."

"Shh." I pointed to the television. "She's talking about Zenigenic."

> **". . . is expected to occur tomorrow at Zenigenic's headquarters in San Francisco and comes on the heels of an explosive interview there with Quin McAllister, son of convicted murderer, George McAllister. As many of you know, the younger McAllister shocked viewers with his statements of support for Xander Steele. Steele appears to be capitalizing on McAllister's popularity—especially with a recent poll showing increased approval rates for the pharmaceutical mogul and his newest drug, Docil-E, particularly in the**

> **18-to-24 demographic. Before Steele's recent brush with death, public opinion of him was at an all-time low with protestors regularly stationed outside Zenigenic. Our sources close to Steele hinted that McAllister will likely make an appearance at Docil-E's unveiling in two days and may even address the crowd."**

Edison chuckled. "Looks like Quin might be an A-lister after all." The sound of my own laughter surprised me, mercifully interrupting my thinking, even if it was short-lived.

"So predictable . . . Mr. McAllister and his fatal flaw." Augustus didn't look at me, but I knew his words were meant for me. Because they stung. Because I knew Quin's weakness better than anyone. He trusted the wrong men, trusted them until they broke him. Ryker. Augustus. But Xander? He didn't really trust Xander—did he? I looked at Augustus, wondering, but knowing better than to ask.

"What's that supposed to mean?" Edison demanded.

Augustus shrugged. "I'm just a small-time con man. What do I know?"

"Argh!" Frustrated, Edison dialed up the volume of the television, drowning out Augustus' disdainful snicker.

Next to me, Max gently tugged at my jacket sleeve. "Lex, I need to talk to you." He gestured toward the foyer, his voice barely audible. I nodded and followed him. When we were out of view of the others, he whispered, "Quin was there today. At your house." I just gaped at him, speechless. "He might've seen me . . . recognized the car. I don't know."

I searched for words, any words. "What—why—was he—what was he doing?" I finally spit out.

"He was with Xander most of the time." After a quick glance to assess my reaction—somewhere between relieved and appalled—he added, "It's good, right? It means he didn't blow his cover."

"Why didn't you say anything?"

"I wanted to tell you first. To see what you thought."

*What do I think?* My brain seemed to be all out of thoughts. There was only blank space and a dull ache.

# CHAPTER FORTY-FOUR:

# HOME, AGAIN

Fortunately for me, Edison and Elana had plenty of thoughts about Max's revelation.

"We have to go to your house," Edison announced without pause. We were sitting in his bedroom while Augustus dozed downstairs under Barry's watchful eyes. Mr. Van Sant was holed up in his office trying to find out something—anything—about the fate of Carrie, Emma, and my father.

I shook my head. "I agree, but—"

"No buts." Edison's voice was firm. "We have to." He looked to Elana for support.

"Lex, I think he's right. We need to know what they took from your mom's lab. Plus, what if Quin left something behind? Like a message?"

"And we can look for Artos," Max added.

"But," I began again, "what about your dad?"

"Let me handle him," Edison said. "Since the trial, he's actually starting to listen to me." I raised my eyebrows, skeptical. "Or at least he's gotten better at pretending."

A few hours later—and some gentle persuasion from Edison—Mr. Van Sant green lighted our plan. Early the next morning, we were on our way, Scooter tailing us in Mr. Van Sant's car. Through the Marina, past the Presidio, those familiar red cables broke through the clouds. They were the link between one world and another, the way home.

"Never gets easier," Edison murmured as we approached the Golden Gate. Still skittish about bridges, his pride outweighed his fear, and he reluctantly agreed to drive. I heard him inhale sharply when the car shifted in the battering wind. He slowed to a crawl.

"Just remember your breathing," Elana prompted. "In through the nose. Out through the mouth."

"Trying." It sounded like his teeth were clenched, air escaping through them like whistling steam.

Max snickered. "At this point, we'll be there in a week or so. Oh wait, we might be dead by then."

"I'm going as fast as I can, Max."

"Sorry, Grandpa."

"Are you okay back there?" Elana asked me, probably trying to distract them both. "We're almost at the checkpoint." Hunkered beneath a tarp in the backseat, I felt her hand on my head and nodded. With Xander and the military still on my trail, we weren't taking any chances.

"Ready for this, Red?" Edison asked, a few minutes later. I figured we were close—the span of the bridge mostly behind us—because his voice was relaxed again.

"Ready," Elana replied.

"I hope I'm ready." Now Max sounded nervous. I lifted the tarp and poked my head out. He was fidgeting with his phone, turning it over and over again in his hand. He could deny it all he wanted—and he had vehemently, several times in fact on the way here—but I knew Max was hoping to hear from String. When our eyes connected, both of us caught, he slipped the phone into his pocket, and I ducked back into my hiding place. I felt the van slow to a stop, heard the rush of air through the window.

"Good evening, sir." Edison was so smooth.

"Where are you kids headed?"

"A hot date," Edison answered. I grinned as I imagined him winking at Elana when he said it.

"All three of you?"

Edison chuckled. "I guess I can't be trusted. Her big brother here is our chaperone."

"That's right," Max said. His voice started a little shaky, but grew deeper and stronger as he spoke. "I'm here to keep this guy in line."

Edison jumped in. "These days you can't be too careful. Right, Officer? With EAMs and all . . . "

"Mind if I take a look back there?" My body stiffened when the back door opened.

"Sure. Knock yourself out. Just a few supplies for our romantic afternoon picnic."

"Romantic?" Max sounded every bit the protective brother. "You might want to rethink that word, buddy. Or you'll be getting romantic with this." There was a smacking sound, probably Max's fist against his palm.

Right on cue, Elana began to cry. Her sniffling building steadily to a wail. "Officer," she sobbed, "can't you tell them to get along? Puh-lease."

"Young lady, I don't have time to get involved in domestic disputes."

"But, but—" Elana was blubbering.

"Enjoy your date." The back door shut, and the van lurched forward. Quiet, I waited, still uncertain if it was safe.

At Elana's laugh, I lifted the tarp. Max was shaking his head, smiling at them as Elana eyed Edison. "So, big shot, how come we've never really had a romantic picnic?"

* * *

The house was waiting for us, its shuttered eyes half open, as if nothing had happened. But as we neared the door, I began to feel queasy. It hung loosely from its hinges, barely pulled to. On it was a typed notice marked *United States Military. WARNING: Illegal emotion-altering medications discovered at this location. Property may be subject to seizure.*

Scooter snapped a picture of the notice with his phone. "Mr. Van Sant will want to see that." He tapped the door with his boot, and it swung open wide, rattling a little. Inside it was cold and dark and different somehow—defiled—as if all the unfamiliar hands had left more than fingerprints behind. In the kitchen, a cup of coffee sat, cold, on the table, still waiting for Carrie's return.

"Let's check your mom's lab first," Edison suggested, sending my stomach into a free fall. I couldn't bear the thought of her things rifled through, violated, left with a tangible stain. Reluctantly, I trailed behind them.

As we entered, Elana gasped, and I braced myself. It was worse than I feared. Broken glass covered the floor. Crunching under my feet with every step were the remnants of my mother's career—pieces of her equipment, broken beakers, papers strewn everywhere. No one spoke. They were waiting for me.

I walked to the corner of the lab, positioning a stool under the shelf. Without a word, I climbed up and balanced on its center. Only two boxes remained, neither marked *Dishes*.

"It's all gone."

"What's gone?" Elana asked, extending her hand to me. I didn't take it. Just stood there. From here, the damage was visible in its entirety. I was flying over the battlefield, surveying the casualties.

"All of it. The Crim-X files. Her Resilire research. Her laptop. Everything." I reached for one of the remaining boxes. Its taped seal was already broken, a thick layer of dust disturbed by unfeeling hands.

"It's heavy," I warned, passing it down to Elana. She and Edison hauled it to the counter wordlessly, and I followed. With the precision of an archaeologist, I opened the box. Before thought, before feeling, the tears came. I didn't try to stop them—you can't hold back a river. And that's what it was. With a current so strong, it bowled me over.

"Lex?" Elana stayed a step back, but I felt her hand on my shoulder. "What is it?"

I held it out to her. It was a picture of my mother. She had shown it to me before, a very long time ago when my dad was still around. "This was a few years before you," she'd said. "My first day in my own lab. The one your father built for me." She was giving that slightly irritated smile of hers to whoever was behind the camera, probably my father. It was uncanny how much she looked like me.

"Why did you print it?" I'd asked her. Most of my parents' photos were stored on her computer.

"It was a special one." That was all she said.

Elana took a cautious step toward the box, gingerly placing her hand on the flap, as if asking my permission. "Are there more inside?"

I nodded. "Lots more." I wiped my cheeks with my jacket sleeve. "But I can't look."

"Why don't you and Max check the house?" Edison offered. "We'll look around in here."

I slipped the photo inside my back pocket. "I think I'd rather go alone, if that's okay."

Scooter handed me a radio. "Call us if you need anything." I headed out the door without a second glance. There are some things you don't want to remember. Unfortunately, those are usually the things you can't forget.

## CHAPTER FORTY-FIVE:

# DEATH'S FACE

I made quick work of the house, calling for Artos as I went room to room. I pretended I was a robot—a methodical, mechanical machine. It was easy to spot what was missing. *Nothing.* Aside from my father's office—ransacked—most of the house was untouched. I saved my room for last.

The door was shut as I had left it. Business-like, I opened it without feeling, systematically scanning the room. The curtains were drawn. My Columbia T-shirt hung loosely over my desk chair, which was pushed all the way into my desk, the way I always kept it. My things were in order. The bed was neatly made. *The bed.* My eyes stopped moving and considered it more carefully. At the edge of the covers, there was a slight indentation, as if someone had been sitting there.

"Artos?" I dropped to my knees and peered underneath. Only a box of my old clothing and . . . I reached my hand toward it. It was a crumpled piece of paper I recognized instantly. I unfolded it anyway, eager for the message inside. My heart was human again, beating faster than I would've liked.

*Nothing false and possible is love . . .*

*—Q (and e.e. cummings)*

Quin had secreted it under my pillow last year. We read the poem together in his mother's poetry book, having already practically memorized all the verses in mine. It must've been one of the notes I'd balled up in my hand nights ago. *But how did it get here?* I opened my bedside drawer and removed my mother's book. I turned to the dog-eared page, letting the other slips of paper fall to the bed. Beneath her handwriting was Quin's.

*1-23-43. Another Chicago.*

"Lex!" Scooter's gruff voice barked at me from the radio. "Gotta go. We've got company."

In an instant, I was on my feet and moving, sweeping the notes into the drawer and securing the book inside my jacket. I pulled back the edge of the curtain, just enough to glimpse the driveway. I expected to see a military convoy, the police, Xander, Valkov—anything but what I saw. There were two armed men approaching the front door, both of their faces covered with black bandanas. *Satan's Syndicate!*

A current of fear gripped me—I was electric. Buzzing, I skirted out of the bedroom and into the hallway, just as the first of them stepped inside. I made no sound, took no breath. Still, he seemed to sense me, turning immediately in my direction.

"It's her." His voice was strange, possessed.

There was a flash, then an explosion—gunshots! I backtracked, fumbling with the door as a bullet lodged in the frame. He was coming. *Fast.* Firing his gun without pause, without aim. The cracking cut the air like a whip and seemed to come from everywhere. I lunged for the window, thrusting it open. As I hit the ground, it shattered behind me.

"Go, go, go!" From here, I could hear Scooter. He was crouched behind the Syndicate's car—so close, but too far away for me to reach—waving Max, Elana, and Edison up the street to safety. Only his thinning gray hair and a gun were visible over the hood as he dodged bullets coming from the direction of the lab. I crawled toward the side of the house, planning my escape route. The backyard. That was my target. From there, I could slip through the fences to the street where our cars were parked, a block away.

Suddenly, the gunfire stopped, but the silence was eerie. Remembering my own trigger-happy mania on Emovere, I wondered if the Syndicate was out of ammunition. *And Scooter?* I couldn't see him anymore. I tried not to think about what I couldn't see, like those twin-inverted pentagrams I imagined were close by. Hunting.

I picked up a shard of glass, a jagged piece of my window, and held it tight in my hand. When I reached the gate, I crouched down low and slipped in, the neighbor's fence in sight.

Then I froze.

One of the Syndicate was on the ground a few feet from me. His body was still but broken, a gaping wound on his neck. His head twisted unnaturally, his eyes so wide. I had seen enough death to recognize its face. I turned away and pressed myself against the side of the house, listening.

The wind gusted and moaned a little, playing tricks on me as it whipped around the corner. Closer, there were my own sounds, a frenetic orchestra of breath and beat. Closer still, there was something else, so delicate it was barely discernible, like a feather settling on a stream. The soft, measured padding of boots on grass. I focused hard, until I heard only that—the crunch and rustle of each tender blade. I was being stalked.

Even though I knew it was coming, his dark hand shocked me. So strong, so quick, so intent. I stabbed at it with the glass, slicing a gash between his fingers. I winced at the way it felt to tear flesh, to draw blood, but he didn't pull back, didn't even cry out in pain. He kept reaching, planting his rose-red palm against my shirt, and pulling me around the side of the house.

I dug my heels into the ground and swiped at him again, cutting a deep chasm in his cheek and another in his arm. Still, he didn't let go. Instead he reeled me toward him. As I raised my hand for another strike, he grabbed my wrist, and for an instant, we were deadlocked, the glass shard suspended between us.

His lips curled in a devil's grin as my muscles weakened. "I'm going to enjoy this." If his voice was a color, it would've been black. Black as the ash of a funeral pyre. Black as a stone set upon an unmarked grave. *Onyx-black.* I watched the tendons in his hand contracting, strangling, directing the glass back to me.

Under the weight of him, I fell to my knees, then onto my back. The length of my arm, roughly two feet, was all that separated us—me and him, me and Onyx, me and a razor-sharp knife of glass. My arm was already shaking, my hand bleeding from my unrelenting grip. I wriggled my legs, willing them to move, but I was pinned. Surrender seemed certain. Death, inevitable.

It wasn't at all what I expected. I felt anesthetized, resigned. I let my mind go somewhere else. *Anywhere else.* And it went to Shelly. I could see her on the bedroom floor, Valkov standing over her, murdering her again and again. *Fourteen times.* Once would've been enough. She would've pleaded with him, knowing the first time that cold edge slipped through her how it would end. She would've clutched her stomach, shielding the baby inside her. It was the last thing she would've done before her world snapped shut, closing her somewhere no light could touch.

The glass was poised above me. I squeezed my eyes tight. I didn't want to see it coming.

* * *

The growl was the first sign I wasn't dead. It was low and deep. Guttural. Artos had never growled like that before, not even at Augustus. He was sprinting, charging, ears down, teeth bared—and so much sharper than I remembered. When he clamped down on the Syndicate's upper thigh, Artos was nearly unrecognizable. Only his collar gave him away. The dark cave of his mouth opened, the edges frothed with saliva. His eyes were wild and wide.

As Artos pulled, yanking the man away from me with fierce determination, I struggled to my knees. I pushed against his arm until I was back on my feet.

"Get off!" he yelled at Artos, still gripping my wrist with one hand. He shook his leg back and forth and pounded Artos' body with his other fist, but the teeth only went deeper. His nose scratched and bloody, Artos maintained his focus, snarling with primal conviction.

I knew I had one chance, and it was now. I opened my fingers and let the glass fall to the ground. The Syndicate watched it with excitement, with desire. He thought *my* chance was *his*. But he was wrong.

I reared back and hit him in the throat, stunning him. Paused but not stopped, he doubled over, still reaching for the glass. Artos briefly released his leg, only to take another harder bite. Before he could recover, I secured the shard and plunged it into him. I'm not sure where—I was already running.

"Artos! Let's go!"

I kept my eyes straight ahead, kept my legs turning, all the while expecting the bullet—the blow, the sudden jerk that would end me. Halfway back to the van, I met Edison. He was hurrying toward the house, gun in hand.

"Lex! We thought you made it out before us." He immediately reversed course, jogging alongside me. "But you weren't here and . . ." He didn't finish the sentence, but I could hear the leftover panic in his voice. Over his shoulder, I saw Elana in the passenger seat, recognized the relief in her eyes. That was the second sign. I was still alive.

## CHAPTER FORTY-SIX:

# YOURS

"Where's Scooter?" Out of breath, my voice sounded more like a gasp.

Edison pointed to the back of the van. "He's wounded. Get in!" I slid into the backseat, making room for Artos. Next to me, Scooter laid on the tarp, clutching his shoulder. His fingers were wet and red, his face pale white.

"We have to get him to a hospital," I said as Edison revved the engine and floored the accelerator. "Marin General is about ten minutes from here."

Scooter was shaking his head. "Too many people. Not safe."

"I'll be fine," I assured him. "I'll just wait in the van." Even as I said it, I doubted I was safe anywhere.

"What happened back there?" Max asked, looking at the gash on my hand. He ripped his shirt at the edge and wrapped the soft cotton around my palm. I hardly felt it until now, but it was starting to burn. Artos was sitting at Max's feet, panting. I rubbed his head, trying to soothe us both.

"Satan's Syndicate happened," Edison replied. He glanced at me in the rearview. "Since I'm pretty sure none of us are part of the Oaktown Boys, I'm guessing they were there for you."

"No coincidence, I'll bet." Max said the words that were already blaring in my brain. I nodded, shuddering a little. *Xander sent them for me.*

"Artos . . . he just came from nowhere," I said. "He saved me." Leaning back against the seat, I inhaled slow and deep. Then I giggled. There was something about skirting the precipice—a near miss—that made me strangely giddy.

Edison slammed the dash with his palm, sobering me instantly, as he sped toward the hospital. "I should've known better," he muttered, his voice biting with vitriol. "Finally, my dad trusts my judgment and look what happens." Elana reached for his arm, but he shrugged her away.

"You couldn't have known this would happen," I said. "No one did. Your dad will understand that." Edison shook his head, unconvinced, and drove even faster.

Elana sighed, conceding defeat for now. "Did you find anything?" she asked me. I'd almost forgotten.

"Yes." I reached in my jacket for my mother's book. Opening it to the dog-eared page, I passed it to her. "It's from Quin."

She read it silently, frowning, as Edison screeched to a stop in front of the hospital. "Help me get him inside," he said to Max. Partitioned between them, Scooter could barely stand. He was mumbling words of protest, still insisting we take him back to the house.

After they passed through the doors, Elana turned to me, somber. "We found something too. It . . . " She pursed her lips together, blocking the rest of the words before they could escape. " . . . maybe we should wait to talk about it."

"Seriously? What is it?"

"Promise you won't freak out."

It seemed like a dangerous promise to make, but I was exhausted. Hardly capable of a proper freak out. "I promise."

Elana held out her hand, a photograph pinched between her fingers. "We found it in your mom's box, buried at the bottom."

I took it from her and held it carefully by the edges, close to my face, already rethinking my vow. My mother looked radiant, eyes shining, the way they always did before my father left. She was wearing a white lab coat, *Knightley* embroidered on one side, *United States Government, Crim-X Program,* on the other. There was a man next to her, outfitted in military garb, his arm wrapped around her shoulders. He was the same height as my mother with a receding hairline and a thick beard. I didn't recognize him right away, though he really hadn't changed that much. It was the soft expression on his face, the way he regarded her adoringly that made him so alien to me. I had seen it before—Quin looked at me that way sometimes—but never on that face. It was as if there was only one star still burning in the universe, and it was her.

I lifted my eyes to Elana. She was watching me for signs of implosion, but I gave away nothing. Gently, she tapped the back of the picture, encouraging me to turn it over. There was a date in the corner—2025, Crim-X Test Group Release—and a handwritten inscription.

*Congratulations, Victoria,*

*Your achievements continue to astound me. Though I must confess, it's not fair for someone so smart to look so lovely.*

*Yours,*

*Jamison*

## CHAPTER FORTY-SEVEN:

# FRUIT LOOP

By the next morning, there it was.

> **"Marin County police confirmed there was a gang-related shooting yesterday afternoon at the home of the late Dr. Victoria Knightley, well known as the researcher who created, then rallied against, Emovere. Early reports suggest at least two fatalities."**

*Two?* I sat up, waiting for more. *Which two?* There was still no word on Scooter since Edison's last text to Elana, a few hours before the curfew last night: *He's in surgery. My dad is here taking charge as usual. He didn't seem too upset with me, but he's probably saving it for later.*

Only Barbara Blake and I were awake. Even Artos had fallen into a fitful slumber. His head rested on Elana's lap, his paws twitching in a dream or nightmare. Sleep seemed impossible with my hand throbbing and my thoughts scattered everywhere. Usually organized like books in a library, the stacks had tumbled down, burying me under an avalanche of confusion. Elana had driven us back to San Francisco—me, secreted under the tarp and contemplating a new reality. *Jamison Ryker had been in love with my mother.*

> **"The identities of the victims are being withheld at this time pending further investigation. Because the shooting is believed to be Onyx-related, the military has responded with increased searches and EAM testing at**

**the mandatory checkpoints tonight. Authorities have been tight-lipped with the media, but an SFTV source tells us that Dr. Knightley's ex-husband, William Knightley, was recently arrested for resisting orders. Additional charges may be imminent after illicit substances were discovered in the Knightley compound."**

"*Compound*?" I muttered under my breath. Artos' ears pricked, but his eyes never opened. As usual, SFTV's reporting was far from neutral. They didn't even mention Langley's first-person account—already gone viral—accusing the military of false arrest.

**"The Knightleys' daughter, Alexandra, has also been in the news, identified as a person of interest in Peter Radley's death. In an exclusive statement obtained by SFTV, she described her mother as "regretful and disgusted" by Zenigenic."**

*That didn't take long.*

**"But our sources suggest Radley may have obtained Emovere from the youngest member of the Knightley family just prior to his fatal jump."**

"Sounds like you and your father had quite the change of heart about EAMs." *Augustus.* Of course, Augustus was awake.

I rolled my eyes at him. "You're one to talk. Leader of the Resistance? Drug czar? Drug dealer? Which one is it exactly?"

Augustus chuckled. Next to him, Barry sputtered awake. "Ms. Knightley, no one role defines me."

"How about lunatic?" Barry suggested with a straight face. "Madman? Nut job? Fruit loop?"

I guffawed. Instantly, Elana was awake.

Augustus shook his head at Barry. "I assure you I am perfectly sane." He directed his eyes back to me. "I simply don't chain myself to one person, one cause. I evolve and adapt. Your mother, she was the same way."

"You don't know anything about her," I began. "She was nothing like—" I stopped myself when I realized Augustus was right. My mother was the queen of reinvention.

> **"In related news, large crowds are expected at Zenigenic's headquarters later today for the unveiling of Docil-E. In an email to SFTV, Xander Steele confirmed there will be increased security in light of the shooting at the Knightley home and the escalated incidents of EAM-related violence throughout the Bay in recent months. In fact, Steele cited Dr. Knightley in his comments, writing, "I believe Victoria Knightley would be proud of what we've done with Docil-E. We hope this launch will restore the public's belief in Zenigenic as a pharmaceutical company that cares." Of course, SFTV will be there live this evening with exclusive coverage of the event."**

Sneering, Augustus tossed a pillow at the television, where Xander's powder-white face loomed large. "If you're looking for a fruit loop, look no further. Mr. Steele would gladly sell his soul for favorable profit margins and a nod of approval from his mommy."

"You're just mad because he cut you out of the deal," Elana fired at him. Augustus' silence seemed like tacit agreement. But no matter how many times, how many ways I'd asked him, he still wouldn't admit his not-so-secret ambition to sell Onyx on the streets.

A key turned in the lock, and our heads swiveled simultaneously. Ears pricked, Artos pranced to the door, waiting.

"They're awake," Mr. Van Sant said as Edison and Max filed in behind him. They all looked beleaguered, Max especially so. His spiky hair was flattened. Half-moons of darkness shadowed his eyes. Even so, he managed a slight smile when Artos licked his hand.

"How's Scooter?" Barry asked.

Frowning, Mr. Van Sant put a hand to his shoulder. "Guarded condition. Hopefully, we'll know more soon." He whispered something else to Barry, shifting his gaze to Augustus.

"Let's go, Mr. Porter." Barry tugged on Augustus' arm, leading him back to the kitchen.

"Oh goody. More quality time with my favorite buffoon."

"Just walk."

Edison scooted in next to Elana, resting his head against her shoulder. "Are you okay?" she asked, gently palming his cheek. "You look tired."

"Exhausted. But we've got bigger problems."

"A lot bigger," Max added.

Mr. Van Sant collapsed into the armchair, closing his eyes for a moment. Then he took a breath and withdrew his laptop from his briefcase. "They're charging your father with maintaining a drug house and holding him without bail. Emma and Carrie are also being detained."

"Can they do that?" I asked. "Docil-E is not even a banned substance . . . yet."

Turning the laptop's screen toward me, Mr. Van Sant shook his head in frustration. "According to the military, these are the substances that were found in your mother's lab." I scanned the list. *25 units of Emovere. 5 units of Agitor.* I felt my face warming in outrage. *50 tablets of Euphoractamine.* My mouth opened, and I gasped. *100 units of Onyx.* No Docile-E.

"This is ridiculous."

"I know. I know. But right now, it's their word against his—"

"Which basically means it's *their* word." Edison finished his father's sentence.

"There's something else," Max said, looking at me apologetically. "Quin was at the hospital." I went from indignation to all-out panic in one second flat.

Elana covered her face with her hands, muting her voice when she spoke. "Is he okay?"

"Geez, Red." Edison rolled his eyes and chuckled. "You sure know how to make a guy feel special. McAllister is fine, but . . . "

"You should have started with that," she scolded. "And really? You're going to pick right now to be jealous?" Edison's cheeks reddened, and he raised his hands in surrender.

"Why was Quin there?" I asked.

Max shrugged. "We didn't really have time to discuss it. He pulled me into one of the empty hospital rooms when I was in the hallway checking my phone. It seemed like he knew about Scooter. He asked me if we found the note." Max gestured toward me. "I told him you found it."

"Did he say any more about what it means?" Elana wondered.

"That's the bigger problem," Edison warned. "He told Max that Xander is planning something. Something catastrophic. Something like Chicago. And it involves the military. He stole a key card to Xander's office, but Valkov hasn't let him out of his sight—even with a broken arm."

"That's not exactly what he said," Max corrected, his frown deepening. "He said *Guardian Force*. It involves the Guardian Force."

* * *

Mr. Van Sant was tense, pacing like a lion in a cage. "Augustus . . . " He paused, tasting the bitterness of his words before he spit them out. "We need your help. Again."

Augustus grinned broadly, amused. "I'm listening." Ever since Barry had shuffled him back into the living room at Mr. Van Sant's request, he couldn't contain his self-satisfied smirk.

Mr. Van Sant gestured toward me. "Alexandra, show him what you found." I reminded myself of what we had discussed. We were running out of time. I hesitated. "Go ahead."

I retrieved the book from my jacket and opened it to the dog-eared page. Somehow it seemed wrong—sacrilegious, even—to let Augustus touch it, so I walked to him and leaned over his shoulder, showing him myself.

"Hmm . . . interesting . . . yes . . . " There was something about Augustus' sounds of contemplation that made me suspicious. I knew I was being paranoid, but I started to wonder if he'd slithered away, rifled through my pockets, and already read the note, while everyone was sleeping. "Another Chicago," he read aloud. "Sounds tragic."

"What do you know about it?" Mr. Van Sant demanded.

Augustus stroked his chin where his stubble was growing thick and gray. "That depends."

"On?"

"What you're willing to pay for it."

Chest puffed, Mr. Van Sant strode toward Augustus. He stood over him, his jaw tightening. "I thought we already reached an agreement about the benefits of your cooperation."

"Cooperation is a strong word. As I remember it, I agreed to provide information to assist you in solving a cipher code, the accuracy of which appears to have just been confirmed. Now this . . . " He waved his hand toward me. "This is a separate transaction. And I do believe, a much more valuable proposition."

Mr. Van Sant's face reddened—and I braced myself for another primal yell. "Are you trying to extort me?" His voice reached a crescendo one octave away from explosion.

"You sound surprised."

Brooding, Mr. Van Sant stalked from the living room into the foyer. He selected one of the porcelain vases from the table in the entryway and headed out the front door. My own trepidation was reflected in Elana's watchful expression. Edison only shook his head. A few seconds later, came the crash, the exclamation point, the sound of something expensive and breakable meeting with an untimely end.

Augustus raised his eyebrows at me. "And you think I've got problems."

"Nobody asked you," Barry said, moving a step closer to Augustus.

Without explanation, Mr. Van Sant returned, calmly shutting the door behind him. Aside from the tiny porcelain splinters that sprinkled his loafers, there were no other visible remnants of his tantrum—though I suspected he was molten lava beneath his hard exterior. "So how much is this transaction going to cost me?" he asked.

"Well, you've already guaranteed my freedom, but even a free bird needs a little spending money."

Mr. Van Sant walked toward Augustus until he was standing over him. "Name your price."

"Five hundred thousand."

"Ha!" He laughed, but there was no joy there, only disdain. "No deal."

Augustus shrugged. "Okay. How much is it worth to you?" In the silence that followed his question, there was a noticeable shift, the rearranging of power in Augustus' favor. He was about to pluck something slimy from his dark belly of secrets. "Is it worth say . . . 500,000 dollars and your reputation?"

I swallowed a lump in my throat and backed away, taking a seat on the other side of Elana. I didn't want to stand in between the two of them any longer. It was feeling more and more like a war zone better left to Barry to manage.

"My dad's reputation is none of your business." Edison started to get up from the sofa, but Elana pulled him back.

"Funny you should say that," Augustus replied, shrugging off Barry's hand from his shoulder. "Since you're the very reason his reputation is in jeopardy."

"What are you talking about?" Mr. Van Sant demanded. Rage was seething under his skin, forcing tiny beads of sweat onto his forehead.

"I'm talking about Connor. Connor Rosenthal. Unfortunate, ill-fated, *dead* Connor." Next to me, I felt Elana stiffen, her breath stopped. I looked at Edison. His face was white, his hands clenched in his lap. He seemed incapable of speech. Reveling in their shock, Augustus didn't hesitate. "The Connor Rosenthal who had the very bad luck of getting into a car with a drunk. Your son."

"You keep your mouth shut about my son." It was inevitable, from the moment Augustus and I rang the bell. Destined or not, watching Mr. Van Sant pummel Augustus' face was jarring.

The first punch was a wild right to the jaw. Mr. Van Sant clutched his hand afterward, grimacing. "Probation," Augustus muttered through clenched teeth. "He got probation."

The second punch, an upper cut, left Augustus looking dazed, but he didn't hit back. Barry would've stopped him, and Augustus was on a roll, landing his own brutal blows. "You paid off the judge, didn't you, Nicholas?"

"You can't prove anything." At his father's words, Edison fled, heading toward hid room with Elana on his heels. Artos trotted after them, stopping at the base of the stairs. He cocked his head at me, his face as sad and confused as my own.

Wiping blood from his nose, Augustus was nearly giddy. "Are you sure about that? It's funny the things you learn as drug czar."

A hook, ugly and unrestrained. That was the last punch, the one that silenced him.

# CHAPTER FORTY-EIGHT:

# DEAL

Barry tapped Augustus' cheeks, rousing him. "Mmmm," he groaned, then drifted away again. His face was already swelling. A spray of his blood dotted the chair's leather arm.

"What just happened?" Max asked, disbelieving.

Mr. Van Sant emerged from the kitchen, his hand in a bucket of ice. "I'm sorry you both had to see that. It's been a long time since I felt compelled to resort to physical violence."

"We've seen worse," I assured him, exchanging a dumbfounded look with Max. "Should we check on Edison?"

"I'm fine." Head hanging, Edison shuffled down the stairs, a teary-eyed Elana at his side. "Dad, what did you do?" Neither looked at the other. In the profound silence, I realized Edison wasn't referring to Augustus' damaged face.

"You were looking at serious jail time, Eddie. What choice did I have?"

"But you disowned me." Edison approached his father, still avoiding his eyes. "Why would you risk your career for me?"

Mr. Van Sant removed his bruised hand from the ice and took Edison by his shoulders. As we waited for his father to speak, a wet palm print formed on Edison's shirt. Finally, with the answer to his question still unspoken, Edison stepped toward his father, giving him an awkward side hug.

Augustus cleared his throat, his eyes half open. He sat up and maneuvered his purpling jaw back and forth. It cracked a little. "What a touching moment."

Barry pointed his gun at Augustus' chest, pinning him to the chair. "Just say the word, Boss."

Mr. Van Sant shook his head. "It's okay. Let him be."

"No, really, I'm touched." Augustus began again, his voice superficially earnest. He offered his most innocent expression, even as I glared at him. "Father and son. Loyal to the end. It's a beautiful moment."

"What would you know about loyalty?" Max asked bitterly. "The only person you've never betrayed is yourself."

"How right you are, Mr. Powers!" He gestured toward Artos, sitting watchfully on the sofa. "Loyalty is a trait admired in dogs, and I'm more of a cat, I suppose."

"Which is it?" I asked, shaking my head at him. "Bird or cat?"

Augustus didn't answer. Instead he addressed Mr. Van Sant. "I'm prepared to revise my offer."

Mr. Van Sant sighed wearily. I understood his exhaustion. Augustus' games were draining, life-sucking. "Tell me."

"Two million dollars. Final offer."

I scoffed. "How is that a negotiation?"

"Please, Ms. Knightley. I haven't finished detailing my proposal."

I exhaled, feeling as worn-out as Mr. Van Sant. "By all means."

"Five hundred thousand to tell you what I know about Xander's plan. The other 1.5 mil to give you exactly what—or should I say who—you need to exonerate George McAllister." Augustus paused, letting his words drop and detonate like bombs. "I'll throw in my silence on the felony bribery . . ." Gingerly, he touched his wounded face. " . . . and first degree assault for free."

Mr. Van Sant didn't ask our advice. He didn't even pause to take a breath before he shook hands with the devil. "Deal."

* * *

My eyes were watching Augustus. He was sitting proud, like a king on a throne, issuing his half-truths as proclamations. But my mind was back in time, at Resistance headquarters almost two years ago—the first time I saw him. *The Augustus Porter.* I remembered the way the crowd parted for him, how he moved through them, among them with ease. Now I understood. Without obligations, commitments, worries, loyalties, loves, he wasn't tethered like the rest of us. He'd always had the charisma of someone completely unburdened. He was right about one thing. *Free bird.*

"So you're saying Xander is planning a bombing." Mr. Van Sant typed furiously on his laptop, trying to follow Augustus' breadcrumb trail. "In order to increase sales of Emovere and Eupho on the black market."

Augustus nodded. "That was his plan from the beginning. When I was appointed drug czar, Mr. Steele contacted me. He knew about my history with Jamison Ryker and used it against me. I reluctantly agreed to a partnership. What choice did I have? Steele supplied me with the drugs—Eupho, Agitor, Emovere—that Zenigenic manufactured in a few underground facilities, like the one in the Paramount. As drug czar, I was conveniently immune from suspicion, so I hired dealers like Sebastian to sell them on the streets, even resold the EAMs we confiscated. But compared to Steele's take, I survived on a pauper's wage. He always talked about how a disastrous event, something like Chicago, would be just what he needed to boost sales. I was against it, of course. I thought it was unnecessarily ruthless."

"What about Onyx?" I asked, wondering if Augustus would finally confess.

He turned to me with eyes like ice. "Haven't I already made myself clear, Ms. Knightley? I did not sell Onyx."

"But you wanted to," Elana added.

"No!" Augustus smacked the arm of his chair like he was swatting a fly. "If I wanted to sell Onyx, I would have. And I certainly would've done it better than Mr. Steele."

"Where does Ryker come in?" Edison asked as Augustus fumed. I bristled at the sound of his name, still trying to reconcile the adoring Ryker in my mother's picture with the other one, the one who ended her.

"I don't know." Augustus answered with the voice of a surly teenager. "I suspect he and Steele were partners all along."

"Partners, how?"

Avoiding Edison's question, Augustus stood and spoke only to Barry. "Take me to the kitchen. I'm tired and hungry." He brought his fingers back to his swollen eye. "And my head hurts."

"Wait a minute," Mr. Van Sant protested. "We've got a ticking time bomb here. Pun intended. You can't just call time out whenever you feel like it. And what about the information you promised on George McAllister?"

"George *who*?" Turning his back to us, Augustus sauntered off to the kitchen.

"Unbelievable," Edison muttered. "That guy is unbelievable."

"Yep, that's Augustus," I agreed. "And you're right, we shouldn't believe him. He's playing us, making Xander look like the only bad guy here."

Mr. Van Sant nodded. "Very astute, Alexandra. Unfortunately, he's our best hope for now."

From where we sat, we could hear rumblings from the kitchen, the sounds of Augustus and Barry arguing. "I told you . . . pimento. Only pimento."

Edison rolled his eyes. "So you're saying the fate of San Francisco and George McAllister rests on that guy?"

"Son, unless you've got a better idea, that's exactly what I'm saying."

"Now that you mention it . . . "

## CHAPTER FORTY-NINE:

# UNVEILED

I felt nauseous. The thick, cold blood of unease crawled under my skin. Even the sky was a sickly shade of gray. Up here, far above the street with the wind swirling about my face, there still wasn't enough air to breathe. I lowered Mr. Van Sant's high-powered binoculars, taking my eyes off Zenigenic's main entrance to glance at my watch. 4:50 p.m. Ten minutes until Xander Steele would emerge from those doors. Ten minutes until he would tell the world about Docil-E. And just ten minutes until Edison would sneak inside their headquarters on a stealth mission of his own.

I peered over the ledge, careful to stay out of sight. The crowd was its own beast—alive, pulsating, growing beyond expectations—already too big for its cage. The stanchions erected by Zenigenic security had toppled to the ground, trampled underfoot.

Barbara Blake and SFTV secured premium real estate near the podium while a few independent Internet news stations—including *Eyes on the Bay*—were relegated to the sidelines. I raised my binoculars again, finding Langley behind the camera. I half expected to see my father there, curious and eager. But of course, he wasn't. That thought weighed heavy, a boulder of worry and regret, but I pushed it from my mind. I had to focus.

Protestors and supporters alike elbowed and shouldered their way toward the red-carpeted entrance where they were stonewalled by a dense line of soldiers. A few daredevils scaled the large metallic *Z*, claiming a front-row seat atop it. My ears, and then my eyes, were drawn to an emphatic group at the periphery.

Their chant was familiar—*We are the New Resistance! Not afraid to feel!*—but their attire was unnerving, reminiscent of the 2040 rallies before San Francisco was evacuated. They all wore red bandanas, the color of the Resistance, tied on their arms or covering their faces. Signs in hand, they were advancing, riled and insistent. While everyone else was pushing forward, moths to the flame, I located Elana's auburn hair at the edge of the crowd. She was watching, unmoving. I picked up my radio.

"Any sign of him?" I'm not sure why I was whispering. I was eight stories off the ground, on the roof of one of the abandoned office buildings opposite Zenigenic's headquarters. Even if I screamed as loud and as long as I could, my cry would've been lost, joining all the others coming from the belly of the beast below.

"Nothing yet. But this is insane." The sounds of the jostling mob nearly covered her voice. "The New Resistance, soldiers in riot gear, and I just got tested."

I lifted the binoculars back to my eyes, finding a group of soldiers at the periphery. White strips in hand, they were swiping wrists just as Elana reported. It should've reassured me, but it didn't. Not even close. Not after what happened with Emma. I settled back to the ground and resumed my position. Waiting. I couldn't help but look for Quin, though I already knew I wouldn't find him. Wherever he was—with Xander, probably—his unveiling would be as orchestrated, as public as Docil-E's. Edison was counting on it.

"I saw Percy," Elana added, giggling a little. Leave it to her to bring him up at a time like this.

"You did?" I quickly scanned the crowd with my binoculars, searching for his close-cropped, raven-colored hair.

"He asked about you, *Lexi*."

"Bleh!" Only Quin could make that nickname sound appealing. "What did he say?"

"He was quite concerned actually. He wanted to know if your dad was really an EAM dealer. And if you were on the run."

"He thinks I'm a criminal?"

Elana chuckled. "He thinks you're a super sexy fugitive. As in, he wants to be the Clyde to your Bonnie."

Partly flattered, partly horrified, I laughed. "What did you tell him?"

"That you are every bit the femme fatale he thinks you are. I'm pretty sure he's already planning a second date somewhere on the lam with you."

"Elana!"

"Kidding, kidding."

Behind me, the steel door to the staircase rattled open, and Mr. Van Sant stepped onto the roof. A sudden gust of wind blew him back a little, but he held his ground and made his way toward me. In blue jeans and a Harvard sweatshirt, he was nearly unrecognizable, far from his usual buttoned-up attorney garb.

"Bird's-eye view, huh?" he said, lowering himself to the ground, armed with a second set of binoculars.

I nodded. "You were right. It's the perfect spot."

"Good thing I never tossed out those old keys." Before San Francisco's evacuation, Mr. Van Sant's law office was located on the third floor of the building. "I came up here a lot when I needed to clear my head." For Mr. Van Sant, I imagined that meant a lot of stomping, cursing, and red-faced yelling.

"I think it's starting," I said as the crowd began to buzz with tangible anticipation. Gina Tan emerged from headquarters and strutted to the stage, backdropped by the pallid sky, exploding with bursts of color.

"I should've expected fireworks," Mr. Van Sant muttered. "Nothing understated about Steele."

"Or Zenigenic." I fought off the memory of my mother and her ambivalence as she watched the fireworks meant for her.

"There's Steele." Mr. Van Sant spotted him, just as I did. He was as slick as always, in a dark, pinstripe suit. Any bruises—there had to be bruises—were expertly covered by his make-up team. A sharp-dressed Quin followed closely behind him, then a limping Valkov—his arm in a splint. He could barely keep up. The rest of the security team, accompanied by a troop of soldiers, trailed a few paces back. "I hope Eddie can pull this off." Mr. Van Sant spoke quietly, wistfully, almost to himself. "You know, I've never seen him in his uniform."

I wasn't sure if I was supposed to answer, but I did. "Don't worry. This kind of thing is his specialty."

"He does have a flair for the dramatic." Mr. Van Sant chuckled. "Wonder where he gets it from."

"I wonder." I let myself laugh with him, but didn't take my eyes from the ground below. I centered my focus back to Elana's red hair. She was in the heart of the mob now—just alongside the red carpet walkway where the military presence was thick. Max had taken his position next to her. Edison—the old Edison, Greenhorn 558—stood just a few soldiers down from them. He blended perfectly.

"Greenhorn 558 reporting for duty," he whispered into the microphone, clipped just inside his collar.

Ignoring the jeers, Xander waved to the crowd, sauntering leisurely toward the podium. As the procession passed Elana, Mr. Van Sant's breathing got quiet. Mine did too. Prepare for impact in *one thousand one . . . one thousand two* . . . Quin lurched forward, catching himself with his hands before he hit the red carpet, tripped by Edison's well-placed boot. He reached Quin well before Valkov, but I couldn't see them anymore. They disappeared under the cover of the crowd, only muffled scratching audible from Edison's microphone.

Valkov, angry Valkov, loomed in my lens. As he strained to offer his good hand to Quin, his face contorted with rage at Edison, his roar audible in Edison's mic. "Watch yourself, you grunt!" After their explosive encounter at Quin's press conference, I was relieved Valkov didn't recognize him in his uniform.

Mr. Van Sant scooted nearer to the ledge for a better view. "What if Quin doesn't have it with him?"

I shrugged. "Max said Quin had the key card in his pocket at the hospital. He probably doesn't let it out of his sight."

Quin was back on his feet, just slightly rumpled and facing Edison. His mouth formed words like drumbeats, short and intense. I wished I could read his lips. Between the fireworks and the raucous roaring around them, Edison's microphone was all white noise. Quin straightened his jacket and turned to Valkov, giving him a good-natured pat on the shoulder. Satisfied with himself, Valkov proceeded to the stage without a backward glance. Quin kept moving too, but the set of his shoulders seemed different, less certain.

I eyed the radio, waiting for confirmation from Edison. "Got it." Mr. Van Sant exhaled, but I was far from reassured.

"What did Quin say?" I asked.

"I could barely hear him. It sounded like *Get out of here*. He was probably just playing along."

I didn't say anything else. I let those words swim around in my brain, trying to ignore their sharp, little teeth biting at the back of it. My eyes followed Edison, then Max until both of them were out of view of the stage, heading toward the side entrance.

Mr. Van Sant's cell phone vibrated next to us on the concrete. "It's from Barry," he said. "He's in." Zenigenic's security cameras were now under his control. He could alter their direction and play back archived footage so Edison could pass by undetected.

Xander tapped the microphone. He was positioned at the podium, protected by a plexiglass shield. Merely a precaution, according to Barbara Blake's morning broadcast.

"Good afternoon, and welcome to this historic occasion. I am thrilled to be here today. In fact, since my appointment as Zenigenic CEO last year, this is my proudest moment." Behind him, Gina Tan clicked a remote, lighting up an oversized screen on the wall of the building. On it, a devilishly handsome man held up a vial marked Docil-E. I blinked my eyes a few times just to be sure. *Yep, it was Quin.* I could feel Mr. Van Sant staring at me, but I couldn't look at him. "Let me introduce you to Docil-E, the newest, the best, the safest EAM that Zenigenic has ever created."

A roar of reproach from the New Resistance dwarfed the meager cheers of support. Xander raised his hand in a futile attempt to silence them. "I understand many of you are skeptical, but I am confident Docil-E will secure a peaceful future for all of us."

I directed my binoculars to Quin, but he was looking away, not at Xander. I followed his gaze to the wall of soldiers. Faces blank as parchment, they stared ahead, stiff-necked. "Kindness." Xander spoke the word as if it belonged to him. "Tranquility. These have been in short supply in our great nation, especially here in San Francisco. Our researchers believe Docil-E is the first building block to a harmonious, non-violent world. Docil-E promotes many of the body's naturally occurring hormones, encouraging relaxation and suppressing anger and aggression. Here at Zenigenic, we like to call it the anti-Onyx." Like any skilled spin doctor, Xander was making Docil-E sound good. Really good.

Mr. Van Sant leaned his ear toward the radio and adjusted the volume. Edison's voice was barely a whisper, "I'm in the building. It's quiet as a tomb in here."

"Bad choice of words," Max chided. "Remember, eighteenth floor. You've got about ten minutes. I'll be outside the entrance if you need me." I could hear Edison's steady breathing and the heel-to-toe clicking of his boots as he moved. Then, silence.

"Hold it, Greenhorn. What is your purpose here?"

"Uh . . ." *C'mon, Edison. Showtime.* "Well, sir, it's a little embarrassing."

"Go ahead."

"I've been demoted to inside detail."

"Why is that, Greenhorn?"

"I tripped Quin McAllister, sir." Mr. Van Sant met my eyes, and we both grinned. "Mr. Valkov told me to get out of his sight. He said the only thing I was good for was guarding an empty building."

"Alright then, try to stay out of trouble."

"Absolutely, sir." The radio went quiet for a while, then Edison snickered.

"Still got it," he boasted. "I'm in the elevator."

Mr. Van Sant pumped his fist. "That's my boy!"

Meanwhile, Xander droned on. "All our research has shown, unlike its predecessors, Docil-E is virtually free of negative side effects and is non habit-forming. As soon as we receive final approval from the government, Docil-E will be available for purchase at ZenigenicCorp.com in easy-to-swallow pill and injection forms. Each package will contain information regarding our recommended daily dose based on age and weight. I assure you that I will be using Docil-E regularly."

Mr. Van Sant was shaking his head. "Phew, he is laying it on thick."

I nodded. Xander was as likely to use Docil-E as I was.

"The applications for this drug are endless and extend well beyond the consumption of the general public. Imagine Docil-E as a tool for defense." My ears perked a little. Now we were getting somewhere. "In this regard, we are proud to announce our partnership with the specialized military force deployed to help manage our fine city in the wake of the banned-EAM crisis. They are now equipped with vials and spray canisters of Docil-E to quell any potential violence with minimal use of force."

Mr. Van Sant's eyebrows were raised like my own. I'd never expected Xander to be so forthcoming about the military's use of Docil-E, but his admission worried me. For every secret he revealed, a hundred more remained hidden.

From the radio, came the ding of the elevator. "There's someone up here," Edison hissed. "She's coming this way."

"May I help you?" The woman was polite but perturbed, as if she already knew Edison didn't belong.

"Hello, ma'am. Greenhorn 558. I was told Mr. Steele requested military presence outside of his office."

"I don't think so, Soldier. Mr. Steele left specific instructions to keep this floor clear until his return this evening. I'm afraid you'll have to leave." That was the sound of Edison's charm hitting a brick wall.

"Okay, then. I'll be downstairs if you need me." The clomping of Edison's boots was followed by a long pause. "I'm in the stairwell. Time for Plan V."

"Max?" Elana summoned. "You're on."

"Got it. Plan V initiated. Calling now." A few seconds later, in a coarse, punishing voice, "This is Valkov. There's an urgent delivery arriving for Mr. Steele on the first floor. I need you there immediately." Goofball Max was still underneath, but it sounded creepy. He totally nailed it.

Xander continued to address the crowd, gesturing to another graphic displayed alongside Quin's face. It was Docil-E's slogan in bold, black type: *Make the world a little kinder.* "Zenigenic has a storied history. We are the pioneers of emotion-altering medication, and like all pioneers, we haven't always gotten it right. But I assure you, it is our mission to do good—to better the world."

Edison was back on the radio. "She's coming your way, Max. I'm going in."

"Is that String?" Elana asked. My stomach curdled, soured with fear.

"Where?" Max blurted the question before me.

"With the New Resistance." Elana's head was directed toward the edge of the audience, near the side of the building, where the Resistance red was thick. "His face is covered, but I think that's his Mohawk."

I scoured the protestors. Most of their faces were shrouded now—just pairs of eyes visible over their bandanas—but I could see their anger anyway. It was in the tautness of their bodies, the emphatic thrusting of clenched fists in the air. "There!" Hand on one hip, String was the only one just standing, cool and removed, leaning against the building.

"What's he doing?" Max asked.

*What he's always doing*, I answered silently. But aloud, I resisted the urge for sarcasm. "Nothing."

"We'll watch him," Mr. Van Sant assured Max and Elana. But the casual way String stood there, his shades concealing his eyes, made me wonder who was watching who.

I followed Elana with my binoculars as she faced the stage. "Lex—" She didn't have to say anymore. For a moment, I forgot to breathe. Quin was at the podium.

# CHAPTER FIFTY:

# UNMASKED

"Thank you, Mr. Steele. I am honored to be here as the new spokesman for Docil-E." Quin gestured to himself on the screen, his cheeks reddening as the audience erupted in applause. When the roaring diminished, a young girl atop the *Z* called out, "I love you, Quin McAllister!" The crowd giggled along with her. They understood what I knew from the moment he sat next to me on the bed at the Resistance headquarters that first night. Quin was lovable. So lovable.

Edison interrupted my reverie with urgency. "Did Quin mention a code to get into Xander's office?"

"No," Max answered. "Why?"

"Because I need one. Obviously." Edison sighed. "Sorry. I'm just freaking out here. Every time I swipe the keycard, I'm prompted for a six-digit code. Any ideas?"

"Six digits could be a date." Mr. Van Sant pulled out his cell phone and began typing. "Maybe Xander's birthday," he suggested, scrolling through the search results. "It's 11-19-08. Try that."

As the crowd quieted, Quin continued speaking. "As many of you know, I have a history with emotion-altering medications, and it hasn't been pretty. As a former member of the Guardian Force turned Resistance, I understand your hesitation."

"Not it," Edison growled.

"His mother's birthdate?" Mr. Van Sant offered. "12-15-77."

"No!"

"But I believe in Zenigenic. I believe in Docil-E. And most importantly, I believe in Xander Steele." My stomach panging, I studied his face as he delivered his lines. This was a different Quin. His voice sounded confident, but his posture was uncertain. He scanned the crowd before he lowered his eyes to read. "I want you all to know Docil-E is safe and effective."

"How much time do I have?" Edison asked.

"Not much," I replied. "Max is stalling her. Five more minutes, tops." Barely enough time for him to get into the office, copy Xander's hard drive onto the password-skirting device Barry gave him, and get out.

Quin pointed to the large screen where his face was replaced by a table of predictable statistics showing an overwhelmingly favorable response to Docil-E. "Experimental trial results have shown only a miniscule percentage of participants suffered mild side effects. Most experienced none. I've witnessed several successful experimental trials myself." *Exhibit A: Augustus,* I thought to myself. *If only he was still medicated.* I followed that thought, breadcrumb by breadcrumb, and suddenly I knew.

"It's the date!" I yelled into the radio. "The date of the next Chicago! 01-23-43."

"Try it!" Mr. Van Sant urged.

Spokesman Quin reappeared on the screen. "Like Mr. Steele, I will be using Docil-E regularly. And I recommend you all do the same."

I heard an encouraging click. "Brilliant, Lex. Brilliant."

Xander joined Quin, putting a firm hand on his shoulder. "Let's all do our part to make the world a little kinder." They concluded Quin's speech in unison, but only their voices synchronized. Xander's body was tense as he pushed against Quin's arm, trying to move him from behind the podium. Quin stood firm, both of them vying for position.

"Something's wrong." I was whispering again, afraid to say the words out loud. Afraid it would make them true. I wasn't the only one confused. A few hands clapped, but most of the crowd was silent.

Sensing the audience's discomfort, Xander forced a strained smile. "We'd like to thank you all—"

"Gun!" A scream from the crowd sliced Xander's sentence in two, leaving one part unfinished and one part forever unspoken. That word, *just one*, and the beast awakened again, spreading itself in all directions. The *pop-pop-pop* of bullets followed. While watching Xander cower behind the plexiglass shield where there was only room for one, I understood. Quin must have known.

"Eddie." Mr. Van Sant breathed the name. "He's got to get out of there."

"Edison!" Elana was yelling into the radio, already swimming against the current, fighting her way through the mob. "I'll go find Max," she said. "We'll meet you back at the tunnels." *The tunnels.* I instantly regretted our decision to leave the car and navigate the derelict BART underground to get here. It was safer—we wouldn't be seen—but slow. And whatever was happening, I wanted to leave it behind us, far and fast.

"Edison, can you hear me?" I asked. A faint crackling was the only answer.

Mr. Van Sant was on his feet. "Let's go," he urged, heading toward the door, but I couldn't leave—not yet. I fastened the radio to my waistband and crouched near the ledge, still watching through my binoculars.

"Alexandra! Let's go!" Mr. Van Sant was insistent now. He was holding the door with one hand and waving the other with urgency. I stood and took one step backward toward him. I couldn't turn away without knowing Quin was safe. He was hunched at the edge of the stage, turned away from the crowd. He had taken off his jacket to shield his face, anticipating the deployment of Docil-E.

My last look was like a puzzle, a kaleidoscope. Turned one way, the pieces came together with ease: Black and blue. Satan's Syndicate and Oaktown Boys. Gun on gun, bullet for bullet, they joined together in a predictable chaos. Soldiers advanced from the wall, gas masks deployed, spray canisters in their hands. In seconds, a cloud of Docil-E descended over the makeshift battleground.

But turn it another, and it was all wrong. The pieces didn't fit, not at first. Someone didn't belong. String. He climbed up the Z, opposite all the others who scurried down it, helter skelter, like ants—displaced and disturbed. He stood there high above Docil-E's fog, as if this exact moment was the one he'd been waiting for . . . the one he wanted to remember. He wasn't there for the New Resistance, that much I knew. A broken river of red bandanas, they were running away along with everyone else.

String aimed his gun at Quin's back with the studied precision of someone who had practiced.

"Quin!" My scream burned my throat, but it went nowhere. It was a ghost, appearing and disappearing without consequence.

String must have pulled the trigger, but I didn't see it. Mr. Van Sant grabbed my arm and yanked me with him. Like a dead star plummeting toward earth, the binoculars fell from my opened hands.

# CHAPTER FIFTY-ONE:

# COMPLIANCE

"Cover your face." Mr. Van Sant had already removed his sweatshirt. He wrapped it across his nose and mouth as he raced down the stairs ahead of me.

I heard him—even through the white noise roaring in my head—but my feet kept going. If I stopped, I would freeze. And if I froze, I would be stuck, tied to the tracks, a train of panic baring down on me. So I kept my eyes on the concrete steps, taking them one at a time.

"Do it!" Muffled, Mr. Van Sant's yell was still fierce. But only a part of me was listening. The rest of me kept seeing String, Quin, and the space between them. "Alexandra! We're almost to the door." He tugged at my sleeve. "Take this off." Already I could smell it. The air was pungent, sickeningly sweet like lilac.

I pulled off my jacket and let him secure it, tying the leather arms behind my head. "Quin." I couldn't say anything else.

"I know. I'm worried too." I was glad he didn't try to reassure me. "Right now, we have to concentrate on getting out of here." I nodded, letting my legs carry me down the last flight. "Ready?" he asked, his hand on the knob.

He didn't wait for an answer.

The wet, white haze was all I could see at first. I shielded my eyes with my hands, but I could already feel them stinging. I followed behind Mr. Van Sant, palming the building with my hand to guide me. The quiet was a shock. The sudden absence of sound felt brutal, raw. Just when I started to wonder if the earth had opened up and swallowed everything, I saw a neat line of legs through the thinning cloud, guns laid on the ground in front of them. Their silent owners were seated near Zenigenic's entrance. Blue and black. Side by side. Calm and obedient.

"Stay here." Mr. Van Sant headed toward the still-cloaked stage until I couldn't make him out anymore.

*Quin is dead.* The moment I pressed my back to the wall—stopped moving—the thought came in a rush, the way a dam breaks open. String's perfect aim, the bullet's long flight, Quin's last breath. I imagined it all. Inside me, a coil of despair wrapped tight and squeezed. *Stop it, stop it, stop it. Stop. It. Lex.* "Quin is *not* dead." I said the words aloud so I could feel them on my lips. So I could believe them. Concentrating on the cold steel of the building flush against my shirt, I turned on my radio. I pressed it against my covered mouth. "Elana?" I whispered. There was only static.

"Get up." A stern but muffled voice directed the line. In near synchronicity, they stood and began walking, leaving their guns behind for the soldiers to collect. As I watched them march, a breeze shifted the cloud of Docil-E. In the clearing, there was a body and another and another. A dark river of red flowed between them, pooling in the center.

My radio beeped. "Lex?" *Elana.* Her voice was a momentary comfort, an excuse to look away. "Is Edison with you?"

"No. Maybe he's with Max."

Elana's breathing was ragged. "Max is here. We're in the tunnels. Edison never came out of the building."

"Have you tried to radio him?"

"A million times. He must've . . . " She sighed, and I could feel her heart measuring, weighing the possibilities, the way I had. The good, the bad, and the unthinkable. "Oh Lex, I'm worried."

"I'm sure he's okay. He's probably on his way now." *But I wasn't sure at all.* In Barry's last message to Mr. Van Sant, he said Edison was in Xander's office when the shooting started. Right after that, he lost the video feed. "We'll be there soon."

I turned off the radio and clipped it to my jeans. Squinting at the stage, I searched for Mr. Van Sant, but the air there was still thick and white, impenetrable. Uncertain, I walked to the edge of the chemical fog. By now I was used to the cloying smell, but my eyes burned a little more with each step. My foot knocked against something hard, sending it scuttling. It was an empty spray canister branded with the words *Docil-E2, Property of the United States Government.* A second version of Docil-E? I picked it up.

When I raised my head, I gasped. There was a soldier directly in front of me. He wore no mask. His eyes were glassy, his expression blank. "Hello." His voice was one flat note. "I'm Greenhorn 935."

"Uh—hi." He stood there expectant, like he was waiting for someone to tell him what to do. "Come closer," I said, testing him. He progressed toward me without question until his face was inches from mine. His sweat was milky white, his breath stagnant with Docil-E. "Not that close."

"I apologize." He stepped back.

"Why aren't you wearing a mask?" I asked him, gesturing to my mouth, still shielded with my jacket.

He put his hands to his face, touching his cheeks and searching, as if he was only now realizing he was exposed. The edges of a familiar tattoo peeked from underneath his uniform sleeve. "It must have fallen off," he said finally, but he seemed uncertain. "Should I find one?"

"It's too late." He cocked his head to the side, confused—but accepted my answer without further explanation. I pointed to the holster at his side. "Give me your weapon." No hesitation, he passed me the gun just as Mr. Van Sant returned. I saw him watching the soldier's movements with curiosity.

"Hello," the soldier repeated, this time to Mr. Van Sant. "I'm Greenhorn 935."

"Sit down," I told him, and he did. I laid the gun down at his feet.

"Well, I have to hand it to Xander. That Docil-E is impressive stuff," Mr. Van Sant said, smiling a little the way my mother used to when she didn't want me to worry. He wiped his eyes with his shirtsleeve. They were red and watery. "There are two more just like him by the stage. Their masks must've come off in the melee."

I nodded, trying to decide on a question for Mr. Van Sant. One I wasn't scared to ask. There was none.

"The stage was clear. No sign of Quin," he said, answering the most unspeakable of them. "Or Steele."

I couldn't decide if that was good or bad. "What about String?"

He shook his head. "There's no one, just the military."

"Edison hasn't shown up at the tunnels yet. Should we wait here?"

Mr. Van Sant didn't answer at first, but his face crumpled a little. He took a long pause. "Let's go," he said. "You can't be seen here." I know it took everything in him to turn his back to the stage, to Zenigenic, to Quin, and most of all, to Edison. I know because it took everything in me to follow.

* * *

"Stop!" The voice was firm and final like the shutting of a door, startling me into stillness before I'd taken a second step. It came from behind us where the Docil-E was finally clearing, the aftermath fully visible now. There were at least five bodies being tended to by paramedics and another five already covered with plastic sheets. Like Greenhorn 935, a few unmasked soldiers wandered, aimless and lost, while the others secured the perimeter.

Mr. Van Sant jerked my arm. "Keep moving. Don't look back."

"I said, *Stop*." I could hear the soldier's footsteps, heavy and booted, behind us. When my eyes met Mr. Van Sant's, I saw confirmation of my own fears. We were being hunted.

"Hey," the man yelled, "I need backup here. That's the girl—"

"Greenhorn 935, shoot him!" Mr. Van Sant barked the order. Stunned, I stared at Greenhorn 935 as he reached for the gun at his feet. *Make the world a little kinder*—I heard Xander's voice in my head. We were already running when he fired the first shot. *A little kinder.* And a second. *Kinder.* I stopped counting at five. With each pull of the trigger, I flinched with a stark realization. Docil-E2 had nothing to do with kindness and everything to do with compliance.

## CHAPTER FIFTY-TWO:

# CUJO

We followed the halo of Elana's flashlight, none of us speaking. The BART tunnel was colder than before and pitch black. I pulled my jacket tight around me, still smelling lilac. Inside it, I could feel the icy metal of the empty spray canister through my T-shirt. There was a constant crunching underfoot. Debris? Gravel? The bones of small animals? I didn't really want to know. Rats fled from the edges of the light as we walked in the direction of the Civic Center stop, nearest Pacific Heights. Almost two miles from the Embarcadero station, this section of the tunnels was never used by the Resistance—the tracks were still in place—but Quin and I ran this far a few times with Artos. Back then, it was an adventure. Scary, but thrilling with possibility. After all, I was with Quin and he was invincible. But then again, so was my mother. Now I only felt lonely here. *Quin is not dead.* It seemed necessary to remind myself. My worst-case scenario kept gnawing through the box I'd put it in. I knew death had no respect for invincibility.

"Somebody say something, please." Max spoke through gritted teeth. He hadn't said anything since Mr. Van Sant told him and Elana what we saw. "Are you sure it was String?" When I'd nodded, he'd gone silent. We all had.

I started to speak, but everything I wanted to say would have only made it worse. So I just shrugged.

Elana put her hand on Max's shoulder. "You know, I wish Artos was here." Max chuckled a little.

"Why?"

She shined the flashlight back and forth between the tunnel walls, sending rats scurrying in every direction. "Got it," Max said, realizing. "He is an expert at rodent control."

In spite of everything—because of everything—I laughed. "And he always knows exactly what to say."

Our laughter played out quickly, and the quiet resettled like dust. After a few minutes, Elana directed her flashlight up ahead a few hundred feet to the marker we'd left at the boarded entrance, the tunnels still shut indefinitely for public safety. We were close now.

From behind me, I heard a pitiful sound, the gasping gulp of a swallowed sob. When I turned around, Mr. Van Sant was on his knees. "I can't . . . go . . . back home. Not without . . . " He buried his face in his hands. " . . . Eddie." The sight of Mr. Van Sant crying was unbearable to watch. His shame radiated as hot and unrestrained as his tears. Elana turned off her flashlight, leaving all of us in complete darkness.

* * *

When we cracked the door to Mr. Van Sant's house, only Barry's head turned. Artos and Augustus were seated across from each other, their eyes locked in a stalemate. I could hear Barbara Blake blaring on the television.

> **"At least five dead and another 15 wounded in the gang-related shooting today at Zenigenic's unveiling of the highly anticipated Docil-E. Authorities on the scene tell us the damage could have been much worse without quick-thinking military personnel who deployed canisters of the wonder drug that promotes kindness.**
>
> **One soldier described two of the warring Oaktown Boys and Satan's Syndicate shaking hands and laughing after Docil-E was administered. We have yet to receive a statement from Xander Steele who was reportedly present for the duration, aiding the wounded."**

Mr. Van Sant picked up another vase from the table in the entryway and aimed it at the television. I cringed, readying myself for an epic crash—but secretly, I wanted him to throw it. It would have felt liberating to see something break open, to watch the pieces scatter with no intention of putting them back together. "Turn it off." His voice was flat as he returned the vase to its resting place unceremoniously. Barry quickly silenced the television.

"Rough day?" A smirk played on the edges of Augustus lips. "Would it be a bad time to say *I told you so*? I told you it was a bad idea, Nicholas. An awful one. Harebrained. But you insisted—*Eddie knows what he's doing . . . Eddie is just as smart as me.* Well that's what happens when you put your fate in the hands of a man-child. Speaking of which, where is the chip off the old block?" Artos' mouth curled in a snarl. His growl was low but threatening like a distant rumble of thunder. "And can we do something about Cujo here? He's been eyeing me like a piece of steak since you left."

"Augustus—" I tried to interrupt, but he didn't even pause. He shushed me with a flip of his hand.

"I know what you're going to ask, Ms. Knightley." His tone was condescending. "Cujo was a little before your time."

"Augustus! Shut up!" Max stomped up the steps, leaving an open-mouthed Augustus in his wake. At least he stopped talking. Sort of.

"Nobody tells me to shut up," he mumbled under his breath, Barry squeezing his shoulder in a vise grip.

Mr. Van Sant followed Max, the slam of his office door punctuating his departure. Suddenly exhausted, I flopped down on the sofa next to Artos. I let him soothe me with long-tongued kisses to my hands.

"What happened?" Barry asked.

"Edison's missing, and Quin was . . ." *Finish that sentence, Lex.* " . . . shot at." I spit out the words, watching Augustus as I spoke. Still twisted in anger, his face never changed. I knew he was listening—and I'd probably already said too much—but I couldn't resist his invitation to sarcasm. "And I'm familiar with Cujo."

He sneered, his tone singsong, mocking. "I do hope Mr. McAllister wasn't shot. A slow and painful death suits him much better. He was protecting you, I presume?"

I shook my head.

"Ms. Hamilton? Mr. Powers?"

"No. He wasn't protecting anyone." Augustus raised a lone eyebrow but said nothing. He wanted me to ask. "Why do you seem so surprised?" I cursed myself for giving him the satisfaction, but I was curious.

"Ms. Knightley, we've covered this ground already. Remember? Quin's fatal flaw? Your boyfriend has a hero complex. Ever since he saw Daddy kill Mommy, he just can't help himself. You, his father, his friends—he'll always be jumping in front of trains for someone."

The clever comeback I was preparing fell flat as a cracker, dry inside my mouth. More than anything, I hated when Augustus was right, especially when I was wrong. And it was undeniable. *That* was Quin's weakness. He'd battled Augustus for my zip drive, chased after Ryker to protect my mother, and now he was willingly inhabiting Xander's lair to secure his father's release.

"String shot at him," I said. "Sebastian Croft. Remember him? Your former employee. Are you happy now?" I wanted Augustus to feel guilty, but it was a lost cause. Snakes have no regrets.

# CHAPTER FIFTY-THREE:

# GUSHING

Elana held her radio on her lap, the volume turned up. On the other end, there had been nothing but static for hours. Then a muted beeping, the battery light issuing its death knell. Now there was no sound at all. Edison's radio was lifeless. Elana refused my attempt to wriggle hers from her hand, clutching it even tighter.

"Where is he?" she asked again. She didn't mean for me to answer.

Barry tried to soothe her. "Don't worry. I'll try again in a few hours." Shortly after we returned, he drove to Zenigenic's headquarters only to be turned away by a military barricade stationed to protect the scene until all the bodies were removed. They told him Edison wasn't among those arrested.

So far Barbara Blake had identified all but one of the known casualties as members of the Oaktown Boys or Satan's Syndicate. No civilians. No Zenigenic employees. No Quin. So far. Per her report, the other casualty—a soldier—was a victim of friendly fire. Friendly and *kind* to hear Xander tell it. I looked at the empty Docil-E2 canister on the coffee table and had a sudden urge to talk to my mother. The urge was so overwhelming, so completely futile that it scooped out an aching hole in my chest. She would know why the soldier acted that way. She always knew why.

Elana's sigh was bordering on hopeless. With a thud, she set the radio on the coffee table, where it stared at us. Then she sunk back down into the couch. Each gesture, a statement of despair. "What am I going to do?" she whispered, turning to me. "What if he doesn't come back?" Her questions were my own—unsolvable. "I always thought I knew my worst thing, that I lived through it. But, what if there's not just one? Or two? What if they keep coming and coming and coming?" Her thumb traced the scar on her wrist.

I enveloped her hand in both of mine, trying to steel my own heart. "No matter how many bad things come, you'll get through them. And so will I." I felt stronger just saying it. "We'll do it together."

"Lex!" Elana sat up suddenly, pointing to the muted television that had been cycling through a reality dating show marathon since the last news report. "Your dad!" I clicked the remote, bringing SFTV back to life. My father's face, cropped from his *Eyes on the Bay* badge, was the first of two images. Under each picture, a different name—William Knightley and Carrie Donovan—but the same caption. *Escaped Fugitive.*

> **"We have just received breaking news that two detainees have escaped from military custody tonight. They were being held at the military base in San Francisco in the newly erected detention facility, built in the wake of the Onyx crisis. The situation is still developing, but our military source confirmed these individuals should be considered armed and dangerous. Stay tuned to SFTV for more information. We will now return to our regularly scheduled programming."**

Augustus was the first to speak. Unfortunately nothing ever seemed to shock him into silence. "Well, well, well, Ms. Knightley, I thought you got your recklessness from your mother. But now it looks like there's another daredevil in the family."

I didn't frown at him, didn't glare, didn't even glance in his direction. My father's freedom, albeit stolen, struck a match inside me. Something like hope was catching fire.

"Someone should tell Mr. Van Sant," Barry said, gesturing up toward his office door. It hadn't opened since he slammed it shut.

I bounded past Barry. "I'll do it." Taking two steps at a time, I made quick work of the staircase, the horned bust of Orillius greeting me at the top. I pressed my ear to the door, listening before I knocked. Nothing. I rapped lightly once, then waited. The door flung open.

"Is there news?" His tone was fragile, desperate, dousing my flame. "Did you hear from Edison?"

I shook my head, and his shoulders slumped. "Oh. What is it then?" I followed him inside. Usually immaculate, his desk was strewn with pictures. "I'm sorry about the mess," he said. "I was just . . . reminiscing." The photo nearest me was Edison in a cap and gown. Mr. Van Sant touched it tenderly. "I missed his high school graduation. That was right before the accident. I was furious with him."

"Why?"

"He'd been caught drinking again at school. Of course, I was worried about my reputation. It was always about me. Sometimes, I think Edison would've been better off with his mother. I was never really cut out for this fatherhood thing." He gave a small, sad smile meant to reassure me, but it seemed only further proof of his brokenness. "I'm sorry. I shouldn't be bothering you with this. You came to tell me something."

I wanted to shout my news, to reclaim that flicker of faith before it turned to smoke, but I just couldn't. "It can wait." I pointed to another photograph, a young Mr. Van Sant holding Edison atop his shoulders. "Tell me about this one."

* * *

"Did you hear that?" Mr. Van Sant stood up and shut his laptop. For the last five minutes, we had been listening to the *Eyes on the Bay* coverage of the escape. There was a reported sighting of the two fugitives in downtown San Francisco—no word on Emma—and the military was referring to my father as the mastermind. It seemed obvious they would come here. *Too obvious.* With Xander and his makeshift Guardian Force intent on finding them, where else would they go? I hoped my father knew better. Mr. Van Sant returned his memories, stack by stack, into his desk drawer and withdrew his gun from a secret compartment behind it.

*Tap.*

*Tap.*

*Tap.*

In the quiet, the sound was easy to locate. I walked over to the window and slipped behind the curtain, just out of view. The backyard was dark except for a small circle of light radiating from the porch. I spotted the next pebble mid-flight. It came from a row of dense shrubbery near the fence, the leaves fluttering a little just before the tap. "Over there," I said. "From the bushes."

"C'mon." Keeping his gun close to him, Mr. Van Sant opened the door to his office and headed down the stairs.

"What's wrong?" Elana asked, nudging Max awake.

He was instantly wide-eyed. "What's going on?"

Elana gestured to the yard. Artos was already at the door, his ears perked, waiting.

"Someone's outside," I said.

Barry pulled his gun from his waistband and tapped it against Augustus' lanky arm. "You stay put." Augustus scooted to the edge of the chair. The tension seemed to invigorate him.

"Yes, sir." He was practically giddy.

So was Artos. His tail was twitching with excitement. Watching it pendulum back and forth, I had a hunch, but I couldn't be certain. Barry went first, turning the lock and pushing the door open wide. He edged, slow and careful, to the opening. When Artos took off over the threshold frisky as a puppy, I knew. And my heart began marking time.

"Show yourself," Barry ordered, still concealing himself behind the doorframe. He trained his gun on the shaking shrubbery.

I tapped his arm. "It's okay," I whispered. "Look at Artos." He was jumping, standing on his hind legs, trying to propel himself over the tall hedge that ran the length of the fence. Realizing it was impossible, he started digging underneath it, dirt flying out from behind his paws. There was laughter from the bushes.

"That dog is as nuts as you, McAllister." Edison emerged first, poking his head through the leaves. As he stepped into the glow of the light, I could see his face was bruised. There was a cut above one eye and a purple dash beneath the other, which was nearly swollen shut. The sleeve of his uniform was ripped. I'm not sure who was faster to get there—call it a tie—but Elana deferred to Mr. Van Sant, letting him wrap Edison in a ferocious bear hug before she pushed her way in.

I saw Quin's hand first, then his shoulder—his rolled-up shirt sleeve revealing the dragon tattoo on his forearm—then the rest of him all at once. Artos wasted no time commencing their long-awaited reunion. He was running circles around Quin's feet. I stayed still, watching Quin watch me. I didn't dare move. But there was a frenzy happening inside me. It felt like wings beating in my chest.

Mr. Van Sant was still holding onto Edison. He rubbed his head, mussing his hair. "You're alive. Alive! Alive!" After the fourth *alive,* Quin snickered. Keeping his eyes on mine, he smiled slow and easy.

Edison's face reddened. He smoothed his hair and straightened his tattered uniform. "Seriously, Dad, you're embarrassing me. Did you really think I couldn't handle myself? Did you think Xander's secretary was going to take me out? Or that idiot Valkov?"

"He did clock you pretty hard with that desk chair," Quin said, chuckling.

"I had it under control, McAllister."

"I know you did." With a wide grin, Quin knelt down and patted Artos head to tail with two hands—as Artos yelped with delight. "Not to steal Eddie's thunder, but I'm the one who got shot at. And I am also . . . *alive*."

Next to me, Max guffawed. "Only you two would argue about who came closest to death."

"Not arguing," Quin answered. "Just staking my claim for an equal amount of gushing." He winked at me, and those wings started fluttering again.

"Your dog is gushing enough for everyone," Edison said, pointing to Artos. He was sitting on his haunches, inches from Quin's feet, worshipping him with soulful eyes.

"What happened to your face?" Elana asked, touching Edison's nastiest bruise. He turned his head to Quin.

"Ask McAllister."

Quin shrugged. "I had to make it look believable."

"It?" Elana sounded as puzzled—but simultaneously euphoric—as I was.

"Let's go inside," Mr. Van Sant suggested. "I'm sure you two have a story to tell. And hopefully a hard drive to crack. We don't have much time."

Edison padded the front pocket of his uniform. "Like taking candy from a baby."

Max and I lingered in the doorway until everyone passed. Everyone but Quin—and Artos. He was Quin's shadow, weaving in between his legs and whining with excitement.

Next to me, Max shifted foot to foot, his eyes trained on the ground, trying to work up his courage. "I didn't know about String," he finally said. "I just wanted to tell you that, in case you thought . . . "

"I didn't," Quin interrupted him. "I never would." Max exhaled, then chortled as Quin pulled him into a playful headlock. "Because if you did . . . "

"Mercy. Mercy," Max squeaked. "I give up." As Quin released him, Max landed a quick jab to his shoulder and scampered inside, still laughing.

"Okay, so what's Augustus really doing here?" Quin asked me after Max left us alone. "We saw him through the window—no sign of Mr. Van Sant—and got worried . . . "

I couldn't help but smile. "Is that why you were hiding in the bushes?" I picked a spindly twig from his sleeve and held it up to him.

Quin laughed. "Sort of. Eddie thought there was a chance Augustus might be holding his dad hostage. We figured a cautious approach would be best." He brushed a leaf from his jacket. "Overly cautious, I guess."

"I like cautious. I want you to be cautious." Gently, I reached for Quin's forearm, tracing the length of it and slipping my hand into his. "I was so worried about you."

Our fingers laced together in a familiar embrace. "I was worried too. With Xander looking for you . . . " He paused, holding something back.

I looked at him with expectation, prompting him to continue.

"Did Xander say anything to you at Coit Tower? About me?"

I nodded, ashamed I let Xander hook me—even for a moment—to doubt Quin. "He wanted me to think you set me up. How did you know?"

"Because he tried to do the same to me. He told me they found a story on your dad's computer about me using Emovere again . . . and you were quoted in it." The thought of Valkov's fat nubs plunking across my father's keyboard sent a spike of indignation through the heart of me.

I shook my head. "That's ridiculous."

"I know." Quin squeezed my hand. I felt even worse for letting Xander inside my head. "He doesn't want us on the same side. He knows we make a great team. An unbeatable one." An easy, devil-may-care smile stretched across his face. It was undeniable. Irresistible. *Sexy.* But his confidence worried me.

"Cautious, remember?"

"Speaking of cautious . . . " Quin's smile was gone in an instant, replaced by a deep furrow between his brows. "What were you thinking showing up there today? You know Xander's after you. I think he's paid people to hurt you. That was really reckless, especially when I didn't even know you'd be there. How could I protect—." He stopped mid-sentence. "Sorry. I forgot. Not supposed to protect you."

I giggled, shaking my finger at him and trying not to think of Satan's Syndicate or the possible bounty on my head. His eyes softened at the bandage wrapped on my still-healing palm. "You're a quick learner, McAllister, but you'll be happy to know, I've changed my mind. Protecting the people you love is just what you do. I used to think you saw me as helpless, but I realized you only do it because you care."

"You're totally messing with me right now, aren't you?"

I shook my head, grinning. "I had an epiphany. An Augustus-induced epiphany."

"I'm not sure I like the sound of that, but I guess I'll take it . . . " He reached for my other hand, the injured one, gently turning it over and bringing it to his lips. " . . . if it lets me do this." That single point of contact—so soft, so tender—was like a live wire against my skin. I gulped, desperate for a distraction.

"So Xander . . . ?"

Quin nodded. "He set up the whole thing. He called it R and D."

"R and D?"

"Research and development."

Thinking of the bodies scattered haphazardly across Zenigenic's courtyard, I shuddered. "I thought you were . . . "

"I know. But I'm not." His soft brown eyes were an invitation. To touch him. To kiss him. To love him. To *anything* him. It was the vortex of Quin and it was unavoidable. I held myself back, teetering on the edge. I knew we had an audience—and after our last kiss, I wanted our first kiss to be like the very first.

I slipped both hands around his waist and pulled him to me, whispering against his ear. "Let the gushing commence."

## CHAPTER FIFTY-FOUR:

# YOUNG LOVE

"What a touching sight." When we came inside, our hands still interlocked, Augustus spoke first, addressing Quin. "Young love is so forgiving. It's almost as if your dalliance with that blonde—what was her name again?—never happened." I had to give him credit. It was a special talent the way he knew when and where to strike. But I was learning. It was a game. And two could play it. While Quin drew in a sharp breath, clearly rattled, I just squeezed his hand tighter.

I met Augustus' keen stare. "Her name is Emma." Elana's mouth dropped open. Max did a double take. Augustus was mute. Declaring myself the victor, I released Quin's hand and sat down on the sofa. Quin stood opposite me.

Mr. Van Sant cleared his throat. "So where were we? Edison?"

"Uh, okay." His eyebrows raised at me, Edison grinned. "When the shooting started—"

"Wait." Quin raised his hand to stop him. "Since when do we trust this nutcase?" His eyes were radiating heat, fixed on Augustus. "How did you get out of those handcuffs?"

A cruel smile played on Augustus' lips. "While you were busy playing spy, drugging and kidnapping me, this *nutcase* plucked your girlfriend out of enemy clutches. So you might want to rethink your hostile position." To Mr. Van Sant, he added, "If you want my help, I stay."

I shrugged at Quin. "Sorry," I mouthed. He huffed, exhaling a short, loud breath in protest. Arms crossed over his chest, he assumed a contrary position near the entryway while Edison resumed his story.

"I knew I had to get out of there. The transfer was only 95% complete, but I couldn't chance it."

"Let's hope the other five percent was Xander's summer vacation photos," Max joked. "Or Valkov's romance novel." We all laughed.

"I headed down the elevator, sure that I was home free—but I never made it past the front entrance. Xander and Valkov came running in, so I hid inside a closet. They were both furious. At first, I thought they were yelling at each other."

"What did they say?" I asked.

Edison and Quin shared a glance. "The gist of it was about String. Like he had done something he wasn't supposed to do yet. I didn't really get it at the time, but then McAllister told me what happened." The spotlight redirected onto Quin.

"Any idea why Sebastian would want you dead?" Mr. Van Sant asked.

"No clue," Quin said. "But I know he's been following me, at least since I got back from L.A. And Lex overheard him say something about tailing my dad."

I glanced sidelong at Augustus. He was preening like a peacock. "You knew about this, didn't you? Why was String following Quin?"

Augustus' serpentine smile was a forewarning. "I wish I could be of assistance, Ms. Knightley. I really do." *Doubtful.* "I'd like to punish that little traitor more than anyone." *That I could believe.* "However, there is the matter of my . . . " He cleared his throat with a purposeful glance at Mr. Van Sant. " . . . compensation. I don't give out priceless information for free."

"Argh!" Max groaned in frustration. "Could you be any more evasive? Is there an evil madman academy where they teach you this stuff?"

"It's called business school, Mr. Powers. Negotiation 101. My favorite class."

"Let me guess, your second favorite was Advanced Fraud," Max replied. "Or was it Accelerated Conning and Manipulation?"

Augustus looked through him. "We had a deal, Nicholas. You pay. I talk."

"Yes, and I will. But you certainly can't expect me to pay you one-and-a-half million dollars today."

"And why not?"

"It's impossible."

"I hate to be cliché, but where there's a will, there's a way." Augustus leaned back and closed his eyes. "Wake me when you have it."

"Porter!" Mr. Van Sant pounded the table with his fist. Augustus didn't even flinch. "We don't have time for this! People's lives are on the line here." He pretended to snore. "Fine. I'll give you $250,000 in cash today. That's the best I can do."

"Well if that's the best you can do." Augustus' smirk returned slowly, as if he was awakening from a delicious dream. "I met Sebastian right after my appointment as drug czar. He was living on the street outside of my office in downtown Oakland. I watched him for a while. He was smart, cunning, independent—a lot like me. So I took him under my wing. I gave him a job. I even bailed him out a few times." A slight variation of String's story. Since neither was known for telling the truth, I wasn't sure who to believe. "That's when he told me he was looking for someone. He wanted to settle a debt. He showed me—"

"Who was it?" Quin interrupted.

"Patience was never your strong suit, was it?" Augustus scowled at Quin. "I was getting to that. It was your father. He showed me a picture of your father. I didn't recognize him at first, of course, until he told me the name. That was before your father got his second fifteen minutes of infamy. When Sebastian said the name *McAllister* . . . well I thought perhaps we could come to a mutually beneficial arrangement." Amused with himself, Augustus chuckled. "I scratch your back, you scratch mine. You find my McAllister, I'll help you find yours."

"But how would String know George McAllister? What would he want with him?" I asked.

Augustus reclined in his chair, his work apparently done. "Ms. Knightley, your guess is as good as mine. But I do know he found him. He was tailing him and—"

Before he could finish, Mr. Van Sant jumped up from his seat, grinning. He put his open palm in front of Augustus. "Give me five!" Augustus gingerly tapped his palm, disdain dripping from the downturned corners of his mouth.

"What are you talking about, Dad?" Edison asked.

"I'm talking about a possible witness. A witness to Shelly's murder. If Sebastian was following George McAllister, then maybe, just maybe, he was there that night. This is the first real lead we've had in a while."

I peeked up at Quin. His eyes were pure excitement.

"Let's just hope he doesn't kill Quin first. Or turn up dead himself," Edison added. *Dead.* Max and I both winced, but that word was a harsh reminder. I still had a few more questions for Quin.

"We saw String aiming right at you," I said. "How did he miss?"

"He didn't." Immediately, the light in Quin's eyes doused. I wondered what he was thinking. "One of the soldiers on the stage pushed me out of the way. He got shot in the back, but he was wearing a bulletproof vest."

"Odd." Mr. Van Sant summed my reaction perfectly. "The military isn't exactly pro-McAllister. Did you know him?"

Quin didn't answer at first. "No, I don't know him." Everyone else moved on. I stayed stuck in the quicksand of what Quin wasn't saying. He avoided my eyes.

"How did Valkov find you?" Elana asked Edison.

Edison shrugged. "That guy is like a sniffer dog. No offense, Artos." Hearing his name, Artos cocked his head and whined a little. "I was being so quiet. He must have heard me breathing."

"So what did you do?"

"Well, Red, I did what I used to do best. I pretended I was plastered out of my mind." Edison and Quin both chuckled. "Valkov hit me with a chair, and then Quin showed up." Edison pointed to his black eye. "He smacked me around a little for old times' sake and convinced the powers that be to let him deal with me. And then we got the heck out of there."

"What did you tell Xander?" I asked Quin. He looked away, uncomfortable. Edison's face reddened. The lightness between them darkened.

"It's okay, McAllister. You can say it." Edison's words of encouragement had a sharp edge, the kind that would make you bleed before you realized you'd been cut.

Quin sighed again. He was used to Edison's razor tongue. "I'd rather not. You know I didn't mean it."

"Yes, you did." Whatever remained of Edison's self-loathing was unearthed. He spit out the words with the sort of bitter vigor he reserved only for Quin. "He said I was a loser. An arrogant, good for nothing—"

"Stop." Quin's voice was soft but compelling. "I was describing myself. My old self. Everything I ever hated about you, I hated about me too." He put his hand on Edison's shoulder, both of them wincing with the effort of it, the admission it required. I saw what I had known since that first night in my kitchen. They were two sides of the same boy. "You're a good guy, Eddie. You're my friend."

Mr. Van Sant nodded. "You've got to stop being so hard on yourself, Son." Considering his words, he amended them. "I have to stop being so hard on you too."

Edison's muscles were tense, his jaw clenched. He was on the verge of something. Good or bad—it was hard to tell. A single, willful tear escaped from his eye before he leveled it with his uniform sleeve. "Alright, alright, alright." He released a shaky breath. Elana wrapped her arm around Edison and kissed his cheek. Disarmed, he finally turned to look at Quin. "I love you too, McAllister. But you know I'm already taken."

Augustus raised his hand like a pompous schoolboy who wouldn't wait to be called on. "Large bills only, please."

## CHAPTER FIFTY-FIVE:

# SECOND CITY

"You're gonna want to see this." Barry called to us from the corner of the living room where he was sitting with the laptop balanced on his knees, sorting through the contents of Xander's hard drive.

On the screen were hundreds of folders, most cryptically labeled. "A lot of these file names correspond to the substitution code. Like this one." He pointed to a numbered folder. "Docil-E," he explained, clicking on it. Barry scrolled through the documents to the very bottom. "Lex, I think this might explain why your soldier was violent." He opened the file. It was an internal email dated November 15, 2042. I read it over Max's shoulder.

*Dear Mr. Steele,*

*As we discussed in our research review meeting last week, the team is nearing completion of the Docil-E2 experimental trials. It is my understanding that the military expects Docil-E2 to be ready for deployment within a month. Though the team has successfully met the requests to alter the chemical composition of Docil-E according to military specifications, I feel it is my duty to apprise you of my reservations, which are based on the trials conducted in our laboratory as well as my five-year tenure at Green Briar Recovery Center treating EAM abuse and dependence.*

*While Docil-E has been proven effective in promoting positive emotions, including kindness and cooperation, Docil-E2's effects are less advantageous. Test subjects in Trials 4 and 5 (who were adminis-*

*tered Docil-E2) showed low levels of activity in the frontal lobe, leading to decreased alertness and self-efficacy, and increased vulnerability to suggestion. Unlike their Docil-E counterparts, Docil-E2 subjects maintained a similar propensity toward violence.*

*In short, these subjects complied with orders to refrain from violence but were also willing to behave aggressively when ordered to do so and, in fact, appeared to have less control over their decisions and limited awareness of consequences. Experimental trials also have shown that subjects who were simultaneously administered Emovere, Agitor, or Onyx demonstrated an unpredictable response to Docil-E2. In my opinion, further testing of Docil-E2 is warranted before its use in real-world military scenarios.*
*Regards,*
*Dr. Layton Ferguson, Senior Researcher*

Max shook his head. "Can anyone say déjà vu?"

"I wish I could say I'm surprised," Mr. Van Sant replied. "I'm willing to bet Dr. Ferguson is already out of a job."

"Or buried in a shallow grave," Max scoffed.

Elana shook her head, puzzled. "It's strange though. Why would the military want to use this on the public? Or even an enemy? It seems too risky."

"That's just it," Quin said. "They're not planning to use it on the public." With all eyes on him, I spoke.

"Research and development." I repeated Quin's phrase and he nodded. An idea, as feathery and formless as a cloud, was beginning to take shape in my mind—the shape of a rain cloud with its dark heart throbbing, signaling trouble.

"It's for internal use only," he said. "Today was just another test. Whatever Xander is planning . . ." Quin detoured, distracted by a newly opened spreadsheet. "Is that what I think it is?"

"2043 sales projections," Barry answered. "By city."

Quin nodded. "For Docil-E?"

"Among other things." Docil-E was clearly marked by name, but there were four other substances identified by number. "This one's

Emovere." As he deciphered the code, he named the others—all banned, of course. "Agitor . . . Eupho . . . "

"I think we all know what's left," Mr. Van Sant said.

"Onyx."

"Looks like Xander's anticipating a big year for Emovere in California." I pointed to the sales graphs for San Francisco, Emovere's line spiking in January and steadily climbing month by month. "And Los Angeles."

"And Boston and New York," Quin added. As Barry scrolled through 100 major U.S. cities, we named ten with a similar pattern.

"Ten?" Mr. Van Sant's sounded dazed and desperate, and I knew exactly what he was thinking. "Do you really think Xander's capable of something like that? That kind of devastation?"

Quin scoffed. "He's selling drugs on the black market. He's supplying gangs with Onyx. He framed my dad for murder. What isn't he capable of?"

"Quin's right, Dad. He'd bomb twenty cities if he could." Edison let out an exasperated sigh. "But this isn't evidence. We can't prove anything."

"Then we have to keep looking." I directed Barry to another file with a logo I recognized. *Guardian Force Rehabilitation Program.* "Carrie was right. She said Zenigenic was funding part of the program." Inside the folder were hundreds of day-by-day Recovery Analysis charts exactly like the one Carrie showed me and my father. I scanned the dates looking for charts dated after her resignation. "There. That one." *July 2041.* "And that one." *January 2042.* Barry opened them, revealing a long list of former Guardian Force. Like Carrie's list, there were many red circles. But on this one, there was something else. Asterisks. And Greenhorn 387 had both.

"Uh, Sherlock?" Edison tapped me on the shoulder. "What exactly are we looking for here?"

I put my finger on Greenhorn 387. "This is Peter Radley—about eight months before he started doing those rallies with Quin's dad."

"What do the marks mean?" Elana asked.

I shrugged. "I'm not exactly sure. Carrie's chart was different. No asterisks. She said the red circles corresponded to an incomplete recovery from EAMs. A damaged brain." The moment my words took a life of their own, I wished I could take them back, squash them inside me like they deserved. *What was I thinking?* I studied Quin's face. Even though I expected it—his instant self-doubt—it still was painful to watch.

"Does anyone ever really recover?" Max asked, rescuing me.

Mr. Van Sant made a noise of agreement. "There's a lot of red on that page. Reminds me of law school, my first legal briefs. Those were a bloodbath."

"Dad. Focus." Edison turned to Barry. "Is there a way to find out what those asterisks mean?"

"Let's go fishing," Barry suggested. He right clicked on the screen and typed * into the search bar. Hundreds of results appeared, but one stood out. It was an entire folder, titled only with an asterisk. "Looks like we caught a whopper."

"Open it," Mr. Van Sant urged. The folder contained hundreds of documents, each labeled with the identifier of a Greenhorn or a Legacy.

Quin's eyes widened. "I'll look for it," he blurted, quickly tilting the screen toward him, squinting hard. His face tensed. *Was he holding his breath?* No one else seemed to notice. After a minute or so, he tapped his finger against the screen. It was a letter addressed to Peter Radley.

*September 1, 2042*

*Congratulations, Greenhorn 387,*

*You have been selected as a qualifying candidate for the Guardian Force Elite Team. This team has been assembled to carry out a series of special missions, the details of which will be disclosed to you after you sign the enclosed contract.*

*As a reminder, your signature on this document confirms your withdrawal from the Guardian Force Rehabilitation Program and reinstatement in the United States Guardian Force as a member of the Elite Team. As always, your discretion is demanded. Should you accept these terms, please report for duty at the main entrance of the Presidio in San Francisco, where you will be issued further instructions.*

*We thank you for your service to your country and wish you success as a Guardian Elite.*

*Sincerely,*

*General Anton Maze*

"Un-be-lievable!" Mr. Van Sant jumped to his feet and began pacing. "Guardian Force Elite Team?"

"Carrie said it was happening again. That's the general she wrote requesting her resignation." I found Quin's eyes looking down at his tattoo, disgusted. It was different now, of course, but what it represented was indelible, inked onto Quin permanently.

His gaze distant, he rubbed his arm. "Maze was fourth in command behind Ryker."

"Do you think Radley was still working for the Guardian Force when he spoke at the New Resistance rallies?" I asked him.

He didn't answer. "Quin?" His sigh was long and brittle, the way regret might sound, if it made one.

"Of course he was." He said it to himself. "How could I have missed that? He always acted a little strange, but I just thought it was the drugs—the long-term effects." He wandered away and sat on the arm of the sofa, putting his head to his palms. I followed, taking the place alongside him. In the space between us, I could feel his angst squatting like a toad. I laid my hand on Quin's back and let it rest there. He didn't move away, but he didn't acknowledge me either.

"Did you know about this?" I asked Augustus. He was lurking in the corner, a briefcase of Mr. Van Sant's money—as requested, large bills only—tucked under his seat, so quiet I almost forgot he was there.

"To what exactly are you referring, Ms. Knightley?"

"Any of it? And why do you always answer a question with a question?"

"What makes you think I would have access to privileged military information?"

I rolled my eyes at him. "Because I know you."

Augustus preened in the spotlight of my unintended flattery. "I do know one thing," he said. "Steele couldn't stand it, the way the public despised Zenigenic and, by default, *him*. His father was similar, always looking for a way to sway opinion. A staged assassination attempt might do the trick." As far-fetched as it sounded, none of us disagreed.

For the first time since we walked through the door together, Quin looked at Augustus. "You're right." Augustus' eyes widened, as if he was waiting on a bolt of lightning to follow those words. "I can't believe I didn't realize it sooner. Barry, is there anything on that drive about what happened in Chicago?"

"You don't think . . . " I let the rest of my words fall away, not ready to say them aloud.

"That's *exactly* what I think."

"Okay, Holmes and Watson." Edison nodded his head toward Quin and me. "Would one of you please enlighten the rest of us?"

"If Zenigenic is willing to bomb cities to increase sales now, what would've stopped them from doing it six years ago?" Quin's question descended like a bomb in its own right.

In the aftermath, Edison answered. "Nothing."

Barry motioned toward the screen to a folder that wasn't numbered. Its label was innocuous. *Miscellaneous.* "This is the only folder with anything from 2037. It hasn't been opened in a while."

There was only one document inside, dated October 30, 2037. "That's three days after the bombings started. Three days after Chicago," I said. "That can't be a coincidence." It was a memo—one sentence—addressed to Xander's father, then-CEO of Zenigenic, Jackson Steele.

*As you requested, all files related to the Second City Project have been destroyed.*

"Second City?" Elana asked.

Mr. Van Sant nodded gravely. "It's an old nickname for Chicago."

## CHAPTER FIFTY-SIX:

# VANILLA

Ten minutes later, I was still peering over Max's shoulder into the bright light of the computer screen. Like a moth to flame, I found it hard to look away, even though the rest of me was somewhere else. *Chicago. Zenigenic. My mother. Did she know?* It was two years after her resignation, but that picture of her with Ryker reaffirmed what I already knew. My mother had a hidden life, a buried labyrinth that knew no bounds. It was easy to get lost there. But I didn't want out . . . only to understand why. Still, I kept stumbling into new rooms, each darker and emptier than the last. I could feel Quin's heat next to me. He was lost inside his own thoughts, his eyes as distant as mine. His thumb rubbed my index finger methodically, strumming something electric inside me with each stroke. I focused on that—the way his touch played the vibrato strings of my body—to the exclusion of everything else.

Edison burst into sudden laughter, and I jumped. "Click the one at the top. *Dear Mother.*" He read aloud.

*My Dearest Mother,*

*I hope this letter finds you well. I am writing to offer my sincerest gratitude for your support. Despite your reservations about my appointment as CEO and leader of our family's greatest legacy, Zenigenic Corporation, I assure you that I will do everything in my power to secure the success Father worked so diligently to achieve. I promise I will not disappoint you.*

*Your loving son,*

*Xandi*

"Xandi! Ha!" Edison doubled over laughing.

Mr. Van Sant—who was perched on the sofa, drafting an email to Langley—shot a stern glance. "We're taking all of this to the media," he said after we found the Second City memo. "And not Barbara Blake. The *real* media."

Quin tugged at my hand, pulling me away from the spot where I was anchored, weighted by the heft of all that was unknown and unanswered. "I have to go soon," he mouthed, glancing down at his watch. It was over an hour since he and Edison returned. Xander and—worse—Valkov would be looking for him. Quin was going to leave me again. It was inevitable. The room felt airless. The wings fluttering in my chest since I saw him went still. "Can we go somewhere to talk?" he asked.

I nodded, letting him guide me up the stairs and into the first open door, one of Mr. Van Sant's countless guest bedrooms. Quin closed the door behind us, shutting out the light from the hallway. He reached for the lamp on the nightstand, but I stopped him. Knowing I might cry, I was okay with only the glow of the moon through the window.

Quin sat on the bed and patted the spot next to him. He lay back, using his hands as a pillow. "What a day." He was trying to be cool, but I could tell he was nervous. I was too. I sunk back into the soft mattress, painfully aware of the space between us. I tried to keep my breath steady and even. Slowly I turned toward him, hoping—not hoping—hoping—not hoping—to find his eyes. He was staring at the ceiling. My fingertips brushed his.

"Hey," he said, curling his hand around mine.

"Hey, yourself." Our familiar back and forth was a comfort, like returning to a favorite childhood place and finding it just as you remembered. For the first time in days, I felt safe.

"I want to ask you something." He rolled over onto his side and scooted nearer to me, putting his hand firmly on my hip. "What is it that you think happened between me and Emma?" And there she was, the elephant in the room. Although really, Emma was nothing like an elephant. Not even close. She was more of a fox. Sleek, cunning, but pesky.

I propped myself up on my elbow, releasing his hand. "A dalliance?" I parroted Augustus.

Quin rolled his eyes. "First of all, please don't ever quote Augustus. And second of all . . . "

"Second of all?" I prompted, preparing myself for the worst.

"I kissed Emma one time after she came to L.A. She always wanted to be more than friends—but you know that already—and I wanted to try to forget you."

"And?"

"Do you really not know?" I started to answer him. That day she taught me to ride, Emma reluctantly admitted the same—one kiss. I carried those words in my pocket like two wishing stones. Even now, I wanted—I needed—to hear him say it. "I felt nothing."

"But Emma is so . . . I don't know . . . exciting. With her tattoos and her motorcycle—and her braid that's always changing color. Maybe I'm too vanilla for you." I looked down when I said it, following the moon-cast shadows on Quin's chest.

He gently lifted my chin. "If this is vanilla—if *you* are vanilla—then I'm crazy about vanilla. I adore vanilla. I'm pretty sure vanilla is essential to my survival." I half smiled at him.

"Seriously, Quin."

"Okay, seriously. Kissing her only made me miss you more. But in a way, I was glad. I don't want to feel this way about anybody else." I thought of my uninspired kiss with Percy and understood completely. It was dreary, dull, drab—nothing like the first-day-of-summer feeling Quin gave me.

"That night at Coit Tower, I had a dream you said you loved me."

He swallowed hard. "That wasn't a dream, but you were supposed to be asleep."

"Why?"

"I didn't know how you felt. If you'd say it back. So I figured it was probably best just to keep it between me and . . . well, me."

I wrapped my arm around his waist, resting my hand just near the hem of his untucked shirt on a slice of bare skin. It was so warm that it left me capable of only one thought. *I don't want to ever stop touching him.* He reached for my hand and pulled my arm tighter around him. "Do you want to say it again?" I asked, his lips nearly on mine.

He cleared his throat ceremoniously. "I love you, Alexandra Knightley. I never stopped. I don't think I can. I don't want—"

Before he could speak it, the rest of his speech tumbled into my mouth. Our bodies picked up the dialogue where the words left off. It was like a half-delirious, talk-all-night conversation so intense you can't sleep afterward, don't want to. I was flush against him, his fingers tangling in my hair. I ran my hand under his shirt, pressing hard against his back—his muscles solid, tightening like a taut rope beneath my palm as he moved—then lower along his waistband, letting my fingers dip dangerously below it. His lips were insistent, needful, asking. So were mine, replying.

"That would've been my answer," I whispered as our kisses slowed to a lazy back and forth. "That, and I love you too."

I could feel his grin beneath my lips. "That's one helluva answer." He trailed his mouth along my jaw, then buried his face in my neck, inhaling me. His stubble prickled against my skin, but I leaned in anyway, listening to his breathing in my ear. I was transfixed by its contradiction—all at once calm and urgent. "But I want you to trust me," he whispered. "Do you trust me?"

I was prepared for this. It was the riddle I always came back to in the dead of night after all my other thoughts fell away, exhausted. I was still mulling over my mother's secrets—how she kept them and why. And my insatiable need to know—the push and pull of it. With Quin, it was no different. "I think that's the wrong question."

"So tell me the right one."

"Do *you* trust *me*? You've said it yourself, you're a closed book. And I understand why. You want to know—really know—I can handle it. Hiding Augustus from my dad was like that. I didn't think he would understand. But I was wrong. I had to trust him. I had to give him a chance. Quin, I need you to let me in. All the way. I can handle it."

"I know you can." He paused, then sighed. "But I guess I've always been worried you would stop loving me . . . maybe return this closed book to the library." I shook my head, laughing, but Quin silenced me with a tender kiss. He pulled me to him, his chest pressed firmly against my back. It was his favorite way to hold me—no space between our bodies but avoiding my eyes. "When I was in L.A., I went to see one of those Prophecy Program researchers." I felt myself stiffen. "They tested me." I couldn't speak, so I just laid there in the blaring silence.

"Lex?"

"Mmhmm."

"I decided I don't want to know the results." I shifted under the weight of his arm, turning to face him. He didn't look away, his brown eyes so bright in the moonlight, they warmed me like the sun.

"Okay," I said. And it was. Whatever was inside of Quin—pumping through the secret, world-worn chambers of the heart I loved, deep in the marrow of his bones—was no different than anybody else. It was mother, father, good and bad, and everything in between. It was whatever he chose it to be. I didn't need a test to tell me that.

"And I do trust you. I trust you completely, more than anybody else. That's why I wanted to talk to you alone. There's something I need to tell you, something nobody else can know."

"What is it?"

"That soldier who saved me—he was my brother. It was Colton."

## CHAPTER FIFTY-SEVEN:

# KEEP RUNNING

"What—how do you know—are you sure?" The words shot out of mouth in a run-on sentence. I sat up too quickly, spinning a little from the rush.

"I'm sure." Quin sat up next to me. His voice was absent of any doubt.

"But how?"

"I noticed him watching me during Xander's speech. He looks just like me at seventeen. And then I saw him up close when String started shooting at me. Colton had this birthmark on his neck, a red splotch just below his ear. This soldier had one just like it. It's him."

"Did he say anything to you?"

Quin shook his head. "They pulled him off me, and he disappeared into the crowd with the other Guardians. But he slipped this into my pocket." Quin handed me a piece of paper—folded and unfolded so many times that it felt like cloth. I opened it with care.

It was a photocopy of a newspaper article dated November 5, 2028. *McAllister Sentenced To Life In Brutal Slaying, Young Son Finds New Home.* In the margins, there were drawings, some pencil scribbling, and handwriting in faded ink that read *Colton ~~McAllister~~ Masterson.*

> *George McAllister's sons, ages six and two, were present in the home when their mother was killed. Los Angeles County Child Protective Services confirmed today that the younger of the two boys was recently adopted, releasing a statement that read, in part, "We are happy to report he has been permanently placed with a loving family."*

*CPS also confirmed McAllister's oldest son remains in their care and custody. There has been an outpouring of support for the two boys, with many offering to adopt or foster them. However, child psychologist and trauma expert Margot Denam cautioned, "In cases like this, even under the best circumstances, we expect deep emotional scars. Research tells us children who witness one parent murder the other have increased difficulty forming attachments with new caregivers. Adopting a child who has suffered this type of trauma is a serious commitment."*

"It's . . . " Strange, but in that moment, I felt the most bitter melancholy. "Wow. This is incredible. We should look in the asterisk folder, see if we can find him. Maybe—"

"I already did when I was looking for Radley's file. He's not in there. But I didn't think he would be . . . " Following Quin's finger, I turned my attention back to the well-worn piece of paper. Taped to the bottom was a picture of Quin, printed from one of the recent Zenigenic Internet ad campaigns.

"Look underneath," Quin said. I scratched at the edge of the tape until it lifted. More handwriting—freshly inked this time.

*Big brother, I've been looking for you since I was 12 years old, the day I found this article in my parents' bedroom drawer. After our dad got arrested again, there you were on the Internet defending him. So I came to San Francisco to find you. But I got recruited—or should I say persuaded. General Maze told me he knew you and that he could reunite us. He lied. Once I enlisted, nobody would tell me anything—just that you went AWOL. They won't let me leave. Half the time, I'm doped up on Emovere. Maze told me he wants me for a special mission. I don't know how you got out, but I want out too before they make me do anything else I regret.*

Quin made a small sound, cocooning his face in his palms. *Was he crying?* "I wanted him to have a better life, a real family. But all of it was for nothing. He's exactly where I was. Because of me." When he lifted his head and opened the curtain of his hands, his eyes were wet.

I wanted to tell Quin I understood—the rejections, the scars, the labels, all of it—the immeasurable price he paid counting on Colton's escape. It wasn't fair. Mostly, I just wanted to catch him on his way down, like he had done for me so many times. Tell him we would figure it out together. But I never got the chance.

The thin rectangle of light at the base of the bedroom door disappeared. Downstairs, I heard a collective shout.

"Did the lights go out?" Quin asked, sobering quickly.

The answer came—fast, heavy—and not from me. Bullets pinging the house, windows exploding, Elana's wailing scream. It was the sound of a monster spitting fire in a dream, but we weren't dreaming. This monster was real.

Quin grabbed my arm and jerked me to my feet. "The window," he said, already pulling me toward it. Jarring it open with one hand, he stepped out onto the roof. I followed. We couldn't see much, only the fenced backyard. Backlighted by the moon, tendrils of gun smoke rose up from the front of the house. "This way." Quin shimmied down the second-floor overhang to the edge. I scooted after him, the hard tiles scraping my thighs even through my jeans. Ten feet below us was a pool of glass from the picture window.

"We have to jump, then run like crazy," he said, not giving me a choice. "Ready?" I nodded against all instinct—*where's Emovere when you need it?*—and pushed myself into the sky. Mid-flight, I felt the burn of vomit rising in my throat. Barely a breath later came bone-juddering impact. No time to assess the damage. No time to look back. A bullet cut the air next to my ear, and my legs were churning as fast as Quin's. We busted out through the gate and onto the street.

"Keep running!" Quin implored, as if I planned to stop. His voice was muted by the pulsing ring in my ears, my frantic half gasps for air. *Keep running.* I trained my eyes on his back—tunnel vision—matching my pace to his. *Keep running.* It wasn't until he pointed up ahead that I realized his words weren't meant for me. I named them all, counted them in my head. Someone was missing. *Keep running.* And we did.

## CHAPTER FIFTY-EIGHT:

# CHOCOLATE-COVERED ANTS

It was so cold my skin hurt. Teeth chattering, I tucked my hands further under Artos' warm belly. His head lay on his paws, but his eyes were open, alert, watching a small bird hop in the corner of the room. Artos had been here before. So had I. In another life—a life without Onyx, without Valkov, without Xander Steele. A life before I found my father and watched my mother die. A life before I gave my whole heart to a tattooed boy with mischievous brown eyes, a boy who was gone . . . again.

"Are you sure no one else knows about this place?" Edison asked, scowling at Augustus. He returned his chin to rest on the top of Elana's head. She was pressed snug to his chest, his arms blanketed over her. I never felt so jealous. "Why should we believe you?"

"You have a better idea, I presume?"

"Here we go again," Max muttered. Edison and Augustus had been going at it, jab for jab, since we arrived at the abandoned Resistance headquarters over an hour ago. Augustus led us here through the pin-drop silence of the BART tunnel, past the lab, the control booth, and the Map Room to his old office. He swiped at the cobwebs in the doorway with his long fingers and produced a key from his pocket, lips turning up in a satisfied smile as he fit it inside the lock. I imagined it was much as he had left it when he fled here over two years ago. Hanging above the wall on his desk was a diploma from New York University,

Stern School of Business. *Real or fake?* Wondering was a convenient distraction.

"You just happened to have a key to an office that's been deserted for two years? Am I the only one who finds that disturbing?" *No. Right here. Me, definitely disturbed.* But I didn't say anything. My tongue sat thick and useless in my mouth. I felt numb and not just from the cold. Barry was dead, shot in Mr. Van Sant's living room by Satan's Syndicate. No one told me, no one spoke the words out loud, but I knew.

If I closed my eyes, I could pretend Quin was here with me. "Lex." I could still feel the puffs of his breath tickle my cheek when he'd whispered my name outside the boarded tunnel entrance. He shivered against me, his body saying *I love you,* while he mouthed other words in my ear. "Don't trust Augustus. There's no way he got out of Coit Tower on his own." His hand slipped under my shirt to the small of my back where he carefully tucked his gun into my waistband. I watched Quin walk away from me until his silhouette was part of the shadows. I was practiced at goodbye, and yet—every single time— it split my heart like a melon and scooped it hollow. Love should come with a warning label.

"He'll be okay." Max nudged me with his elbow, reading my dark thoughts as clearly as if they were scribed in stone. "Remember when we first met?" He half smiled. "I told you Quin is kind of amazing."

Being in this place brought it all back, and in spite of everything, I beamed back at him. "I think your exact words were *moody, but strikingly handsome.*"

"And was I wrong?"

"Truer words were never spoken." I leaned against Max and put my head on his shoulder. "I'm sorry about String."

Max sighed, then chuckled. "That's what I get for trusting a guy with better hair than mine." But there was no mistaking the sorrow behind his jest.

"I trusted him too."

"We all did," Elana added.

Max sat up straight and turned to look at me. "Is it crazy I'm still worried about him and furious at the same time? I just want to look him in the eye and ask him *why.*"

"And punch him in the face." I tried to make him smile again.

He didn't. "That too."

"He was probably just following Xander's orders," Elana suggested.

Max nodded. "Probably." But when his eyes met mine and quickly cut away, I wondered if he was convinced. The way String slowed time to savor the moment just before he pulled the trigger, I had no doubt. Whatever he had against Quin, it was personal.

"Are you *sure* he never told you?" I asked Augustus. He pretended not to hear me, his eyes shut in a sudden and unconvincing portrayal of sleep. Quin's warning repeated in my head. *What am I supposed to do, Quin?* Frustrated and unnerved, I turned away. Across from me, Mr. Van Sant sat rigid in Augustus' dusty office chair. He was a statue, stony and unspeaking. I was afraid if I looked too long, he might crumble, dissolve into sand and silt. He'd spoken just one sentence, a forlorn proclamation. "The email to Langley never sent." Of all the things he could've said, it seemed the least devastating, but the tremble in his voice—and all he withheld—made it sound irretrievably dire.

"I'm hungry." Augustus stretched his legs, repositioning himself atop his golden egg, the briefcase stuffed with his $250,000 payment. I rolled my eyes but couldn't deny the growl in my own empty stomach. What little we had with us—Elana's now-lifeless cell phone, Mr. Van Sant's gun, and a pack of chewing gum Max found squished in his jacket pocket—was laid out like a feast in the center of the room, lit by two kerosene lamps from Augustus' closet. I took comfort in my secret, the gun's icy metal against my back. I planned to keep it there.

"I'm—"

"We heard you the first time," Edison snapped. "Why don't you call for a pizza? Tell them it's the first moldy, rat-infested tunnel on the left. I'm sure they'll be right over."

"He's right, Son." Mr. Van Sant was hoarse, each word scraping his throat. And for a moment, I felt an indescribable shock as if I had expected him to stay mute forever. "We need supplies. We need electricity. We need a computer. I have to send that—"

"Dad, wake up! The email to Langley is the least of our problems. There's a gang chasing us. A gang with the symbol of the devil on their necks. The devil! Oh, and by the way—*like they need it*—the devil-worshippers are taking Onyx. Bombs are going off somewhere tomorrow.

Lex's dad is on the run. We're trapped down here with this—" He waved a dismissing hand at Augustus. "—this lunatic and . . ."

"And Barry's dead." Finally, Mr. Van Sant conceded it. And for a while, there was nothing else to say.

When I found my voice again, it was as scratchy as Mr. Van Sant's. "There might be food left in the kitchen." We had passed it on our way here, too afraid to stop. "And we should check the other rooms too."

"I'll go," Max said, already on his feet.

"I'm coming with you." The words tumbled out before I considered their meaning—willingly walking into the unknown. But I couldn't just sit here with our collective grief hanging heavy, covering me in its shroud. I stood and Artos followed.

"Take the gun." Mr. Van Sant directed Max to the pile at his feet. "And a lamp."

Elana shifted nervously in Edison's embrace. "Be careful."

"Allow me." Augustus unlocked the rusty deadbolt that stood between us and anything that wanted in. He bared his teeth in a smile, and I could only guess about the source of his gratification—when we walked out, he would shut the door behind us, securing it with a scrape and a thud.

* * *

"This is spooky." I shuddered as Max held the lamp up to the control booth. Its windows were covered in a thick layer of grime, making it impossible to see inside.

"Why, whatever do you mean, Ms. Knightley?" Max asked in his best vampire voice, punctuating his question with a sinister cackle.

"Not funny." I rubbed the center of the glass, revealing a bit of red paint, the familiar mark of the Resistance. It reminded me of something—a trace of memory, receding like a will-o'-wisp as I chased it. A knot tightened in my stomach.

"I can't believe this is the same place." Max directed the light down the tunnel where Artos was letting his nose lead him, sniffing his way from room to room.

I turned my face back toward the glass to the red mark. I could see my fingerprints in the dust. "That day I first met String, you said he wanted to go to one of those New Resistance rallies, right?"

Max froze, then spotlighted me. "Yeah. We saw Quin and his dad there."

"Did he ever say anything about it?"

"Not really. We left early before most of the speeches finished." Max hung his head. "That was a Eupho night."

I nodded, taking a step in the direction of the kitchen. Max's hand stopped me and pulled me back. "You can't just ask me that and not tell me why."

"I don't know why. I'm just thinking out loud. Something about String in that red bandana, standing up there on the top of the world with his gun, all wild-eyed, it reminded me of . . . "

"Quin?" I was relieved Max said it first. *Maybe I wasn't crazy.*

"It was straight out of the *Book of Quin*," I said.

"The what?" He smirked at me.

"His Guardian Force file. There was a photo from that rally in San Francisco, the one where Quin was disguised as a member of the Resistance, the one where he . . . well, you know."

Max started speed walking ahead of me. "Lex, that's crazy." *Maybe I was.* "How would String even know about that? Why would he care?"

I dismissed myself with an exaggerated shrug. "You're right. I think this trip down Resistance lane is getting to me." That was true, at least. Neither of us spoke until we reached the kitchen. Just outside it, hanging by a few threadbare wires, was one of the intercom speakers. On the door—informing me I was, yet again, doing what I shouldn't be—was a sign: *Property of the United States Government, No Trespassing.*

"I wonder if these doors even open," Max said. "Most of them were automated."

"Well, there's one way to find out." I tugged at the handle of the kitchen door. Set in a metal track, it was meant to release with the click of a button. It squeaked a little in protest and didn't budge. "Help me pull." Max set the lamp at our feet and held on next to me.

Before we began, he gasped. "What was that?" I'd heard it too, the faintest rustle, like a snake in the leaves. I looked to Artos for a signal—safe, not safe. He was busy stalking a pair of crickets.

"Cujo's not concerned," I teased. "It's probably just a rat or some other animal."

"Comforting."

I repositioned my hands. "One . . . two . . . three . . . pull." The door groaned with our effort. "One . . . two . . . three . . . pull." It inched forward in the track, leaving a small opening. Artos squeezed his head inside, the rest of him slipping through with no effort.

Max laughed. "Hey, Artos, can you bring back some food?"

I wrinkled my nose at the sour musk of rot. "That doesn't smell edible—whatever it is."

Heaving against the door with his boot, Max widened the opening. "Well, we're about to find out." The instant I sidestepped the threshold, I wanted to turn back. The air was dead, suffocating. There was a constant buzz that got louder and louder as we approached the center of the room. Even before Max raised the lamp, my stomach lurched at the sound. Flies. Swarms of them, writhing in a shapeless black mass on the table, beating their tiny wings as they delighted in the decay.

"Let's try the pantry," Max suggested, ushering me ahead. Riding a wave of nausea, I kept my mouth closed, afraid I might gag. He swung open the metal cabinets one by one, taking a quick step back each time. Empty. Empty. Empty. "Jackpot!" Max stood on tiptoe to reach a jumbo-sized bag of chocolate bars hidden on the top shelf. "It could be worse." He grinned, then dropped the bag in horror, kicking it away from us.

"Chocolate covered ants?" I asked.

Poker-faced, he repeated my words. "Not funny."

# CHAPTER FIFTY-NINE:

# JACKPOT

Empty-handed, we traced our steps back to the kitchen entrance, Artos trotting alongside. "I'd say that was a colossal failure," Max said, averting his eyes from Fly Mountain. As we neared the exit, the lure of stale-but-breathable air quickened our pace. I stopped short of the door.

"Hey, wasn't there a portable TV down here somewhere?"

Max snapped his fingers, invigorated. "You're right! A few of us snuck it in. Augustus didn't want us exposed to *propaganda*."

"Go figure."

Max opened a few drawers, scattering their contents—mostly silverware, tarnished by the damp air. "Dare I say it? Another jackpot?" He held up a small battery-powered television, wiping a film from its screen.

"Don't get too excited, high roller. It probably doesn't work."

Max's finger hovered over the button for a small eternity.

". . . number one source for television news, SFTV. Reporting live, I'm . . ."

"Now can I say it?" Max asked, not waiting for my answer. "Jack. Pot. Yes!"

I grinned back at him, never so enthused to hear Barbara Blake's canned introduction. But a sudden rumble from Artos ended our celebration. Next came a crash, the sound of delicate glass cracking against the floor. Artos barked, then darted back into the cave beyond the kitchen doorway.

"Someone's here," Max mouthed. Though I knew it, his pronouncement tripped the wire of panic already rigged inside me. I could feel my heart pinging in the hollow of my chest, my nerves firing off like tiny bombs. I steadied myself against the nearest counter and gripped Quin's gun in my waistband, squeezing it so tightly that my hands stopped shaking. We took one step and then another and another, making methodical progress until we were poised at the mouth of darkness. The lamp's meager light was a cruel trick. The tunnel seemed to stretch on forever.

"I think it came from the lab." Max gestured ten feet ahead with his gun, where Artos waited, uncertain.

"The door is already open," I whispered, horrified at the gap wide enough for a large man to fit through. Setting the television and the lamp just outside the entry, Max put his finger to his lips, then pointed at the ground. The light illuminated a trail of glass, beckoning like breadcrumbs in the woods. I stopped my breathing and listened, but it was impossible to hear anything but the thumping *whoosh* of blood in my ears.

Max held up his hand to caution me. He spun fast, aiming his gun inside, then waved to me. Artos headed past us, giving the broken glass a cursory sniff before trotting toward the back of the room, where the light barely reached. It was stacked high with the remains of the Resistance—carcasses of supply boxes, picked-over skeletons of lab equipment. Guns raised, Max and I followed him.

To either side of us, the walls were blank sheets of white, the perfect stage for our dancing shadows. The large-screen computers that once lined the tables were gone, probably dismantled and removed by the government. Only the hanging diagram of the brain remained, its colors muted by age and dust.

Artos whined a little, his ears at attention. He seemed curious, his eyes trained on a tower of boxes, piled haphazardly in the corner. With a nudge, I drew Max's attention to the top of the pile. The highest box was shaking ever so slightly, like a petal flitting in the breeze.

"Hello? Who's there?" I made a move to cover Max's mouth or clock him myself—*what was he thinking?*—when I realized the voice, feeble and trembling, wasn't his. But it was one I recognized.

"Dad?"

Wide-eyed, Max kept his gun pointed ahead. Behind the boxes, soft footsteps and a figure emerged.

"Mr. Knightley?"

"Dad!"

"Lex?" My father—still clad in a jail-issued khaki jumpsuit—was holding a broomstick and a shard of glass. His face was dirty, his eyes still pleading as if he half expected to be wrong. Dead wrong. Artos approached and sniffed him with earnest recognition as my father lowered his makeshift weapons and turned back toward his hiding place.

"It's safe," he said. "You can come out." Carrie emerged as tentative as a hunted animal. Unsteady on her feet, she teetered as she met my eyes.

"Safe," she repeated. Like she didn't believe it. Like it wasn't possible. Like there was no such thing. Then she collapsed in a heap at my father's feet.

## CHAPTER SIXTY:

# THE SAFEST PLACE

The small television screen reflected my face back to me. My hair was plastered to my forehead with a paste of dirt and sweat. I pushed it back, looking up at myself with bloodshot eyes. My unflinching assessment: haggard. But Carrie was much worse off than me, than any of us. She had been curled in the corner, unmoving since we returned. My father told us she'd refused to fall asleep at the jail, afraid to close her eyes, afraid of what might happen. Not surprising, her skin looked worn, her cheeks sunken in. Beneath her fluttering eyelids, her flesh purpled like a bruise.

"Lex." Max elbowed me. Everyone was waiting. I pressed the button bringing the television to life.

> **" . . . Van Sant is well known for representing San Francisco's elite, spearheading the successful defenses of many wealthy, influential, and infamous clients, including Preston Abbott—better known as the Financial District Fiend who was acquitted in 2040 on multiple charges of corporate racketeering, fraud, and solicitation to commit murder. Van Sant recently suffered a rare defeat in his pro bono representation of George McAllister, convicted in October for the brutal murder of his wife Michelle and their unborn child.**
>
> **Police have yet to identify any suspects in today's shooting that claimed the life of Van Sant's 48-year-old**

**bodyguard, Bernard Nelson. However, our sources suggest emotion-altering medications were discovered inside Van Sant's multimillion-dollar villa in Pacific Heights. He and his son, Edison, have been missing since the homicide was discovered . . ."**

"Off." Mr. Van Sant turned his face away, but not before I saw his disgust. He was too defeated for anger.

Edison reached to stop my hand with his own. "No, Dad. We have to watch it. We need to know what's going on out there."

Mr. Van Sant shrugged, then let his shoulders droop. "What more do we need to know?" I understood how he felt. Somehow the closer we came to Xander, the Guardian Force, and the bombings, the further away it all seemed. Now in the early morning hours of January 23, 2043, we were as close and as far as we'd ever been.

"A lot more," my father answered. "I'm willing to bet what Carrie and I saw is the tip of a very large, Titanic-sinking iceberg. San Francisco is just the beginning. You know that."

"How many?" I demanded, glaring at Augustus. His cheeks were round as apples, stuffed full and chewing a stick of jerky from the supplies Carrie and my father found stashed in the lab. I watched him swallow with effort. Then his lips parted in a saccharine smile.

"Give me a break, Ms. Knightley. That was only my second piece."

"How many *bombs*?"

"Oh. That. I haven't the slightest."

A frustrated sigh caught in my chest and was interrupted by the television, the story we'd been waiting for. I turned up the volume.

**"The Department of Transportation announced that, starting tomorrow, the newly constructed Bay Bridge spanning between Oakland and San Francisco will be available for motorists to travel. The rebuilding of the eastern span of the historic bridge, which was redesigned in 2013, comes just two years after it was bombed by Resistance forces."**

Augustus sneered. "Still pinning that one on me, I see." I didn't want to give him the satisfaction of my agreement, but he was right. It was unnerving how pliable the truth was, how SFTV could twist it into any size and shape that fit their agenda.

> **"Repairs were funded primarily by Zenigenic CEO Xander Steele, who is scheduled to be among the leaders observing the inaugural procession across the bridge from San Francisco to Oakland. Social media is abuzz with rumors he will likely be accompanied by the newly appointed Docil-E spokesman, Quin McAllister. Large crowds are expected for the 9:30 a.m. reopening—with police and military personnel on hand to quell any violence. In an exclusive interview with SFTV, General Anton Maze denied safety concerns at the event and confirmed troops will have access to Docil-E should bystanders become unruly."**

"My God . . . " My father's voice was haunted. Back to the wall, he was sitting cross-legged like a young boy, but his eyes were older, harder than I remembered. He was watching the rise and fall of Carrie's chest.

"You were right," I told him. He nodded, solemn.

"I didn't want to be. But what else would the military be doing with a scale model of the Bay Bridge and a ton of fertilizer?" After leaving their cells, Carrie and my father had escaped through a heating vent. Crawling through the air ducts, they'd seen a lot—bomb components, a model of the bridge, and canisters marked Docil-E2. "We have to warn people, call the police, something."

Mr. Van Sant shook his head. "Easy, Knightley. If we do that now without any proof, Steele gets away again. And Zenigenic keeps right on rolling."

"So we just do nothing? Let all those people die? You really are the moral paragon I thought you were."

"Dad!"

He shrugged at me. "I call it like I see it."

Chest puffed, Mr. Van Sant wasn't about to back down from a challenge. "Call it like you see it, huh? Is that why you rolled over for Steele like a spineless jellyfish the minute he demanded you interview Quin with his scripted book of questions?"

"Listen here, you . . . you . . . lawyer." My father was obviously a novice in the art of insults. Augustus snickered as I cut my eyes to Edison, searching for an ally on the battlefield.

Edison held his hand up. "You're both right. We can't just do nothing, but we can't trust the police either. We'll figure out how to get there, find the bomb, and expose them ourselves."

Max looked skeptical. "Just that?"

"Getting there shouldn't be hard," Elana said, frowning at Max. "We can use the tunnel. It's not far from the Embarcadero Station to the bridge."

"And then?"

Elana winked at me. "We improvise."

"Exactly, Red." Edison grinned broadly. Still glowering at each other, Mr. Van Sant and my father momentarily retreated to their respective corners.

"What about Augustus?" I asked. "He doesn't exactly blend in a crowd." I talked over Augustus' disdainful muttering. "And my dad and Carrie. They're all fugitives." *So am I.* I didn't say it aloud, but it was obvious I was just as much of a target.

"They can hide in the tunnel," Elana said. *I'm not hiding. I'm not leaving Quin on that bridge alone.* I didn't say that out loud either.

"You were right about a lot of things," I said to my father softly so that only he could hear me. "Like me being reckless . . . " I stared at his wrists—red, raw reminders of his captivity. "I'm sorry, Dad."

He shook his head. "I wasn't right, not about that. Reckless means not caring, and you've always had caring in spades. You care too much sometimes, but I can't fault you for that. So did your mom, by the way." There were questions burning my tongue—*Did he know about the picture? Was my mother in love with Jamison Ryker? Did she have an affair with him?*—but I let them simmer, unasked for now. I wasn't sure I would ever be ready to say them aloud, not to him. Even unspoken, I could feel their heat. I knew how badly they would burn.

I nudged my father. "Did you find out anything more about Radley?" I'd almost forgotten about his last assignment. His eyes brightened.

"I interviewed his mother. Turns out she knew String." At the mention of the name, Max spun toward us, his curiosity as undeniable as gravity's pull. "He'd been to the house a few times."

"And?" I prompted.

My father shrugged dismissively. "They were happy to have him. I guess Peter had a hard time making friends. He'd been cyberbullied in high school, dropped out, and had some mental health issues. That was just before he was recruited for the Guardian Force. Anyway, she called String *a nice young man, a real charmer*. Apparently, Peter met him in a Guardian Force survivors' chat room."

Max sighed as our eyes met. "Shocker."

"And . . . " My father paused. I could tell he was preparing all of us for something unexpected, something monumental. "Radley's father was a part of the Crim-X program."

"What?" My question led a chorus of gasps. Even Mr. Van Sant was speechless.

"I didn't believe it either at first, but his mother convinced me. She had a brief relationship with Inmate 490, James Sorensen, before he was incarcerated for murder. Nine months later, Peter was born. But by that time, Sorensen was in prison. She lost track of him for a year or two, didn't even know he had been released as part of the Crim-X program until he contacted her. They stayed together for a little while, but when that first research group of inmates was forced to return to prison, she ended it. Never heard from him again. She told Peter he'd died."

"Does the military know?"

"He wasn't classified as a Legacy, but I'd be shocked if they didn't."

"So Emma and Radley, two Legacies at risk for the Prophecy gene, were recruited for the Elite Team." I silently added Colton to that list. "I wonder how many of the asterisks in that file were at risk for the gene."

Mr. Van Sant nodded at me. "You may be on to something. With a gene that supposedly predicts violence, they would certainly be a lot easier to scapegoat."

Next to me, Carrie stirred a little, her breathing quickened. "Emma." Her voice grew darker, deeper, as she thrashed about. "Emma! No!" My father reached to shake her awake, but she was stuck halfway between this world and another. "Emma!" Then her eyes opened—white and wide—like twin saucers. "Emma," she said again, this time to my father, despairing. "How could we leave Emma?"

* * *

Carrie took an unsteady breath before she spoke again. "Have I been asleep for long?"

"An hour or so," I told her. "Are you hungry? Thirsty?" I passed her a bottle of water from the box we hauled back from the lab. She twisted off the cap, gulping it in one long swallow and set it down next to my own half-empty bottle.

"What happened?" She blinked, blinked, blinked at Augustus.

"You don't remember?" I asked.

"Uh . . . am I still dreaming?"

Augustus stared back. "A pleasure to see you too, Ms. Donovan."

Tentative, Carrie opened, then closed her mouth. I patted her arm. "Don't worry about him." She frowned a little but didn't argue. "Do you remember being in the lab?"

Uncertain, she looked again to my father, then nodded. "We were there searching for supplies. Then we heard a voice—and a dog." She petted Artos' head, realizing. "We hid behind the boxes. That's when I started to feel woozy. I heard Bill say it was safe. That was the last thing I remember."

"You passed out," he said. "Exhaustion, I guess. We brought you back here."

"Here," she repeated, finally taking in her surroundings. "Is this . . . " She tried not to look at Augustus. " . . . your office?"

"Has it been that long, Ms. Donovan? Surely, you recall."

Carrie didn't answer him. "What are you all doing here?" she asked me.

It was Max who broke the uneasy silence with a joke, the way he always did. "We missed this place. The sounds, the smells, the evil dictator."

Carrie laughed. We all did. Even Augustus forced a smile. Afterward, I gave her the simplest, truest explanation, marveling at the paradox in my words. "This was the safest place we could find."

# CHAPTER SIXTY-ONE:

# FLOWN

"So what happened to Emma?" I finally asked Carrie after we explained all that transpired since I drove away on Emma's motorcycle three days ago. My father had been unable to answer the question, only knowing what he saw: his computerized cell door popping open yesterday evening, a soldier looking the other way as my dad walked past. Carrie was already out. She'd said nothing about Emma, skillfully dodging my father's questions like a prizefighter.

Carrie shook her head, her eyes filling to the brim. "She . . . she stayed behind." She lowered her head, wiping her eyes on the sleeve of her jumpsuit. "I should've never let her do that."

"Did she help you escape?"

"I can only assume it was her. She kept saying she owed me for what I did for her, and she knew one of the soldiers assigned to the control room. He recognized her from the rehabilitation program. But I think they were pressuring her too. They knew she shot that commander on the bridge."

"So they were still trying to recruit her?"

Carrie shrugged. "It certainly seemed that way. She was being interrogated longer and more often than your father and me. That night when the door opened, Emma wasn't in her cell. I waited, but . . . " Her voice broke a little under the weight of her guilt.

"Emma's smart," I said, ignoring the swift turn of disbelieving heads in my direction. "I'm sure she had a reason for staying behind."

"You're right." Carrie gave me a sad smile. "I just hope she can handle it. She's been through so much. She's more vulnerable than you think, especially if what you said about Docil-E2 is true."

My father cleared his throat, signaling a pronouncement. "So what are we waiting for?" With a grimace, he maneuvered to his knees and began to stand. "C'mon." Surprised at his assertiveness, I raised my eyebrows at him but followed.

"What?" he asked. "Your mother's not the only one who can rail against the establishment. Let's go find that bomb."

A quick look at Max, Elana, and Edison confirmed what I was thinking. "Dad, we need to slow down and make a plan. The last time we rushed into things . . . " There it was again—that bright bloom of blood on my mother's chest. " . . . people got hurt."

Edison motioned to our meager stockpile. "We're going to need a few more guns."

Augustus shifted on his briefcase throne. "I may be able to help with that."

"What do you mean?" I asked.

"The armory."

Max shook his head. "The armory was bolted shut. We tried to get in."

Augustus only grinned, sauntering to his desk and reaching inside the top drawer.

"Let me guess," I said. "You have the key." He jingled it in reply. "Well, you're not going alone."

"I wouldn't dream of it. Mr. Powers, would you like to accompany me?"

"And Artos," I added. At the sound of his name, he wagged his tail at me and came to my side.

"Of course. Cujo is more than welcome." Max took one of the lamps and Quin's gun from the pile. He waited as Augustus unlatched the deadbolt.

"After you, Mr. Powers." Summoning Artos with a pat of his leg, Max stepped back into the tunnel. Augustus remained as rigid as a pillar in the doorway.

"We'll see you back here in ten minutes," I said, ushering him out.

"Not so fast." He reached down, securing the handle of his briefcase with a desperate grasp as if he expected me to pull it from his clutches. "There's no way I'm leaving this behind."

* * *

"It's been fifteen minutes," I said. "Fifteen and counting." Dread crawled further up my spine, tickling my nerves like a snake's tongue. Slither and hiss, slither and hiss.

"I'll go look for them," Edison said.

"I'm coming with you." Elana and I spoke the words together. I couldn't wait any longer, wondering. But before I put my hand to the door, I heard a sound from the other side of it. A desperate whimper. It was familiar in the worst possible way, like a recurring nightmare. As I pried the bolt loose, I tried to focus on my fingers, on the rusty squeaking of metal on metal—anything but the noises wrenching soft places inside of me. I opened the door already knowing what I would find.

Artos could barely open his eyes. He squinted up at me, rubbing his face with his paws. "Dad! Take him inside. He's got something in his eyes." My father scooped up Artos, cradling him like a baby as I ran to catch up with Edison and Elana, following the light from their lamp down the tunnel.

The armory was just past the lab. The door was already open, a dark invitation. "Max?" Edison called out as he kicked the door a little wider, swinging the lamp left to right and peering inside. Augustus didn't lie. The armory was as stocked as I remembered. Rows of handguns and high-powered rifles were mounted on each wall, ammunition stacked to the ceiling.

"Look." Elana pointed straight ahead to a flicker of light casting shadows on the wall. "There's one missing." Five slots—each labeled, *Sniper Rifle*. One was empty. Max's lamp was overturned nearby, and a few bullets were scattered from an open box on the floor. I ran toward the chaos, hoping to find him there.

"Lex! Watch out!" I froze, my right foot teetering on the edge of something like oblivion. I caught my balance and took a step back before I looked down. In the center of the floor was a manhole. A rickety access ladder extended down into murky brown water—I couldn't tell how deep. The walls were covered with graffiti.

"Max!" I yelled down into the hole. Only my own voice returned to me, distorted by the echo.

"What's down there?" Elana asked.

Lamp in hand, Edison dropped to his stomach, the light illuminating a small corner of the darkness. "It's an emergency overflow. It probably empties out into the ocean. These were San Francisco's sewers about a hundred years ago." Elana wrinkled her nose in disgust.

"Secret tunnels under San Francisco?" I asked. "I thought that was a myth."

Edison shrugged. "Looks pretty real to me."

I rolled my eyes, annoyed, mostly with myself. *Leave it to Augustus to escape via an urban legend.*

I lowered myself to the cold ground. Elana lay next to me, staring down, down, down—her red hair falling around her face like a shroud. She didn't move until she gasped. "It's Max." I followed her gaze across the water to a dry section of concrete barely within reach of the light. I watched until the lamp flickered just so—and for a breath, the glint from the rocks reflected the eyelet of a boot. Max's boot.

"Max!" The abyss swallowed our collective voices and spit them back at us. Feet first, I reached for the ladder and started climbing the mossy green rungs to the muck below. To my relief, it only went up to my shins. I trudged forward, Elana and Edison right behind me. From somewhere unseen, I heard water trickling. It sounded like a whisper. *Help me. I'm dying.*

I could see Max, crumpled on the mud. There was a gash on his forehead—an angry, red knot growing around it. A rock, just the right size for Augustus' hand, sat guiltless in the dirt. I exhaled when I saw Max's fingers twitching with life. "He's alive."

Max groaned as we tried to move him. He half opened his eyes. "Pepper spray . . . and a big rock," he mumbled before closing them again.

Fueled by indignation, I snatched the lamp from Edison and plowed down the tunnel, where the muck was deeper and colder. *Find me. You'll never find me.* The water was talking to me again. "Augustus!" I screamed his name so loud my throat burned. Even if I couldn't see him, I wanted him to hear me.

"Lex!" Edison caught up to me faster than I expected. "What are you doing?"

"I'm going after Augustus." I turned my back to him. "He had this whole thing planned from the beginning. He took us where he wanted to go, and we followed. I can't just let him . . . " I took one step forward and found myself waist deep in water. " . . . leave."

Edison grabbed me by the elbow and pulled me back up. "We have to." I stared down the tunnel, where the walls, the shadows, and the water became one. Something moved, shifted, pulsed.

"He's there," I insisted. "I see him." Edison put his hand to the lamp, raising it with mine. But there was nothing—just my mind's tricks and more darkness.

"Hey!" Elana called to us. "Max is awake."

It wasn't a choice—I had to turn back—but it felt like one. The hardest one. My pride hurt to swallow, choked me on the way down. And the water was saying *I won.*

Max was glassy-eyed but standing. He pointed at the wall when we returned. I held up the lamp to see a small bird etched in the rock. A bird had been here alright. A free bird. Augustus had taken flight . . . again.

## CHAPTER SIXTY-TWO:

# ARMORED

Mr. Van Sant and my father met us halfway down the tunnel. My legs felt heavy, weighed down by the muck dripping from my clothing and Max's right arm draped around my shoulder. I passed them two handguns from my waistband. We'd each taken as many as we could carry.

"Where is that snake?" Mr. Van Sant asked, grimacing at the bruise on Max's head, the perfect complement to his bloodshot eyes. Putting his hand to his own face, Max winced.

"Gone." I was glad Edison answered because I didn't want to admit it. "There's a secret tunnel in the armory. Augustus pepper sprayed Max and Artos. When Max tried to come after him, he got a rock to the head."

"And he took a sniper rifle with him," Elana added.

Mr. Van Sant pounded the wall with his fist. He sighed, then began the trudge back to Augustus' office. "We should've known. That pepper spray was probably in his desk drawer."

"This is my fault," Max said, relinquishing his grip on me and slogging ahead on his own. "He knew I was the weakest. That's why he asked me to go with him." I reached for Max to stop him, but he brushed my hand away. "He probably figured I'd be distracted, worrying about stupid String."

Elana shook her head. "That's crazy. You're one of the toughest people I know." He shrugged and kept walking, unconvinced.

"What did he say to you?" I asked, suspecting one of Augustus' mind games.

"Nothing I didn't already know." There was a hard stop at the end of that sentence. Max was done talking for now.

"Any idea where the tunnel goes?" my father asked. I was grateful for his well-timed diversion.

"I thought all those abandoned sewer lines had been sealed off years ago," Mr. Van Sant answered.

"Apparently not," I said.

Dejected, we traipsed back toward Augustus' office, finally catching up with Max. "Try the Map Room," he grumbled, half-heartedly. I remembered the panoramic map spanning the length of the wall, plotting the citywide course of the BART tunnels.

Elana looked confused. "There were never any secret tunnels on that map."

"Before you joined the Resistance, there was another map on that wall," Max said with a little more vigor. "It had the sewer tunnels on it, the ones that lead to the water treatment plants and the ones that lead out."

"What happened to the map?" I asked.

"Augustus commissioned a new one, but the old one is still there underneath."

"Let's go." I felt a surge of energy and let it carry me. We couldn't catch him, but at least we would know where Augustus was headed with that rifle. Next to me, Max matched my pace stride for stride. There was visible tension in his hurried gait. "Augustus told me something," he finally said. "Something I didn't know." His sudden announcement stopped us all. "But I don't want to believe it. I don't want to say it out loud."

I put my hand on Max's shoulder and watched his resistance give way. "Tell us."

He breathed deep, staring down as he spoke. "He said String knows who killed Shelly. He's known all along. He saw the murder." Watching Max's face twist in the agony of ambivalence, I wasn't sure how to feel either. *Betrayed? Elated? Worried? Enraged?*

Only one of us seemed certain. Mr. Van Sant pumped his fist, lit with excitement. "A witness!"

* * *

The last time I saw the inside of the Map Room, I was a different girl. Naïve, I'd sat at the table and pleaded with the Council to let me leave Resistance headquarters. Now that table was covered in a blanket of dust, and my heart was armored. I knew better than to demand fairness from the world.

"I can't believe your mother sent you here alone," my father said, his eyes darting to the corner where a rat's thick tail slipped just out of our sight.

I laughed. "It wasn't quite this scary back then, Dad."

He put his arm around me. "I know. Still, you were braver than I would've been." I placed my hand on the back of Augustus' chair, the leather already cracking with neglect. I could picture him there, could still feel the table shaking when he pounded it with his fist.

"I wasn't that brave."

"Yes, you were," Elana whispered. The map was there too, yellowing a little at the edges and peeling back from the wall in spots. Max and I tugged at the corners until the paper gave way, revealing the other version underneath. Mr. Van Sant held the light up as Max traced his finger along the blue line, marking the BART tunnel at Embarcadero Station.

"Here it is." He pointed to a thinner line drawn in pencil. "It looks like it ends at . . . " I followed it with my eyes.

"Pier Twenty-six." I finished for him. "Right underneath the Bay Bridge."

## CHAPTER SIXTY-THREE:

# TYPICAL

Carrie was waiting at the door. Artos sat near her, still rubbing his eyes with his paws. "Thank God!" she exhaled. "I was beginning to think I was on my own here." We made our way back inside and bolted the door behind us. Carrie looked from Artos to Max and back again. "Looks like you both got a taste of pepper spray."

Max lowered himself to the ground, glowering again. He didn't answer. Carrie gestured toward the television set. It was turned on—the usual reality show reruns—the volume down low. "They're looking for your . . . friend," she said to Max, settling on the least awkward word. I cleared my throat, hoping to stop her. "String, right?"

"Carrie—" I started to interrupt, but Max stopped me.

"Who's looking for him?"

"The police. I guess they figured out he shot at Quin because they've charged him with attempted murder. See, there it is." Carrie pointed to the scrolling bar—*BREAKING NEWS*—at the bottom of the screen. My heart unsettled, I followed the words as they streamed past.

> *SUSPECT IDENTIFIED IN ATTEMPTED SHOOTING OF ZENIGENIC SPOKESMAN, QUIN MCALLISTER . . . SEBASTIAN CROFT, AGE 18, HAS A LENGTHY JUVENILE RECORD THAT INCLUDES ARRESTS FOR PETTY THEFT AND LARCENY . . . XANDER STEELE OFFERS $100,000 REWARD FOR HIS CAPTURE . . . UNNAMED ZENIGENIC SOURCE POINTS TO POSSIBLE LINK*

> *BETWEEN CROFT AND WANTED FUGITIVE, AUGUSTUS PORTER.*

I watched Max's face. It was a bellwether—his frown deepening, his blue eyes stormy, tempestuous.

"Typical Xander," Edison muttered. "He's always blaming someone else. From what I overheard in the closet, he was well aware String was going to shoot Quin, and he didn't seem to have any problem with it. But he didn't want it to happen that night."

"No!" Max's voice was a forceful gust of wind blowing with the strength of all his bottled frustration. "It's typical String. He deserves this. He let George McAllister go to prison and never said a word. He's probably been playing both sides. Playing me too. Laughing at us. I hope they catch him. I hope I catch him. A hundred thousand dollars is way more than he's worth, but I'll take it."

"Max—you don't . . ."

"Don't tell me I don't mean it, Lex. Because I do."

"I'll split it with you," I said, waiting for him to laugh. It took longer than I expected, but eventually the corners of his mouth turned up in a melancholy smile.

"Seventy-thirty," he replied.

## CHAPTER SIXTY-FOUR:

# IMPROVISE

The sun was a glowing yellow ball, lost behind a dense thicket of clouds. But after the pitch black of the tunnel, even the muted brightness stung my eyes. From the Embarcadero, the bridge towered up against the morning sky like something out of a dream. A long line of cars extended back into the city, their path congested by spectators filing up the highway from the newly erected mandatory checkpoint. I looked at my watch again. 9:10 a.m.

Keeping my head down and my jacket collar turned up, I walked at the edge of the crowd, convinced someone would recognize me. My jeans were still damp from the overflow tunnel—and the four bottles of water I'd used to clean them. They felt even tighter with the gun tucked inside my waistband. With every step, I smelled the faint odor of dank water and heard the refrain of my father's goodbye. He and Carrie were safely hidden in the BART tunnel with Artos. "How is it possible I've nearly lost you so many times, when I've only just found you again?" I knew exactly what he meant, but I'd only shrugged my shoulders under the weight of his embrace, afraid I might cry.

A soldier with a canister of Docil-E strapped to his belt spoke into a megaphone as we approached. "Ladies and gentlemen, please be prepared for random EAM testing. If you are selected, kindly step to the side so others can pass. Positive tests are subject to arrest and will be denied entry."

"Great. Just great." I was certain the soldiers had my picture in a plastic sleeve, my face lined up alongside Augustus, one criminal to another.

"Just act natural . . . normal," Edison teased. "Tell yourself, *I haven't just spent the night in the BART tunnels. I haven't crawled through sewage. I haven't cheated death twice in one week.* No problem, right?"

I masked a chuckle with my hand as we passed the first line of soldiers. "Was that normal enough for you?"

Edison chuckled. "*I haven't been duped by a psychopath . . . again. I haven't made out with a B-list celebrity. I haven't—*" Elana ended Edison's comedic monologue with a sharp elbow to his side. A thick-browed soldier stood in our path, unsmiling.

"Young man, step to the side please." He ushered Max away from us, then covered his nose with his uniform sleeve. "Phew! You stink!"

"Sorry." Max shrugged. "I must've forgotten to wear my soldier-approved cologne."

Humorless, the man hastily swiped Max's wrist with the plastic applicator. I slowed down but kept walking—afraid to stop—and listened for the sound of his stern voice. "Clean," he finally said, stoically, seemingly oblivious to the contradiction in terms.

"What's the verdict?" Edison teased as Max caught up to us.

"Clean—but malodorous."

As we reached the entrance to the bridge near Bryant Street, I nudged Elana. "Xander." She nodded. Even from here, he was unmistakable. Sharply dressed and prancing about the observation booth, he was hobnobbing with the mayors of Oakland and San Francisco. A tall, well-muscled military officer joined them. I was too far away to see the name stitched on his uniform, but I was willing to bet it was General Anton Maze.

Valkov was there as well, his broken arm resting in a sling against his chest. He wasn't speaking to anyone, just frowning indiscriminately. Barbara Blake was at the front of the procession, holding a microphone, ready to give the go-ahead while the rest of the media was cordoned off behind the checkpoint. Mr. Van Sant was headed there now to find Langley.

Elana pointed to an older woman approaching the booth. She shared Xander's jet-black hair and ice-cold eyes. "Who's that?"

"His mom?" I guessed. "She looks like him."

As the apparent Mrs. Steele preened in one of the car's side mirrors, ignoring the throngs of people attempting to sidestep her, Max snickered. "Those two are definitely related."

"Well, *Xandi* did say he wouldn't disappoint her, and he certainly has a big show planned for today." Elana meant the joke for Edison, but he didn't respond. He was clinging tight—white-knuckled—to the bridge railing behind us.

"Are you okay?" she asked him.

At first, the only reply was the shaky inhale, exhale of his breath. But then, "What do you think? Of all places, why a bridge? Why?"

"Where's Quin?" I could hear the worry in my voice. *He's supposed to be with Xander.*

Elana clutched my arm. "There."

Quin was in the driver's seat of an ostentatious piano-black convertible, one of the first cars in the motorcade. The hood was ornamented with a metallic Z. A banner on the back fender trailed behind: *Make the world a little kinder.* I felt my knees buckle, and I gripped Elana tighter. *He's supposed to be with Xander.* I willed him to look at me, but his back was turned to us, signing an autograph for a giddy teenager.

"I thought he would be with Xander." Max echoed my concern, making it that much more difficult to ignore.

"Me too." It was a simple equation. With Xander, Quin was safe. But now, he was just as vulnerable as we were. Maybe more so. Max leaned in and patted my arm.

"We'll find it," he said. *It. The bomb.* I was glad he didn't say that word aloud. "We'll stop it." I tried to make a face of optimism, confidence even, and began scanning the cars behind Quin.

"What exactly are we looking for?" I asked.

"It's probably in a van or a truck," Edison answered. "Something big."

The crowd was much larger than I'd expected. By now, the sides of the bridge were overgrown, unwieldy, teeming with people. But my gaze kept returning to the checkpoint. Just beyond it was a group of motorcycles and their pentagrammed riders—Satan's Syndicate. Though it seemed unlikely they could see me, every time I looked, I shivered with the certainty I was being watched. I forced myself to focus on the cars instead, considering them one by one, a process of elimination.

"Got anything?" Edison asked.

"Nothing yet."

I nearly missed it. Three cars back from Quin. An antique convertible—Resistance red—with an oversized trunk big enough to store explosives. It was the driver who first caught my attention. He wore a bandana over his mouth and another on his forearm. But as he shifted his hand on the wheel, it slipped a little, revealing the inked edges of a Guardian Force tattoo. Sitting atop the white leather backseat—at first glance—were five more bandana-clad protestors. At second glance, "It's Emma," I whispered, horrified. I couldn't take my eyes from her black braid, afraid to look at the boy sitting next to her. I recognized him too, though I'd never seen him before. Quin's brown hair. Their mother's eyes. The hard set of their father's jaw. It was Colton.

I swallowed hard before speaking, knowing I couldn't take it back. "It's in that car." I lowered my voice and breathed the word, the one that would make it real. "The *bomb*. They're going to blame it on the New Resistance."

"Are you sure that's her?" Edison asked, squinting as we walked closer to the car. "Why would Emma—"

He stopped mid-sentence when Emma, Colton, and the others started chanting. "We are the New Resistance. Not afraid to feel." Their voices were methodical, passionless. And yet, protestors in the crowd joined in, quickly covering their listlessness.

Edison and I exchanged a look. "Docil-E," he said.

"Docil-E2," I corrected, noticing the microphones tucked inside their ears. "Someone's giving them orders." I silently measured the distance between their car and Quin's. Thirty feet, give or take. *Way too close.*

My watch beeped, signaling 9:30 a.m. Barbara Blake tapped her microphone, her face looming on two giant television screens that offered a live feed of SFTV's coverage of the festivities. Xander and the other dignitaries took their seats.

"Ladies and gentlemen, it is my pleasure to welcome you to the opening of the repaired eastern span of the Bay Bridge between Oakland and San Francisco. Before we begin, I would like to take a moment to recognize Zenigenic's CEO for his generous donation to this project. Without Xander Steele, we would not be gathered here today. To honor Mr. Steele, newly appointed Zenigenic spokesman, Quin McAllister, will be driving the lead vehicle in the procession this morning." Quin gave a small wave to the crowd's delight. "Mr. McAllister, please start your engine."

The line of vehicles roared to life and began a slow crawl up the freeway ramp toward the bridge. "What are we going to do?" I asked, on the verge of panic.

Edison grinned despite the fear in his eyes. "Improvise."

# CHAPTER SIXTY-FIVE:

# STREAKING

If there wasn't a bomb in that car, if it wasn't about to explode, if we were anywhere else but here, I would've found it impossible to stop laughing. Elana's cheeks were flaming red. Her face turned a deep shade of crimson as she peeked through her half-covered eyes at Edison. "I'm creating a diversion," he explained, completely straight-faced, while stripping down to his underwear. "Use it wisely."

"Oh my!" Barbara Blake cried out as Edison tossed his boxers in her direction. He sprinted to the front of the procession, weaving between the cars and swiping the microphone from her hand. "Hey! Come back here with that!"

Quin's brake lights flashed red, and the cars behind him ground to a halt as the spectators laughed and pointed. With high-heeled Barbara and two soldiers in pursuit, Edison tossed the microphone in my direction and kept running, ducking behind a van. His throw came up short. The mic hit the ground and bounced, announcing me with a resounding *thump, thump, thump*. It scuttled into the forest of feet lining the bridge. I scampered after it, searching until a spindly arm extended toward me, mic in hand. I followed it—elbow, shoulder, neck, pale face—blushing, hair as black as a beetle's shell.

"Percy!"

He looked at me with awe, the kind of distant reverence usually reserved for girls like Elana. "Hi, Lexi . . . *Lex* . . . ugh. I always forget." Captured by the mic, his voice resonated.

"It's okay." I took it from him and faced the masses of people, surprised at how quickly they turned their attention to me. I zeroed in on Quin, focusing on the surprised *O* of his mouth.

"Hello," I said. All those curious eyes, and I wasn't even sure where to begin. "My name is Alexandra Knightley." *Relax, Lex. It's not a valedictory address.* "My mother was Victoria Knightley. She spent most of her career creating emotion-altering drugs for Zenigenic. And then she died trying to stop the military from using them against us."

Xander was already on his feet. "Arrest her!" he commanded. "She killed Peter Radley. She's on something!"

*There's a bomb in that car!* I wanted to say it, to scream it, but I needed more time. If I said it, they would run, never knowing, and I had to tell them—everyone—who put it there and why. My mother's ill-fated mission to upload the video at Alcatraz made more sense to me than it ever had. I heard the gasps as I withdrew the gun from my waistband and waved it at the approaching soldiers. Masks already deployed, they hung back, unclipping their Docil-E canisters.

"But the public never learned the worst of it—how the military experimented with Onyx, how their experiments went horribly wrong. The military hasn't stopped using people. Neither has Zenigenic. They've been selling Emovere, Eupho, and Onyx on the streets for months. And Xander Steele . . . he's probably not even clean himself."

"Ha!" Xander's eyes darted from his mother to the crowd as if he couldn't decide who to convince first. "She's crazy. A complete nutso." He stomped down from the booth. "Spray her!" he directed, covering his mouth with a handkerchief from his pocket.

"No!" At his mother's protest, the soldiers lowered their canisters. "There's no need for a public spectacle, Xandi. If we react to her nonsensical claims, we only give them merit. It's not good publicity. Think of Zenigenic!"

Xander took her words like a slap to the face, cowering, then turning away. Valkov sneered, first at Xander's mother, then at me, his lip curling like a worm over his teeth. "I don't take orders from her." He advanced toward me, calling my bluff. "Shoot me."

I aimed the barrel right at his chest, but my hand trembled, giving me away. "If she won't, I will." Quin climbed out of the driver's seat and stepped in front of me, his gun pointed at Valkov.

"And if he doesn't, I definitely will," Max said.

"That makes three of us." Elana fell in line next to them.

"Four!" Percy shouted from the crowd. And in an instant, a fervor rolled through them like a wave. "Five!" a man yelled from the car behind Quin.

"Six!"

"Let'er talk!"

"Seven!"

"Sit down, Steele!" Then the chanting, "Not afraid to feel! Not afraid to feel!" The energy—electric—spurred me on.

"The military wants you to believe they disbanded the Guardian Force, but that never really happened. They've been recruiting soldiers, the most vulnerable ones, to blow up a bomb here today so we'll all be afraid, and Zenigenic can keep profiting from our fear." SFTV cut the mic at the word *bomb,* and I tossed it to the ground. Like a startled pack of animals, the crowd began to move. A few, including Percy, fled. A few stayed put, holding up their cell phones as silent witnesses. Most just skittered about, waiting for someone in charge to tell them what to do next.

The general joined Xander, his nostrils flaring with outrage. From here, I could read *MAZE* in bold black letters on his right pocket. I expected him to proclaim innocence and tell me—loud enough for the cameras—just how wrong I was. But he didn't. Instead he turned to Quin.

"Quin McAllister, you've got a lot of nerve pretending to be a hero. I've kept quiet till now as a favor to Mr. Steele, but people should know exactly who you are and what you've done." A knot tightening in my stomach, I watched the back of Quin's head as he stood there, unyielding. The way the ends of his hair waved a little in the wind reminded me of the first time I saw him through the library window. "Quin McAllister is a murderer and a traitor. He took an oath for our country for the Guardian Force. Then he shot and killed people for the Resistance—in cold blood. Hard-working people like Jack Croft. In fact, Victoria

Knightley is the only reason we didn't arrest you, Quin. For treason. She made a deal with Jamison Ryker for your freedom."

I felt my world spin off its axis and tumble away. It broke, irrevocably. "That's a lie," I said. "All of it." I tried to gather the pieces—*Jack Croft?—A deal with my mother?*—but I couldn't think fast enough to put them together. "Most of it," I corrected when Quin's guilty eyes met mine over his shoulder. "Quin was ordered to kill those people to make the Resistance look bad. I saw it myself in his military file."

"Really? The file that's been missing for years? Let's see it." In my mind, I held my breath and swam to it at the bottom of the ocean. Fished it out of the sand, where it was buried deep. "Your mother promised Ryker she would let it all go—the Guardian Force, Emovere, everything. But she broke her deal, and she ended up dead. She's no hero either, just a liar."

"You don't know what you're talking about." My protest was half-hearted. Everyone—even complete strangers—seemed to know my mother better than me. "She would never agree to that."

"Think about it, Alexandra. We saw Quin in your neighborhood, at your house. We even sent our investigators to talk to your mother. I think you were there that day, weren't you?" *The blacks suits.* "Did you really think we'd give up so easily?" *How could I have been so naive?* I didn't want to believe it, but it stung like the truth. My mother must've changed her mind after watching the Onyx training video.

"Where's the bomb, Steele?" Mr. Van Sant demanded, still several car lengths away. Pushing his way through the unruly crowd, he was marching with Langley, her video camera rolling and a foil-blanketed Edison in tow.

Doe-eyed, Xander directed an exaggerated shrug at his mother. "I haven't the slightest idea what he's talking about."

General Maze pointed to Quin's convertible. "I wouldn't be surprised if there was a bomb in your car, Quin. That is your car, isn't it? The one Mr. Steele bought for you."

I watched as Quin seemed to contemplate a response, a defense. Then, gun still drawn, he aimed for the general, sending my heart into overdrive.

"I wouldn't do that if I were you." Looking smug, General Maze directed his own gun toward the backseat of the red car, his target a stone-faced Colton. "Unless you're prepared to have his blood on your hands." Quin stopped cold.

"Put your guns down! All of you!" Detective Katherine Brewster and a small band of officers charged toward us from the checkpoint, dodging the cars retreating back down the freeway, where a melee had broken out between Resistance and Zenigenic supporters. As two soldiers approached the chaos—ready to contain the fight with a single spray—the crowd turned on them, finally united in a cause. A canister of Docil-E went flying, ricocheting off the hood of the red convertible. Its medicated occupants followed it with their eyes but sat in frozen silence.

"Detective," Xander began, his tone cloying. "We have reason to believe there is a bomb in Quin McAllister's vehicle."

"What about that car?" I asked. "The red one. That's the one with the bomb." Even as I heard myself say the words, I felt sick. All the things that made sense to me were unraveling as fast as unspooled thread.

"Give me your gun, Quin." Detective Brewster spoke in the voice I remembered. So calm that it was sinister, like a doctor poised to stab a needle in your arm. "We need to search your car."

Quin shook his head, gesturing to General Maze. "I'm not putting mine down until he does. Search all you want."

"I will." Her voice was an indictment, already presuming what she would find. With reverence—as if she was raising the lid of a coffin at a funeral—Detective Brewster opened Quin's trunk. I couldn't see what was inside, but her face told me what I needed to know. And whatever it left unsaid, her words finished. "Mr. McAllister, you're under arrest."

"Katherine, let's talk about this. It doesn't make any sense. Why would he blow himself up?" Mr. Van Sant extended his hand, imploring her, but met with her stiff arm. "Don't say anything, Quin. We'll figure this out."

At Detective Brewster's direction, an officer confiscated Quin's gun and patted down the length of his body, checking his pockets and the inside of his jacket. "Where is the detonator, Mr. McAllister?"

"I don't know. I didn't—"

"It's in Xander's pocket," Max blurted. I opened my eyes wide at him, hoping his posturing was more convincing to the detective.

"Uh-um-uh-that's ludicrous." Xander puffed his chest but turned to his mother seeking refuge. She responded with fire.

"How dare you accuse my son! You should be ashamed of yourself, young man."

"It's not an accusation," Max replied, daring to look Mrs. Steele in the eyes. "It's a fact. See for yourself. Ask him to empty his pockets."

"I will do no such thing," she said. "Xandi is not a common criminal. And turn off that camera!" Langley placated her with an agreeable nod but kept filming.

Detective Brewster paused and considered Xander. He stared back at her steely-eyed. To me, he never looked guiltier, but she converged on Quin first. Conceding defeat, he winced as she and two officers forced him to the ground. Valkov chuckled to himself and limped back toward Xander and General Maze, victorious. I couldn't look—not at any of it—it all was unbearable. I covered my face expecting tears, but they were finally dammed inside me behind a wall. A wall I had been raising since I watched my mother die. A wall built brick by brick with helpless outrage. I understood what Elana meant when she wanted to step into the fog, when she thought there was no way she could live in this world. And I wished, if only for a moment, the bomb would explode, returning me to stardust.

"Will you at least check the other car?" I tried not to sound desperate. Determined, I marched back down the freeway toward it—Langley filming me—passing the space left by one sports car, already sped away by its owner. Only two antiques remained—a shiny yellow pickup truck and a powder blue sedan—both abandoned.

I glanced back, relieved to see Detective Brewster and her officers following. Two of them led Quin by the arms, his hands cuffed behind him. As they approached the trunk of the red convertible, the driver swiveled his head, setting his vacant eyes on the detective. I watched Emma's hands tense on her lap as General Maze covered his mouth. *Was he giving them orders?* I felt a stir, a twinge in my stomach. I recognized the feeling like an old friend. It was fear.

"Stop." A voice emerged from the mob still tussling near the checkpoint. It was slick. It was smooth. It was String.

## CHAPTER SIXTY-SIX:

# THE REAL STORY

String was strutting up the freeway entrance, one long-legged stride after another. His eyes were hidden, as usual, unseen behind his dark sunglasses. But the pistol in his hand wasn't subtle. He raised it, directing it at Quin. "I'm here to turn myself in," he announced. "For the murder of Quin McAllister."

"Don't come any closer." I pointed my gun back at him. Quin jostled with the officers, trying to take cover. "I mean it, String." I positioned myself in front of Quin as String ignored my warning.

"This isn't your fight, Lex. Move out of the way." He swept the barrel of his weapon from left to right and back again. "The same goes for all of you. You too, Detective."

"What about me?" Max asked. He lowered his gun. Handing it to me, he took a decisive step toward String, arms raised. "Are you gonna shoot me too?"

"If I have to." String was convincing. He always was.

Another step by Max. "So what are you waiting for?"

String's jaw quivered. He gritted his teeth, shifting his aim just over Max's shoulder. He looked away, then fired into the air.

"Is that the best you can do?" The rest of us ducked, taking cover behind the hood of the red car, but Max didn't flinch. He was an arm's length away now, close enough to touch the gun if he wanted. But instead he wrapped his hand around String's wrist and trained the gun on his own heart.

"Max!" Quin shouted at him, straining against the officers' hold.

"It's okay, Quin," he said without turning back. "He can't do it. He won't do it. Not because he cares, but because he's a coward."

Even with his eyes covered, String looked wounded. "That hurts, Maximillian. It really does." There was a hint of sincerity in his voice, but I'd stopped believing String so long ago, the feeling was hardly recognizable, easily ignored. "If you knew what I know, you'd shoot Quin yourself."

"What is it that you think you know?" Max asked, pressing the gun harder against his chest. "Did you hear it from Xander or Augustus? I'm not entirely sure which hypocrite you're working for nowadays."

String's dark lenses rested on Xander. "I don't work for anybody anymore."

"Really?" Max asked. "Because Augustus sure sounded like he knew you pretty well. He had a lot to say about you—how you used me, how you never really cared about me, how you hid things from all of us . . . life-altering things. If you trust what you hear from these psychopaths, I guess I should too."

String raised his sunglasses, setting them atop his head. The darkness in his eyes was deep and undeniable. It made me wish he'd cover them again. "Okay, okay," he admitted. "I wasn't exactly honest. You know me—you can't really be surprised. But I do care about you, Max." He curled his fingers around Max's arm, his light touch strangling Max's resistance until they both lowered the gun together. "And what I know about Quin, I saw with my own eyes."

I could barely hear the din of the crowd anymore. There was only the insistent wind of my own breath and the crash of my heartbeat like water battering the rocks. I watched Max say the words. "I'm listening." And we all were. I couldn't do anything but.

"When I was fourteen, your buddy, Quin—the one you're ready to take a bullet for—shot my dad." *Jack Croft. Finally, something made sense again.* "My dad was just a blue-collar guy, working his fingers to the bone to support us after our mom left. He met me after school that day like he always did. We were close, him and me, so close he liked to joke there was a string attached between us. Get it? The nickname. Anyway, we passed by this rally, where this crazy guy in a

Resistance T-shirt was standing on top of a car with a rifle in his hands. And just like that, he started shooting. I ran faster than I've ever run in my life. I thought my dad was right there with me." He raised his weapon again with new conviction. "But Quin shot my dad. He killed him."

"I already know what happened at the rally," Max said. "We all do." String looked at me, and I nodded. "But it's not what you think."

"Not what I think? He bragged all the time about killing my dad. That's what I heard."

"Who told you that? Augustus? Xander? I never did that." Quin looked from String to me and back again, his voice was almost pleading. "What I did to your dad is part of the reason I wanted out of the Guardian Force. I couldn't stand who I was becoming on Emovere. I'm sorry. I'm so sorry."

As Quin's words settled onto String's face, Xander began slinking away, pulling his mother along with him. After a few steps, he snuck a glance back over his shoulder.

"Not so fast, Steele." String redirected his gun to Xander. "I thought you wanted to see this."

"I don't know what you're talking about. I don't know you."

"That's funny. I could swear I remember you telling me you'd let me kill Quin when the time was right. *Help me, and we'll both get what we want*—isn't that what you said when I helped you clean up the mess with Radley? Isn't that what you said the night I saw—"

"Get down!" Quin yelled as Valkov rapid-fired at String. Stumbling, staggering, clutching at his chest, String veered haphazardly, grasping at the hood of the red car to steady himself. The driver, now alert, put a hand to his ear, listening. He reached down out of view and raised a weapon, methodically aiming it at String. "String! Watch out!" Quin launched himself at String's legs, both of them landing hard behind the bed of the yellow pickup.

As we took cover, Detective Brewster and the other officers returned fire. I hit the ground, bear crawling until I was completely concealed by the hood of the blue sedan. "Requesting immediate backup! Officers down—" Detective Brewster fell forward. The radio cracked against the pavement. Her blood spread like wine over the white leather seats from the wound on her shoulder. Abandoning her camera, Langley ran to help her, dragging her behind one of the truck's front tires.

"Spray them! Spray them!" Xander ordered. The soldier nearest him fumbled with the canister, nearly dropping it before he aimed it in the wrong direction, spritzing Xander's mother with a fine mist of Docil-E. "Not her, you idiot! *Them!*" Valkov redirected his gun at the errant soldier, dropping him with a single bullet.

Gunshots pinged off the metal, bounced off the concrete around me. In seconds, all four tires were flattened. I leaned forward, peering around the front fender to Quin and String, a car's length away. There was a hole in String's shirt. No blood. String met my eyes and lifted the edge of his T-shirt, confirming my suspicion. A bulletproof vest.

"Hurry!" Elana yelled to Edison. She ducked behind the door of the blue sedan—narrowly dodging a bullet that shattered the window—and fired back at Valkov and General Maze. Edison and Mr. Van Sant scrambled to help String drag Quin, still handcuffed. His palms were scraped raw from his abrupt landing on gravel. He scooted himself next to me, straining to free his hands.

"Are you okay?" he asked me. "Can you see Emma and Colton?"

Edison answered for me. "Yes, no, and no. Wait—who? Who's Colton?"

Quin groaned. "I wasn't talking to you, Eddie."

"Really, McAllister? You want to do this now?"

"I can't see them," I told Quin, waiting for a break in the gunfire to try for a glimpse of the convertible's interior.

"Your long lost brother, Colton?" Edison asked.

"Can you put some clothes on?" Quin replied. "I can't take you seriously in that foil blanket." From her pocket, Elana produced the now-infamous boxers and tossed them to Edison. He concealed himself beneath the cover and slipped them on, rolling his eyes at Quin.

"I'll take that as a *Thank you for saving my life, Eddie.*"

Staying out of sight, I raised my gun over the hood and fired a few shots in Valkov's direction. Elana did the same. With Valkov on the defensive, I snuck a fast glance at the red car. The driver was collapsed over the steering wheel, his head disfigured. One of the soldiers was draped over the door, a Docil-E canister still in his hand. Emma was lying on top of Colton, not moving. The others must have been slumped beneath them.

"I couldn't see them," I said to Quin, wishing I hadn't.

"Go! Get out of here, Mother!" Xander barked. I inched over so I could see her. A vacant smile revealed porcelain white teeth in a red lipstick frame. "Anything you say, Xandi." He gave his mother a little shove and fired at our hiding place as she ran. As awkward as a newborn fawn in her heels, she gathered momentum, not grace.

Mr. Van Sant watched with me. "There goes our last hope of talking any sense into this loon. If he's got the detonator, we're in big trouble."

"Detective Brewster called for backup," I said, optimistic. "Surely, they'll be here soon."

"Uh . . . Lex?" String was pointing around the side of the car, his face pained. "I don't think we should count on that backup." A row of motorcycles formed a sinister black barrier at the checkpoint. As one police car approached, then another, Satan's Syndicate opened fire. String was right. We were on our own.

## CHAPTER SIXTY-SEVEN:

# FLOOR IT

I jumped as a bullet skirted under the car just missing my hand. "Do you have any ammo left?" I asked Elana. She nodded. "On three, go for Valkov." We scooted down so we were nearly flat against the highway. "One . . . two . . . three . . . " Turning onto my side, I followed Valkov's stocky leg under the red car, squeezed the trigger, and prayed. On the second shot, he went down with a groan.

"Nice shot," Edison said. "Now what?"

"The detonator," Max called to us from behind the other car. "Without it, we're toast."

Edison guffawed. "Literally. Burnt toast."

"On three again," I said. "But this time, we aim for General Maze. As soon as he goes down, we run for Xander."

"One—"

"Hold on." String stopped me. He rested his gun on the pavement and peered around me at Quin. "Look, I didn't know the whole story about you. I still don't. Maybe Max is right. Augustus told me what he wanted me to believe. But you saved my life. So in case I don't make it out of here—it's hard to say this out loud because it sounds really bad. But I used to think an eye for an eye, you know?"

Mr. Van Sant turned to String, suddenly excited. "You followed George McAllister, didn't you? You were going to kill him. You saw what happened that night—you saw who killed Shelly!"

String nodded. "It was Valkov. I saw the whole thing. He would've killed me too, but I convinced him I could help Xander because I wanted the McAllisters for my own reasons."

"Can we talk about this later?" I asked. "Burnt toast . . . "

Quin strained again, pulling at his handcuffs, gritting his teeth with the effort. He leaned back against the car, exhausted. "Go without me. I'm no use to anybody like this."

"No way. I'm not leaving you."

"I'll be safer here," he insisted. "You can handle this. I trust you, remember?"

I put my hand on his knee, keeping my focus there. "Stay down, okay?" I was afraid to raise my eyes to his. Afraid of what I would find there, afraid I couldn't turn away, afraid that look would be the last. My breath caught in my throat making a small, pitiful noise.

"Alright, alright," String said, shaking his head at us, exasperated. "I can't take any more of this star-crossed-lovers bit. Here." He produced a tiny key from inside his vest and freed Quin's hands. I raised my eyebrows at String, and he shrugged.

Shaking his head, Quin rubbed his wrists. "I knew Augustus didn't spring those cuffs by himself."

With fresh hope, I signaled to Elana. "One . . . two . . . three!" This time we both angled beneath the car and the General fell, clutching his knee. Our small army advanced on Xander, but there was another army gaining ground. A platoon of masked soldiers was running past the checkpoint toward us. The row of motorcycles parted, allowing them entry as Xander ran zigzag down the freeway. Just before I ducked behind the hood of the red convertible, a bullet—not ours—pierced his side and he fell.

"Where did that come from?" I asked, doing a low spin around on my heels. Another shot. Xander's body writhed, then went still. Valkov fired at us from behind the trunk of the car. I couldn't see him or General Maze, but I could hear his raspy, growl of a voice.

"If anybody's gonna blow, it ain't gonna be me."

"Well it's not gonna be us either, if that's what you're thinking," Max retorted, pinging a few shots off the concrete.

"Don't be so sure about that," General Maze shouted as the soldiers' boots and the rumble of a military jeep announced their imminent arrival. Several of them stopped to attend to Xander. The general paused there too, removing something from Xander's pocket. *Don't be so sure about that.* I couldn't shake those words. They stuck like burrs in my brain. The other soldiers pressed on—and I could already smell it. Lilac. Forced surrender and whatever came after. It reminded me of the fog, the way it rolled in, white and wet.

"Cover your face," I said. I stretched my T-shirt over my nose and mouth, but the odor was overwhelming. I dove into the passenger seat of the red convertible, averting my eyes from the mangled driver. The dead soldier draped across the door was still warm. I unclasped the mask from his face and secured it on my own. My breathing sounded unfamiliar, unnatural inside it. Quin did the same, affixing a mask discarded in the melee. Max, Elana, and String hadn't covered in time. They were sitting quietly with their backs to the car watching the commotion. Langley and the detective fared no better.

"What now?" I asked. I sounded like a robot, my voice dead-ending inside the mask. I watched Quin's back, waiting for him to turn and answer me. Behind him, Valkov limped to the waiting jeep, repeating an artificial *thank you, thank you, thank you* to the two soldiers offering him their shoulders. General Maze followed, his face protected by a camouflage rag.

"Quin?" Finally, he faced me. I staggered backwards, horrified by the small crack in the mask's plastic—like a fissure in a lake of ice—and his stupefied smile.

"I'm going to rest for a while," he murmured. "Fighting is exhausting. Can't we all just get along?" I started to argue, but I knew it was futile. As he joined the others, I watched the jeep drive deeper into the chemical cloud until I couldn't see it anymore. Like thunder came the rolling rumble of Satan's Syndicate speeding away. *They're all leaving us. They're leaving us here to die.*

On the pavement to my right, the foil blanket covered two shapes. To come out now would render Edison and his father just as useless. I was utterly alone. I crawled into the backseat, scooting around Emma's body to examine the open trunk. A brittle sound from my throat reverberated inside the mask. I had never seen a bomb before. More rudimentary than I'd expected, its simplicity was menacing. Just like the General's cryptic threat. *Don't be so sure about that.*

And that's when I noticed.

Emma.

Colton.

Their faces masked. *Not dead.* Very much alive.

Buzzing from their earpieces, General Maze's voice. "Stay low. Keep your mask on. Await further instruction. Stay low. Keep your mask on. Await further instruction. If necessary, activate the alternate detonator. If anyone approaches—"

I snatched the mic from Emma's ear, then Colton's—pushing them aside—then from the other soldiers piled beneath them. I slammed my foot down onto the floorboard, smashing the tiny buds like insects.

"Edison!" I stepped out of the car, took off my jacket and waved it wildly, clearing a space in the Docil-E fog. Under the blanket, movement. There wasn't much time now. Each second passed with the promise of obliteration. I raised my mask and yelled again. "There are two bombs! Maze has one of the detonators. As soon as they get far enough away, he's going to push it. We have to drive both cars off the bridge." It sounded completely insane. Like something Quin would say. Or worse—my mother.

Edison lifted his cover a little, looking out at me with shell-shocked eyes. "My dad." That was all he said. When he stood, I saw a small pool of blood forming under Mr. Van Sant.

"Go get in the other car," I directed him, surprised at the ice in my tone.

"Lex, I can't do it. The bridge—I can't."

"Yes, you can. You have to." More seconds passed, and we were—*one thousand, one thousand two, one thousand three*—closer to death. I held the car door open. "Emma!" She raised her eyes to mine, then lowered them in submission. "Give me your mask and get out." She complied, passing it to me with a sweet smile. *If only she was always this way.*

"Colton! Out of the car!" He joined Emma and they watched me, waiting. "Out! All of you!" Two other soldiers filed out behind him. The fifth lay face down, unmoving, his jacket pierced with bullet holes.

I passed Emma's mask to Edison. "Put this on." He snapped it in place and stood up. I pointed to the spot where the edge of the road ended, and the clear sky began, the spot just before the guardrails. "Floor it and jump out," I told him as he marched somber toward Quin's sports car—like he was walking the plank.

I took a last look down the freeway ramp, toward the checkpoint. Three shapes. Three gut-wrenching shapes. Artos was running full speed toward us, my dad and Carrie at his heels. *I should've known.* Bill Knightley, the journalist, could never resist the lure of the story.

"No! Go back!" I screamed, but my protest was muffled. My heart—and everything else—seemed on the brink of explosion. I could hardly stand it.

"What?" my father yelled back, running faster. I opened my mouth and closed it again. There was no time to explain. I fished the keys off the floorboard and started the engine. Edison was already in the driver's seat, his ragged breath fogging his mask.

"Floor it and jump out," I reminded myself, like it was that easy. *Who am I?* I was about to drive a car off a bridge. I was my mother's daughter after all. I closed my eyes and pictured her face the day I took that impossible walk away from her into the fog. I heard her voice. *I'm so proud of you, my girl.*

I raised one finger ...

Two fingers . . .

Then three . . .

And floored it.

## CHAPTER SIXTY-EIGHT:

# EDITED FOR CONTENT

"And then I said *Floor it, Lex!* And as soon as I could see the water, I jumped like this!" Edison sprung from his seat into the air and did a clumsy pirouette, landing on all fours. "And boom!" That car exploded behind me like a stick of dynamite. It even singed me a little. But I kept going for my dad." Mr. Van Sant pumped his fist from his leather armchair, where he sat with his wounded leg propped. "I carried him all the way to the ambulance. I owned that bridge." Nearly a month later and Edison was still retelling the tale every chance he got—edited for content, of course.

Max chuckled. "And to think, you did it all in your boxers."

"You gotta do, what you gotta do," Edison replied, winking at Elana.

"Wow. That's some story." Mr. McAllister grinned across the Van Sant's antique coffee table at Edison, then turned to me. "Is that really what happened, Alexandra?"

"More or less." My proud father put his arm around my shoulder. Langley's special report—*Zenigenic CEO By Day, Terrorist By Night*—had topped five million views and landed *Eyes on the Bay* the first non-government sponsored television slot in years. She was in Washington D.C. covering a special hearing on Zenigenic's suspected involvement in the 2037 bombings. With Xander dead and Zenigenic defunct, justice seemed too little, too late. But for the government, late always meant right on time.

Quin nudged me with his elbow and pretended to whisper a secret, speaking loud enough for everyone to hear. "I think String's rubbing off on Eddie a little. You can really only trust about half of what he says."

"Hey," String feigned insult. "That's completely, absolutely, one hundred percent . . . sort of true."

Mr. McAllister chuckled. "Well I'm glad the judge bought the half about me being innocent." I squeezed Quin's hand, and he squeezed mine back.

"Me too," String replied. "That little nugget was my bargaining chip, my ticket to freedom from an orange jumpsuit. And believe me, orange is not my color." He laughed a little, then sobered as he faced Mr. McAllister. "I know I've said it before, but I apologize—"

Mr. McAllister extended his hand to String. "No hard feelings. If you hadn't been following me, you never would've seen what really happened. It's not too often you get to thank the guy who was trying to kill you for saving your life."

"Well, when you put it that way, I guess I am a bit of a hero."

"Okay, *Augustus*," I teased. "Don't push your luck."

"Speak of the devil, I can't believe you conned him and Xander," Max said to String. He sounded equal parts repulsed and wonderstruck. "That's impressive—in a really twisted way."

String shrugged. "Well I did learn from the best. Jack Croft was quite a con man. He taught me—"

"Wait a second," Elana interrupted. "You said your dad was a blue-collar guy."

"Industrious, yes. Blue collar? Nah. He did work his fingers to the bone though. He was a masterful pickpocket. That's why we were at the rally that day. Cleaning up."

Mr. Van Sant's phone beeped, interrupting me mid eye roll. "Dad!" Edison scolded him. "You promised no work tonight."

Grinning, Mr. Van Sant snuck a glance at the text on his screen. "This isn't work. It's Katie."

"Oh! Kaaaa-tie." Edison teased. "Is that what we're calling her now?"

From his position in the corner of the room, Scooter chuckled. "Barry—may he rest in peace—always did say you had a little thing for her."

Splotches of red began to crawl up Mr. Van Sant's neck. As he put it, he and Detective Brewster had become *better acquainted* in the hospital, recovering from their gunshot wounds. Edison snickered. "So what did she say, big guy?"

"Son, you're walking a fine line." His voice was stern, but his eyes were bright. "It's the ballistics report from the autopsy. Alexandra, you were right. The bullets they removed from Xander's body are a probable match for that missing sniper rifle."

"Looks like Augustus got the last word after all," String said.

I nodded. "Doesn't he always? You know what I can't figure out though? Why did he settle for $250,000? It seems pretty unambitious for a free bird."

String guffawed. "Two hundred and fifty thousand? Are you kidding? He had way more than that. That was one of the first things he told me when I started working for him again after you found him on that boat. He wanted a nest egg—and he wanted Xander to fund it. I was siphoning off stacks of cash every week from Zenigenic's illegal EAM sales and hiding it in that disgusting tunnel. He left here with at least two million. Half of which was *supposed* to be mine . . ."

String put his arm around Max. It lingered there for a less than a second before Max shoved him off. "But I'm sort of glad Augustus bailed on me. Aside from my brother, you guys are the closest thing to family I've got."

"So we're third in line behind Augustus?"

String winked at me. "Now that he's out of the picture, you're a solid number two. In fact, I haven't felt this happy in a long time. I just wish I could bottle it."

"Already been done," Edison joked.

Quin pointed at the television. "Turn that up, Mr. Van Sant."

On the screen, Zenigenic's headquarters backdropped a somber Barbara Blake.

> **"Today marks a painful milestone for the San Francisco Bay Area as Zenigenic Corporation closes its doors. In the wake of CEO Xander Steele's tragic death, Zenigenic has faced significant financial hardship. Pending**

**an extensive government investigation, the company has ceased business operations.**

**The announcement also falls on the heels of a wrongful death suit filed by the family of Peter Radley. Radley's mother alleges that her son—as a member of the Guardian Force Elite—was forcibly administered illegal EAMs while carrying out missions favorable to Zenigenic, including a staged assassination attempt to boost the company's approval ratings. This morning, interim CEO Gwendolyn Steele issued the following exclusive statement for our viewers.**

**"'How do you want to feel today? That question has served as our slogan since this historic company began its groundbreaking mission in 2030. At Zenigenic, we have always strived to make our customers' lives better. With Emovere, we delivered mastery over fear—with Euphoractamine, limitless joy. It was my son's hope Docil-E would make our world a kinder place. Unfortunately, our world is anything but kind. He was shot in cold blood by an unknown assassin, likely a member of the New Resistance. So how do I want to feel? Today, I simply desire peace. Some of you may have heard rumors about my son and my late husband. I can assure you those are nothing but vicious lies concocted by Zenigenic's enemies to sully our good name. Rest assured, this great company will rise again, better, stronger—'"**

Then came the knock at the door we were all waiting for. With his best hello bark, Artos bounded over, ready to lead the welcome wagon. "It's them," I said, as Mr. Van Sant muted the television.

I could see Emma looking in through the side window, her new tattoo visible on her collarbone. A stick of dynamite and the words *the bomb.* The girl was clever—I had to give her that. I was surprised she'd agreed to accompany Colton back to the rehabilitation program for detox and counseling. And even more surprised Carrie agreed to pick them up there this morning. "Eventually, we all have to stop running," she'd said. "If I don't stop now, I never will."

Over Emma's shoulder, a face both familiar and new. "I'll get it." I was on my feet, halfway to the door when Mr. McAllister's chair scraped the floor in protest. Even as he stood, his hands shook. He seemed to be walking a tightrope—one side, tears . . . the other, laughter. My eyes met Quin's with complete understanding as his father spoke.

"Let me."

# EPILOGUE

I read our poem aloud to her from her book, the one she gave me, the one she taught me to love. *Tell me about your despair, yours, and I will tell you mine. Meanwhile the world goes on.* Walking the endless rows to the stone that was hers—Quin's hand embracing mine and my father trailing behind us—those words beat as true as my own heart. She'd been gone two years today, but it was the first time I'd come here. To Fernwood, the place where my mother was buried.

There was a picture in my pocket, a picture that asked unanswerable questions but demanded answers nonetheless. *How could you kill someone you loved? Did you love her?* I'd written those words to General Jamison Ryker after he'd refused my visit at Larkhill Federal Penitentiary. I wasn't expecting a reply, not after he'd been sentenced to an additional fifteen years for his involvement in illegal sales of EAMs. In exchange for leniency, Valkov talked and talked and talked. He revealed Ryker's plan to escape prison—Docil-E in the air ducts, and he'd walk right out. Xander's sights on world domination—bombs to explode in nine major cities after San Francisco. And his scheme to use the Legacies—Colton, Emma, Quin, any soldier at risk for the Prophecy gene—to pin it all on the New Resistance. Valkov even confessed to Shelly's murder.

*How could you kill someone you loved?* I'd saved it for the end, hoping to leave Ryker with something that would burn, a lit match to the center of his chest. Sitting here, her book in my hand, her bones under my feet, it wasn't my question after all. *Who were you really?* Sometimes the sharp teeth of those words gnawing in my head were so persistent I wanted to scream them. The worst questions—the ones that drive you mad—are the ones you have to answer for yourself.

I'd lost count of all the things I didn't know. Why did my mother stay so long at Zenigenic? Maybe she had made a deal—sold her soul—to protect me, the way she did for Quin. Maybe the punishing whip of her own ambition drove her. Maybe she'd fallen for a man with real demons . . . a man who was not like my father in every way. Maybe she spent a lifetime pining for the one she let walk out the door, hoarding my father's letters as artifacts of a love lost. For a girl who always asked *why*, the silence was deafening.

I felt Quin's warmth beside me, his hand set upon my shoulder. He let me be alone, but not, which was exactly what I needed. *How could you kill someone you loved?* Quin knew that question by heart. It was written on the slate of his soul, and even his father's best attempts would never erase it. The worst questions are riddles that can't be solved. How does the sky taste? What does red sound like?

"She loved you more than anything, you know," Quin said. There was only one thing I knew for sure about my mother. And that was it. That was enough. It had to be.

I turned toward Quin and leaned my head against his chest. With his arms snug around me, the warmth of the sun on my face, all I could hear was the relentless thump of his heart.

There wasn't a word for it, that feeling—any feeling really. Not *just* one. There was no joy without sorrow, no courage without fear, no hope without regret, no love without loss. For once, I didn't try to have one without the other. I felt everything.

## Coming Soon

Want more of the Legacy Trilogy? You're in luck. AWOL, a prequel novella narrated by Quin McAllister is coming soon. If you would like to receive a notification when AWOL is released, please sign up for Ellery Kane's newsletter at www.ellerykane.com.

# Acknowledgements

Fifteen months and almost 800 pages later, I owe a tremendous debt. To the readers who discovered, read, reviewed, and fell in love with the Legacy Trilogy.

To my editor, Ann Castro, and the team at AnnCastro Studios for fostering my growth as a writer and polishing these books until they shined.

And to Gar. If you want to know if someone loves you, then doggedly-obsessively-passionately-crazily pursue your dream. If he cheers you on, even in the midst of your insanity, you got lucky. If he talks plot with you for hours; censors all your bad reviews; reads your books almost as many times as you have; sits with you on the side of the street for two days straight peddling your books to strangers; and lives this and every adventure with you, page by glorious-awful-terrifying-fantastic page…then you won the lottery. And I did.

CPSIA information can be obtained
at www.ICGtesting.com
Printed in the USA
FSOW02n1606240116
16083FS